NANCY HOLDER

DAUGHTER of the BLOOD

D0172127

Silhouette®

BOMBSHELL™

Published by Silhouette Books

America's Publisher of Contemporary Romance

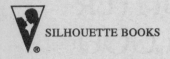 **SILHOUETTE BOOKS**

ISBN-13: 978-0-373-51431-1
ISBN-10:   0-373-51431-X

DAUGHTER OF THE BLOOD

***

Jean-Marc stood alone in a shimmering aura of blue light.

His long, wild hair was caught back in a ponytail.
His dark eyes blazed. A terrible anger came off
him in waves, and she remembered the first rule
she had made for herself when she had met him:
Never piss off Jean-Marc.

He gazed down at her. His lips parted and she
felt his breath on her forehead. Determined not to
betray herself again, she resolutely matched his
gaze, raising her chin and tipping back her head.
An inch closer, and his mouth would press
against hers.

"You can't be here," she told him. "You just had
major surgery."

"I heal fast," he said. "I'm a Gifted."

"So am I." *And if you had died, I would never have
gotten over it.*

Dear Reader,

As I write this note, my daughter, Belle, has just finished her third year as a Brownie Girl Scout, and is now a Junior Girl Scout. To mark the occasion, our service unit put on an elaborate bridging ceremony. I watched my daughter eagerly cross a small wooden bridge—Brownie on one side, Junior on the other—with wistfulness and pride. I, too, have crossed many bridges in my life. Some I burned (!) and some I tripped merrily across. But to be honest, I didn't want to cross a lot of them. I wanted to stay where I was, where I felt safe.

In *Daughter of the Blood,* Isabella DeMarco must cross a bridge from her old life to her new one. I hope that as you read about her journey, you'll remember that you, too, have taken that scary first step many times. That makes you a true heroine in my book. In nearly every instance, once I'm across I'm glad I did it. But sometimes that first step requires a tremendous act of faith. Please write me about your own courageous crossings at www.nancyholder.com, and visit me at bombshellauthors.com.

Be bold!

Nancy Holder

NANCY HOLDER

is a bestselling author of nearly eighty books and two hundred short stories. She has received four Bram Stoker Awards from the Horror Writers Association, and her books have been translated into two dozen languages. A former ballet dancer, she has lived all over the world and currently resides in San Diego, California, with her daughter, Belle. She would love to hear from readers at www.nancyholder.com.

In memory of Jehanne D'Arc, the Maid of Orleans,
valiant warrior and commander.

To my Gifted daughter, Belle,
bridge-crosser par excellence.

Acknowledgments:

With sincere thanks to the Silhouette Bombshell team:
Tara Parsons, Natashya Wilson, Charles Griemsman and
my acquiring editor, Julie Barrett. To all the terrifically
talented, bright and courageous Bombards, my deep
appreciation and gratitude for all the support, advice
and friendship. Deepest thanks to my agent and friend,
Howard Morhaim, who has guided my career and fed me
well, and his assistant, Katie; and to my most excellent
Webmaster and fellow soldier, Sam Devol. Also to
Persephone, buffybuds, litvamp, SF-FWs, bryantstreet,
novelscribes and JoysofResearch, especially
Pat MacEwen, Val and Gerald. To Karen Hackett,
Linda Wilcox, Christie Holt, Ashley McConnell,
Leslie Jones Ackel, Elise Jones, Sandra Morehouse,
Richard Wilkinson, Skylah Wilkinson, Wayne Holder,
Anny Caya, Lucy Walker, Kym Rademacher, Susi Frant,
Terri Yates, Monica Elrod, Barbara Nierman,
Margie Morel and Steve Perry. Deepest thanks to
Susan Wiggs and Gillian Horvath. And a deep bow
to Andy Thompson and everyone at Family Karate,
especially our dear friends Haley and Amy Schricker.

As a grateful citizen, I thank NYPD detective
Edward Conlon, author of *Blue Blood;* and NYPD
police officer Chris Florens, who wore the flower my
daughter gave him behind his ear, and let her wear his
hat. Last but certainly not least, my heartfelt thanks to
Special Agent Jeff Thurman, not only for his friendship,
but for the many years of hard work he has put
into making this world a safer place.
REV, o makunda o makunde.

Chapter 1

New York

The moon was a flickering, low-watt streetlamp threatening to go out any second. Sirens roared in the New York City jungle of burned-out tenements and rusted cars. Bottom-dwelling predators—dealers, pimps, 'kickers and gangbang-ers glided through the misery and poverty of the urban landscape surrounded by snowdrifts, garbage and needles.

It was the last hour of third watch, the end of Izzy DeMarco's very first shift as an NYPD rookie. She and her field training officer, Patrolman Juan Torres, were escort-ing Sauvage, a young goth from Brooklyn, to her boy-friend's place. The building was not very nice, but at least the graffiti on the bricks was random and crude, lacking the trademark tags claiming the building for some gang. Gang territory was worse news than basic low-rent squalor.

Sauvage had promised to stay here until the department located Izzy's former coworker, Julius Esposito, and took him into custody. Sauvage had witnessed Esposito, who had worked with Izzy in the property room, shaking down a corner boy—a street dealer—for money and contraband. She hadn't seen him commit murder, but Esposito was also wanted in connection with the possible homicide of Detective First Grade Jason Attebury, also of the Two-Seven.

Detective Pat Kittrell—what should Izzy call him, her lover? her boyfriend?—had argued that Izzy needed protective custody of her own. Although he had no concrete evidence to back up his case, Pat was sure Esposito was the shooter who had taken aim at Izzy's father in a burning tenement fire—and missed. If he wanted one DeMarco dead, he might want two. Pat was furious when Izzy was assigned to escort Sauvage to a so-called safehouse, and he had half a mind to go to Captain Clancy and tell her so.

Torn between feeling flattered and patronized, Izzy had demanded that Pat stand down and back way off. The last thing she needed was a gold shield lecturing her boss about how to use a new hire.

I'm a cop. Finally. And I sure as hell knew the job was dangerous when I took it.

Besides, Sauvage had declared that Izzy was the only person in New York whom she trusted. With white makeup, black eyes and scarlet lips, costumed in her evil Tinkerbell finery—black-and-red bustier, lacy skirt and leggings topped by a pea coat, with combat boots sticking out underneath—Sauvage cut an exotic figure beside Izzy, who had on her brand-new NYPD blues. Izzy wore no makeup, and her riot of black corkscrew curls were knotted regulation-style, poking out from the back of her hat. Dark brows, flashing chestnut eyes, and unconcealed freckles danced across her small nose—Izzy had never aspired to fashion-model looks, but some men—okay, Pat—said she was a natural beauty. She didn't know about that. But she did look exactly as she had imagined she would look in her uniform, and she was very proud.

"Okay, so where *is* your boyfriend?" Torres thundered at Sauvage as the three stamped their chilly feet on the stoop of the building. Izzy blew on her hands. She had forgotten her gloves. Torres had not. He was bundled up against the night air, and he had a few extra pounds of his own to keep himself warm. And onion breath. Their vehicle reeked of it.

Huffing, Sauvage jabbed the buzzer repeatedly with her blood-red fingernail. About ten minutes ago, back in the squad car, Sauvage had let her boyfriend, Ruthven, know they were on their way, and he'd assured her that he was in the apartment cooking her a big bowl of brown rice and veggies—with a supply of her favorite clove cigarettes at the ready.

"I don't know why he's not answering," Sauvage muttered. "He is so dead."

Let's hope not, Izzy thought, a chill clenching her gut, but she remained silent.

From his jacket pocket, Torres handed Sauvage his cell phone and said, "Call him and tell him to get this door open ASAP."

Sauvage obeyed, punching in numbers. She waited a moment, then looked up from the cell phone and said, "It's not making any noise."

Izzy's anxiety level increased. She turned her head, surveying the street, tilting back her head as she scanned the grimy windows. A few of them had been boarded over.

"Try mine," Izzy offered, pulling her Nokia out of her dark-blue coat and handing it to Sauvage. Meanwhile, Torres was depressing buttons on his cell phone as he exhaled his stinky onion breath, which curled like smoke around his face.

Sauvage took Izzy's phone, punched in the number and murmured, "C'mon, c'mon" under her breath. She closed her kohl-rimmed eyes and pursed her blood-red lips as if she were trying to send her boyfriend a message via ESP.

"Nope," she announced, shaking her head and holding the phone out to Izzy. "It doesn't work, either."

Izzy listened to the dead air and frowned.

Torres said, "I just called in. I'm not getting anything. Let's go to pagers."

They whipped them out. Nothing.

Torres announced, "I'm going to the car."

He jogged about ten feet down the block to their squad car. After about half a minute, he was out of the car and looking in the trunk.

He came back with their twelve-gauge shotgun.

"*Hijo de puta*," he groused. "Computer's out. Radio phone's not working, either."

"How can that be?" Sauvage asked, sounding frightened. "You guys are the police. Your stuff is always supposed to work."

A frisson shot up Izzy's spine. This all seemed familiar in a way she could not define. The cold, the phones not working…

"I think we should get out of here," she said. "Let's take Sauvage to the precinct."

"No, we can't go," Sauvage fretted, hunching her shoulders. She tapped the column of nameplates and jabbed the same button. "He's here. We can buzz someone else who lives here and get them to let us in." She ran her finger up and down the list. "Here's a cool one—Linda Wilcox."

"No," Torres said. "It's his place or we're not going in."

Izzy thought about arguing. Maybe something had happened to Ruthven. Something bad. Maybe it was happening right now. Ten—make that fifteen—minutes ago, he had been cooking something for his girlfriend to eat. Izzy sincerely doubted he'd left to go buy some more zucchini.

"I'm going across the street to call for backup," Torres said.

There was a little mom-and-pop convenience store across the street, signs in the window for Colt 45, cigarettes and lotto tickets.

"Let's go together," Izzy suggested. "Something is seriously wrong."

He said, "I'm only going across the street. You two should keep trying the buzzer."

Then he split, taking full advantage of the lull in the oncoming traffic to jaywalk between parked cars.

Uneasy and cold, Izzy checked her watch again. Forty-eight minutes to go. She knew that Big Vince, her father, was counting each minute, too, waiting for her call to assure him that she had come through her first tour safe and sound. A veteran patrol officer, Big Vince hated that she had become a cop, which was exactly what she had predicted. He wanted his little girl safe and protected from the cold, harsh world, not out in it protecting others.

As soon as this detail was over, she'd phone Big Vince and assure him that he could go back to bed. Then she'd meet up with Pat, debrief, celebrate. Pat Kittrell, a detective second grade in the NYPD, was the man who had helped her fulfill her dream of becoming a cop. Encouraged her, supported her, even helped her overcome her phobia of guns.

He had bought a bottle of champagne to celebrate. They'd go to his place, pop the cork, toast…and then they would make love. As on edge as she was, her body became energized with the thought of his hands on her body, of how it felt when they started the dance. She could smell his musky scent, feel the smoothness of his lips, hear his voice whispering her name in her ear just before he slid into her warm and willing body.

"What is taking him, like, forever?" Sauvage asked Izzy, jolting her out of her reverie. Sauvage tap-danced against the pavement in her combat boots. "I don't like this."

Izzy didn't either like it, either.

"Let's check the store," she said to Sauvage.

"Be careful of the ice," Sauvage cautioned her, as she herself slipped and slid, grabbing Izzy's hand.

When they reached the crosswalk, Izzy reached out to depress the pedestrian signal. As soon as she touched it, the streetlight above them flickered a few times and went out, casting them in relative darkness.

"What the—?" Sauvage muttered, gazing upward.

In the same instant, a black panel truck roared around the corner on the same side of the street as the convenience store and squealed up to the curb. Izzy yanked Sauvage back, hard. The front bumper missed Sauvage's left knee by inches.

Izzy aimed her weapon as the passenger door burst open and a dark silhouette leaped out. She recognized the pomaded hair—Julius Esposito—just as he lunged at her and slammed something against her arm. There was a sharp, painful jolt.

Taser.

Her vision fragmented into gray, shiny dots and there was a scream out in the world or maybe that was the nerves in her ears going haywire. She began to convulse, and she hit the icy sidewalk hard, her arms and legs twitching. For a few forevers, everything shorted out. Then as she swam back, her head began to throb.

Stupid, stupid, stupid, she thought.

It took her a while to wrap her right hand around the grip of her revolver and get to her feet. Her left ankle hurt worse than her head. Bad sprain.

The car was long gone, but Esposito was two blocks ahead of her, dragging Sauvage on foot down the street. She was shrieking and batting at him. Esposito didn't pay her the slightest attention. Neither did the solitary man staggering drunkenly past them in a pair of earmuffs over a do-rag and a black Mets jacket.

Izzy shouted, "Stop! Police! Torres! Torres, get out here!"

Esposito was hustling out of her kill zone—too far away to shoot. And she might hit Sauvage or Mets.

She was surprised that Esposito had taken Sauvage.

Why didn't he drag her into the truck and tell his wheelman to take off? Obviously, he wants me to follow him. Great.

Her best bet was to sic her uninjured partner on him. The mom-and-pop loomed across the street like a journey of a thousand miles. It took her a supreme effort to walk, but she put her pain on hold as she started across the street. She was still holding her gun, but she let her arm drop to her side, concealing it from view.

A bell on the front door of the shop tinkled as she rushed inside. The store smelled of tobacco and floor cleaner, and the clerk, a short Asian man, leaned over the counter at the front and pointed toward the opposite end of the store.

He said, "He go into the alley."

"Did he use your phone?" she asked, as she made her way

down an aisle of canned lychee nuts and Japanese rice crackers. She spread her thumb and forefinger and held them against the side of her face like a phone. "Did he call the police?"

"No call," the man informed her, shaking his head. "No working." He held up his white portable unit as if to corroborate his testimony, and shrugged apologetically.

Why aren't the phones working? What is going on?

"Try again. Call 911! Tell them officers are in pursuit, on foot. Perp armed and dangerous. And tell 'em all the radios are jammed up down here."

"It no working," the man insisted.

"Keep trying!" she bellowed.

She burst through the back door into the alley. There were Dumpsters and trash cans, but no Torres.

She whirled in a circle, shouting, "Torres! Damn it! Where are you?"

There was no answer.

Figuring he'd circled back around, she flew back through the store and burst outside again.

No Torres there, either.

Damn it, she thought.

Esposito had put a lot of distance between himself and her. Alone, without backup, she hobbled through East Harlem, one of the more impoverished neighborhoods in all of New York City. Fifth Avenue to the East River, Ninety-Sixth to One Hundred and Fifteenth Street. Night was a heavy lead weight slung across her shoulders, a sudden dumping of snow flurries slowing her pace as surely as the pain freezing up her ankle.

Esposito maintained at least a fifty-yard lead, despite the fact that he was dragging Sauvage and she was fighting him every step. The young goth's black combat boots kept scooting out from underneath her on the icy sidewalk; now he was screaming at her over his shoulder and brandishing his gun. Izzy wondered how long Sauvage would be able to struggle. Beneath her pea coat, her black-and-red bustier must be constricting her breathing, and her skirts were wrapped around her legs like a shroud.

A handful of curious street people—"skels" in police parlance—materialized on door stoops and alley entrances to watch the excitement. She wondered if she should tell one of them to call for help. Probably the better course was for them not to know that she needed help.

She kept going.

Then a voice inside her head said, *You need to hustle. You're on point. She's going to die.*

And you'll be next.

Izzy jerked, hard, and nearly fell. She knew that voice. It had whispered to her in her nightmares for over a decade, speaking in riddles, promising death. She'd gone to see a shrink about it; her father wanted her to talk to their priest.

But I'm awake, she thought. *I'm awake and I'm hearing it.*

She took her attention off Esposito and looked all around herself—at shadows and the icy falling snow.

"Who's there?" she called.

Allez, vite, it told her. French, which she did not speak. But which she seemed to understand, if her dreams were any indication of her linguistic abilities. For the voice often spoke to her in French. And sometimes she woke herself up, responding aloud, also in French.

Hurry. Stop him. Or they'll die. And it will be your fault.

Then a gun went off. Izzy ducked behind a row of newspaper dispensers. She felt no compression of air, heard no impact, no telltale ping of a casing. Had someone taken a potshot at her? More important, would they take another? Was that the deal—Esposito would lure her into the line of fire and someone else would gun her down?

She inched cautiously around the dispensers and started back up the street. Her mother's gold filigree crucifix was wedged between her breasts, flattened by her brand-new Kevlar bulletproof vest. The facing on her polyester shirt itched against her sensitive skin. She was uncomfortable and she was scared and she was mad as hell.

She had no idea how she crossed the next block without being hit by oncoming traffic, but she did it. Then she saw Esposito and Sauvage at the end of the block, racing catty-corner to a high-rise tenement. On the upper floors, flames shot from blown-out windows, licking and curling at the pitted exterior. Smoke billowed like wavy hair from the roof.

Esposito darted inside.

She got to the curb and raced into the building, yelling "Fire!" She limp-ran past the long row of tenants' brown metal mailboxes and raced down the carpeted hall. There was no smoke yet, and she smelled garbage, marijuana and urine.

"Fire! Call 911!" she bellowed, pounding her fist on the nearest door. She lurched past the cracked, peeling wall to the next door. "Fire! Get out *now!* Leave the building! The building's on fire!"

Through an open door to her right, watery light blinked above a wooden staircase topped with an Art Deco rail. She stopped, cocking her head, and detected a distant shuffling noise—rapid footfalls on wood.

She gripped the rail with her left hand and pulled herself

up the stairs, her Medusa pointed toward the ceiling. Her ankle screamed in protest.

At the second-story landing, she tried the doorknob that led into the hallway. It was locked. She didn't know if that meant Esposito had gone in that way and locked it after himself, and she debated for an instant —force the door open, or go up another story?

She decided to stick with the stairway. If he wanted her to follow him, he wouldn't throw obstacles in her path. He'd make it easy for her.

Just like Torres made it easy for him to attack me. Is he in on it? Where is he now?

Maybe Esposito's objective was to make sure she died in the fire. Something about that tugged at her. Dying by fire. Dying in fire. That had something to do with her. With her heritage.

What heritage? I'm a second-generation cop and my brains have been scrambled by a stun gun, she thought. *I don't know anyone who's died in a fire. I don't even know any firefighters.*

As she climbed, she heard people screaming, and she smelled thick, oily smoke. The fire was traveling rapidly to the lower floors.

On the third floor, the hallway door hung ajar. Beyond it, the hall lights were dim, smoke curling around the sconce directly across from her. Then she looked down and noticed a three-inch piece of black lace—from Sauvage's skirt?— draped across the transom.

Izzy painfully bent down, picked it up and examined it. Had to be. The more important question was, was it Sauvage or Esposito who had left it there for her to find? Maybe Esposito was hiding behind that open door right now, waiting to blow her head off.

Her scalp prickled. Extending her Medusa with both

hands, she kicked open the door and darted into the hallway, sweeping a circle. The hallway was filling with smoke. Apartment doors slammed open as the frightened occupants spilled out of their homes. They began running toward the front of the building—toward an elevator, Izzy feared—a very, very bad thing to do in a fire.

Breaking whatever cover she had left, Izzy shouted, "Stairs! Here!" and made broad gestures to get their attention. The three or four closest to her hurried over, and she waggled the flashlight toward the stairs, bellowing, "Move it! Get out now! Go down the stairs and go across the street! Call 911 when you get outside!"

If their phones would work.

She lurched toward the back. As the terrified civilians swarmed past her, she yelled, "This is the police! Stay calm! Walk to the stairs!"

As she moved in deeper, curls of smoke rolled toward her in waves. She snatched off her hat with her left hand and waved it in front of herself, trying to keep her vision clear. A tiny, wizened man with walnut-hued skin ran past her with a barking Chihuahua in his arms.

"Po-lice!" he yelled, smiling at Izzy. "Po-lice done come! Hallelujah!"

"Take the stairs," she told him, gesturing behind herself. "Don't take the elevator."

He gave her a wink and said, "*Oui, ma guardienne. Merci.*"

Izzy jerked. *What the hell?* That seemed familiar too, being called *ma guardienne*. Part of her life.

She realized with a start that she had seen this hallway before, too. She looked to the left and spotted the fire extinguisher, just as she'd expected to see it in that location. There was the deep, jagged crack in the wall.

Her heart skipped beats as she remembered when and where she had seen it before:

In her vision in the restaurant.

At lunch she had watched her father as if by remote camera, only it was all in her mind. He was on a detail, walking along this exact same corridor—also during a fire. She had been sitting in a deli blocks away, but she had seen him as clearly as if she'd been there with him. She had known someone in the hall was raising a gun and taking aim, and she had shouted, *"Hit the floor!"*

In her head.

And Big Vince had heard her in *his* head, and obeyed. The shooter had missed, and her father had lived to tell the tale, labeling it a miracle from heaven.

Big Vince wasn't here now, but if the rest of the vision held true, there was a perp hiding at a hallway intersection off to her right, his gun pointed at her skull—and she was certain now that it had been Esposito, and that he had lured her here so he could enact the same ritual execution he'd planned for her father.

She dove to the floor and rolled onto her side, aiming her gun at the appropriate angle, aware that there was no safety on a revolver, and the last thing she wanted to do was shoot an innocent bystander.

There! She saw movement…seconds before the sconce in the wall above her head went out. Now the intersection plunged into darkness, but she still knew there was definitely someone there.

She drew another breath, keeping her arms outstretched. Her muscles began to quiver with fatigue. Her Medusa was heavy, fully loaded with six cartridges in the cylinder…

No, there are five, the voice said in her head. *You used it, remember?*

She blinked. She *hadn't* used it. If she had, she'd be facing hours of paperwork and at least a couple of Internal Affairs interviews. Discharging a weapon while on duty was a huge deal.

Despite the darkness, she glanced downward, in the direction of her gun. Her eyes widened and her lips parted in sheer terror as little sparks wicked off her hands.

I'm on fire! she thought, as she rolled over on her side. But she wasn't in any pain. The sparks multiplied. She was *glowing*.

Then the light vanished, and she wondered if she had imagined the whole thing. Maybe it was some kind of taser aftereffect.

A voice called, "Iz?" as a tall, rangy figure stepped from the smoke and shadows, into the light of the central corridor.

It was Pat. He was holding both a flashlight and a gun— a .357 Magnum. His deep-green eyes glittered in the soft yellow light that burnished the planes and hollows of his face.

"Jesus, Iz." He set down the flashlight as he gathered her up with his left arm. "When I heard it was Esposito…"

"I'm okay," she said as he laced his fingers through hers, easing her to her feet as he swept the area with his gun. "I don't know where Torres is. Did he call it in?"

"Must have," he said. "Captain Clancy told me to get my butt over here. She didn't need to tell me twice."

Her leg buckled as she put weight on her injured ankle, and he kept her from falling, his face creasing with concern.

"I'm okay," she said again, then realized that she had to be honest about her injury. They were on a mission. She confessed, "My ankle's sprained. It hurts."

"You stay here, then," he ordered her as he retrieved his

flashlight and clicked it off—a wise precaution, one she would have taken herself.

"No way," she insisted, coughing as the smoke seeped back into her lungs. "I think he took her toward the back."

He gazed at her and shook his head. "Don't go all Jane Wayne on me, Officer. I'm getting you out of here."

"He wants me to follow him. If I don't take the bait, he might shoot her," she argued.

With the stern expression of a detective who could make hardened gangbangers break down and cry after ten minutes in an interview room, Pat said, "You're out, Iz. I'm on it."

Coughing harder, she fanned the smoke away from them both with her hat.

"She's on my watch," Izzy insisted. "I'm thinking the fire escape. Let's go."

As she stepped forward, there was a loud ripping noise overhead. She gazed up, just as an enormous section of the ceiling dislodged and crashed to the floor. The impact threw her into Pat's arms and he dragged her along the hallway as another section cracked free and smashed inches from her back.

An illuminated Exit sign buzzed and winked about ten feet ahead of them. Pat reached it first and pressed his hand on the metal door beneath it.

"It's cool," he reported. Meaning that there was no fire on the other side. Then he yanked it open.

Their feet clanged on metal; they had reached the fire escape, a metal rectangle from which ladderlike stairs angled upward and downward. Reflexively, they both looked up. Far above them, flames danced on the roof.

Then an eerie purplish-black light bloomed from below and streaked toward them like a missile. They both dropped to the floor of the fire escape; as it bobbed dangerously, the black light exploded against the open door and tore it off its hinges.

Bricks broke and flew outward; Pat threw himself on top of Izzy and bellowed, "Cover your head!"

A fragment of brick pelted her forearm. She heard a shower of pieces ringing against the metal floor. Pat grunted.

"Are you hurt?" she cried.

"No, I'm okay." He gripped her shoulders. "Stay down. Here comes another one."

"What's going on?" she demanded, trying to jerk up her head. But Pat was in the way.

"It's Le Fils," he said into her ear. His breath was moist and warm. "Esposito's down there, too. They're attacking, and they have Sauvage."

"Le Fils?" Izzy suddenly felt very dizzy. The world canted left, right, as if the fire escape had pulled from the building and was swinging freely. Le Fils, Le Fils...

It was all there, in an instant. Everything they were doing right now could not be happening. If Le Fils was down there, they could not be in New York. And she had never told Pat about Le Fils. Le Fils du Diable—the Son of the Devil—was the king vampire of New Orleans, terrorizing both Gifted and Ungifted alike. She hadn't known about Le Fils until the day she had left New York...

Oh, my God. I left New York. I never went to the Police Academy. I'm not NYPD.

She felt another wave of vertigo.

The floor beneath them was not metal. It was wood. As Pat shifted his weight, she lifted her swirling head and saw men in tuxedos and women in gowns rushing past the two of them. A leathery creature in a hood bobbed past. It had been at the dinner, when Jean-Marc had presented her to the family.

Jean-Marc...where is Jean-Marc?

Another explosion rocked the floor. She smelled smoke. She heard screaming.

"Let me up," she woozily ordered Pat.

"No, stay down, darlin'," he told her. Pat's face was backlit by a shimmering curtain of blue. The curtain darkened with purple; then another bolt of purple-black burst through and hit the white wooden wall behind them. "He's attacking."

He already did attack. Le Fils and his accomplice, Julius Esposito the voodoo bokor, *attacked us last night. Here, in New Orleans. Why is it happening again? This is more than a dream. Is this a vision?*

With a burst of strength born of determination, she forced his weight off her body and slowly got to her feet.

Surrounded by familiar faces, some standing still as white light poured from their palms, others rushing through the chaos, she and Pat stood on the verandah of the de Bouvard mansion on the outskirts of the bayou—her blood family's home for nearly three hundred years. She was not wearing her police uniform, but the white satin gown embroidered with flames on the bodice she had worn at her presentation.

The flame-shaped brand in her left palm glowed and pulsed, and she remembered the rest: she was no longer simply Izzy DeMarco; she was Isabella Celestina DeMarco de Bouvard, the daughter of the flames. Her biological mother, Marianne, the *guardienne* and titular protector of this House, lay downstairs in a coma.

And this was her battle.

Around her neck, Izzy wore protective talismans: the rose quartz necklace Sauvage had given her, and the chicken-foot gris-gris of Andre the werewolf.

Andre...Jean-Marc... She looked for the Cajun werewolf and Jean-Marc, the passionate magic user who had tracked her down and brought her here from New York. The men who should be here. She searched the throng for Sange, the elegant vampire. She saw none of them.

She reached out a hand to Pat and said, "You're not supposed to be here. You need to go inside."

"No way," he replied. Then his sea-green eyes widened and his lips parted in a silent grimace. Silently, he sank to his knees and fell forward, hard, onto his face.

The back of his jacket was shredded, and blood gushed from an entry wound.

"Oh, my God, Pat!" she cried. She placed one hand over the other and pushed to stem the geyser of blood. It was spraying her face. *Pat's blood was spraying her face!*

"Officer down!" she yelled. "Officer down! I need assistance!"

No one seemed to hear her. Nor even see her.

You're on point, said the voice inside her head. *Get up and kill Esposito. Do it. Now. Or others will die, and this House will fall.*

In a daze, Izzy stared down at Pat. His head was twisted to one side; his eyes were fluttering shut, and his face was a deathly white.

"This isn't happening," she whispered. "This can't be happening!"

But it was happening.

Do it.

"I'm not leaving him," she said aloud, putting her arms

around his broad shoulders. He was gasping like a beached sea creature. His lips were cyanotic.

Shoot Esposito or everyone will die.

"I won't leave you," Izzy promised Pat, as she burst into hoarse, wild wails. "Pat! I won't leave you!"

Chapter 2

Pat can't be dead. He shouldn't even be here. He can't be dead....

"Oh, my God, he bit me, didn't he! That freakin' vampire bit me!" Sauvage cried.

Izzy jerked awake, tears streaming down her cheeks. Sauvage, in her red-and-black goth attire, was sitting about five feet away on a white plastic chair in the corner of the OR, which was located in the lower depths of the House of the Flames. Ruthven, her boyfriend, knelt before her in black leather pants and a black T-shirt, scrutinizing every inch of her exposed flesh for vampire bites.

"Pat," she whispered, knowing already that he *wasn't* there. That he *wasn't* dead. It had been a horrible nightmare—horribly real, but just a nightmare—one of the many that had plagued her of late. New York, Sauvage and Torres, Pat and the apartment building—all that had been a dream—or perhaps another vision of things to come. Since arriving in New Orleans, she had been plagued by dreams and visions. But Sauvage had definitely never been in protective custody, and Esposito had never dragged her through the streets of East Harlem.

But last night, on the verandah, Izzy *had* shot and killed Esposito. In the melee, Esposito had been about to slit Sauvage's throat. Izzy had taken aim, and with one clear shot from her Medusa revolver—an enchanted .9 mm cartridge—she had shot him in the chest.

And he had burst into purple fireworks.

He exploded. Thinking of that, seeing it again in her mind, Izzy trembled. Two weeks ago people in her world didn't die like that; there were no mansions filled with people with magical powers or werewolves or vampires.

Two weeks ago her world had been the borough of Brooklyn, where she lived in a row house with her father and worked as a civilian in the property room of the Two-Seven. Gino, her brother, was studying to be a priest in a seminary in Connecticut. And the little family of three had shared the memory of her beloved mother, Anna Maria DeMarco, who had been dead for ten years.

And then the *real* nightmare had begun. Izzy had learned that she had magical powers, and that she was the missing heiress of the ancient French magic-using family, the de Bouvards—the House of the Flames. Jean-Marc de Devereaux des Ombres, Regent of the Flames, had saved her life, told her who she was and brought her here, to New Orleans, to take over leadership of her family.

Now Jean-Marc lay a few feet from her on an operating table, hovering someplace midway between life and death. He, not Pat, had been badly wounded during the battle.

"Patient's BP still in the basement," someone muttered at the OR table. They moved inside a magical sterile field of white light. Within it, everyone was dressed in white—white scrubs for the surgical team and white gowns and veils for the Femmes Blanches, the legendary de Bouvard healing women, who were as silent as ghosts as they held each other's hands. The two women on the ends of their line clasped Jean-Marc's hands as well. They were transferring their magical energy to him.

As the surgeon shifted to the left, Izzy caught sight of Jean-Marc's sharp profile, and she drew in a sharp breath at the instant, riveting rush of…*intensity* overtaking her. Jean-Marc had searched for her for three years, and once he had found her, a link—physical, emotional, magical—had formed between them. One touch, one smoldering look, reduced her to a fine trembling. Her engulfing attraction to him frightened her.

And then there was Pat. When Jean-Marc had barreled into Izzy's life, she had only just built up the nerve to ask Pat over for dinner. Pat had been interested in her for months, but he had given her all the time she needed to respond to his patient, easygoing flirtation. It was the lack of pressure she savored most; he was a little older than she was, more seasoned, less inclined to see each opportunity that came his way as the last one he would ever have. He respected her boundaries. He never challenged her need to go slow.

Before she left New York, fleeing for her life, she had slept with Pat. In some ways, it had been too soon in their relationship for sex. But Jean-Marc himself had explained that for magic users like themselves—known in their world as the Gifted—sex magic was the strongest type of spell they could employ. He had gone so far as to suggest that she go to bed with Pat, to protect him from harm.

Death was all around them, people she cared about going

down; Izzy had done it…and making love with Pat had rocked her to her foundations. Never in her life had she experienced such transforming pleasure, felt such joy and completion. She had seduced Pat to protect him, but her Texas cowboy had claimed her as surely as if he had roped and branded her. Pat was in her heart now.

And yet, when she gazed at the unconscious man on the operating table, she knew that if Jean-Marc woke up, she would have to face a decision. Pat was Ungifted—not a magic user—and he was back in New York, watched over by Captain Clancy herself, who knew the score. Izzy had no idea what was going to happen to her old life—could she go back? If so, when? Would Pat wait? When he found out who and what she was, would he want to?

Or did her heart's destiny end in the path that led to Jean-Marc? He was her mentor, her guardian. She thought she felt his heart beating inside her own chest. Closing her eyes, she smelled the roses and oranges that signaled his working a spell of protection and comfort around her. She half-suspected that if he did die—and she could hardly bear to even think of it—their link would survive the grave.

Jean-Marc, she sent out to him, *I still need you here. You can't go. You can't die.*

She felt a tiny flutter against her mind. She gasped and shut her eyes, waiting for words, for thoughts, for heartbeats.

It came:

Isabelle.

Her throat closed up with emotion as she replied, *N'as pas de peur. Je suis ici.* Don't be afraid. I am here.

She waited hungrily for more, listening to the shorthand of the surgical team, watching as they combined traditional medicine with strange magical incantations, powders and objects—crystals, a ritual knife called an athame and candles. Unmoving, the fully veiled Femmes Blanches held his hands through it all.

Then the surgeon sighed heavily, and the women bowed their heads.

"Oh, my God, what's happening?" Izzy asked, half rising from her chair.

The doctor looked at her over his shoulder. "Please, madame, stay where you are. We're doing the best we can."

Retaining her seat, she pursed her lips and fists together. The best had not saved her mother. Marianne had flatlined, and nothing they had tried had restored her brain activity. She remained technically alive, but only technically.

Izzy kept vigil, willing a better outcome for Jean-Marc.

Michel de Bouvard, Izzy's liaison to the House of the Flames, poked his head in, saw Izzy and entered. He was still wearing his tux from the dinner. Coming up beside her, he crossed his arms over his chest and watched the medical team for a few moments before he asked, "How's he doing?"

She wiped fresh tears from her cheeks. She'd been crying without knowing it. As steadily as she could, she replied, "He's still alive."

Michel wore a poker face as he took that in. Then he looked—really looked—at her and said, "How are *you* doing?"

"I'm okay. Let's debrief," she said tersely.

He held up his fingers as if to enumerate the facts of their situation. "Le Fils got away."

"Right."

"Andre is still missing."

Aside from Jean-Marc, the werewolf was her strongest ally in this strange new world of passion and deceit. "Could he have survived that jump off the verandah?" she asked hopefully.

Cocking his head, he raised a brow. "A leap off the third story? I don't know. Maybe. He gave you his gris-gris, so he didn't have that protection with him when he jumped. I assume Jean-Marc made talismans for him, so they would help. And werewolves are uncommonly strong and quick to heal," he added. "Like us."

She filed that away, wondering if "us" meant all Gifted individuals or just Bouvards. She wanted Jean-Marc to be quick to heal. She wanted him healed *now*.

"What about Alain?" That was Jean-Marc's cousin. He had been MIA since before Izzy's private jet had landed. Jean-Marc had been terribly worried, sending two security details to search for him.

"Still missing." His voice was flat, as if he was attempting to sound neutral. She knew Michel detested Jean-Marc; she had to assume he had no love for Alain de Devereaux as well. Was Michel involved in his disappearance?

"What are you doing to locate him?" she asked.

"We're scouring the battlefield for residue," he said. "And I sent out an additional search party. We've got one in the swamp and two in the city—one in the Garden District and one in the French Quarter."

"Residue," she said.

"Emanations," he explained. "We may be able to read them for clues."

She still didn't fully understand, but she said, "Maybe I could help."

"Madame, please leave these things to us. You need to meet with Gelineau, Broussard and Jackson." They were the de Bouvards' Ungifted allies: the mayor of New Orleans, the superintendent of police, and the governor of the state of Louisiana. "You should include Sange as well." She was the elegant vampire with whom the House of the Flames had forged an alliance.

He took a breath and reached into his left pants pocket. "And you should put this on."

He opened his hand, revealing the gold signet ring that was the symbol of authority for the House of the Flames. According to Jean-Marc, it was nearly seven hundred years old.

"Where did you get that?" she demanded, flushing with anger. Jean-Marc had been wearing it the last time she had seen it.

"I took it when they stripped him for surgery," he replied guilelessly. "A reasonable precaution, given its value."

Did she dare accept it from his hand? According to both Jean-Marc and Michel, innumerable factions sought to place their own woman—or man—on the throne. Jean-Marc spoke of assassination attempts on his own life, and the regent before him might have been murdered. For all Izzy knew, putting on that ring might be signing her own death warrant.

Where would it leave Jean-Marc? If she wore the ring, did that signify the end of his term of service? So many Bouvards hated him for ruling in her mother's name. He was a Devereaux, an outsider, and though the Grand Covenate, the supreme governing body of the Gifted world, had arranged for his service as regent, the Bouvards had resented his presence from the start.

I don't know what I'm doing, Izzy thought. She shut her eyes tightly and prayed to St. Joan, the *patronesse* of the House of the Flames, known to the Bouvards by her French name, Jehanne.

Jehanne, aidez-moi. Je vous en prie. Jehanne, help me. I petition you.

She heard no answer, felt no guiding intuition. She didn't

hear the voice that often counseled and directed her, which had sounded so clear and real in her dream.

"You must take it," Michel insisted, extending his hand palm up. "*I* can't wear it."

With trembling fingers, Izzy closed her fist around it. It was much heavier than she had anticipated. She turned over her hand and opened her fingers, tracing the dime-shaped circle etched with flames surrounding a *B* for Bouvard. Then she clutched it in her fist again as she unclasped the gold crucifix that had belonged to Anna Maria DeMarco—the woman she had always believed to be her mother—in preparation for sliding the ring onto the chain.

Michel stopped her with a shake of his head. He said, "We have an agreement with Sange that no one wears crucifixes in the mansion. If you put the ring on that chain, she will be highly insulted. We can't afford to alienate her."

The rose quartz necklace Sauvage had made for her also hung from Izzy's neck. She pointedly reclasped her crucifix—continuing to wear it—and unfastened the string of pale pink quartz. Then she slipped the ring onto the beaded necklace and reconnected the clasp.

A sudden burst of warmth pressed against the satin of her gown. She looked down to see a white nimbus of magical energy emanating from the ring.

Michel de Bouvard sank on one knee, lowering his head as he whispered, "*Ma guardienne.*"

"I'm not the *guardienne* yet," Izzy protested, as the light faded.

"You're the closest thing we have," he replied. His voice was softer, more deferential.

"Now we should go to the private meeting room upstairs," he continued, rising. "I'll let the governor and the others know you're ready to meet with them. Jean-Marc and Alain both have assistants, of course. You should talk to them, as well. They're very upset."

"No." She crossed her arms and stood rooted to the spot. "Tell everyone to come down here," she said. "I'm not leaving my mother and the regent alone." Marianne lay in her bed of state in the chamber beyond the OR.

Michel blinked, obviously taken aback.

"Devereaux and your mother are *not* alone."

"Without me, they may as well be," she retorted.

"Madame, these are healers," he reminded her as he opened wide his arm, taking in the other people in the OR. "They honor the code of ethics of healers everywhere—First Do No harm."

Harm was open to interpretation. One of those healers might decide that allowing Jean-Marc to live would harm the House of the Flames. Or that snuffing out Marianne's life once and for all might help it.

Izzy clasped the ring dangling from the necklace, its warmth seeping into her bones. She narrowed her eyes a fraction and said, "They'll come down here or there will be no meeting."

She caught his answering grimace and handily ignored it. Back in New York, in the Two-Seven's prop cage, she had blown off the wheedling and blustering of career police officers and detectives who wanted her to bend the rules in order to make their lives easier. No amount of pressure had ever succeeded in getting Izzy to violate procedure.

Here and now she had no set of protocols for what was happening. She couldn't play it by the book, because there was no book. But she could stand up to Michel de Bouvard and make her decisions stick.

"They come to me," she said again.

"We're in a precarious position," he reminded her. "Now that Le Fils has dared to attack us, the Ungifted will consider us too weak to protect them against the supernaturals in this region."

Maybe they are too weak, Izzy thought, then corrected herself: *Maybe we are too weak.*

"You need to be seen," he continued. "I agreed that we would keep the regent's condition a secret on a need-to-know basis, but you don't have the luxury of seclusion. The people have *got* to know that you're all right."

"Then bring a contingent down here to meet with me," she reiterated. "Would my mother jump if the governor told her to?"

"I have no idea," he replied harshly. "Your mother's been in a coma for twenty-six years."

"You're out of line," Izzy said.

"I'm not!" he shouted. Heads turned. More quietly he said, "I'm not. We're in an emergency situation. Our chain of command puts me in charge after Jean-Marc. But you're here now, and I'm trying to steer you to the best course of action."

Her lips parted, but she let him continue. He needed to get this off his chest, and she needed to know where he stood.

"Let's not mince words," he said. "I honor your status. I truly do. I'm loyal to you. But you just got here, and you don't know anything, and we're practically at war, and not just with Le Fils. I don't how to explain to you just how tenuous our association with the Ungifted is right now."

"Got it," she said.

"So you need to reassure them. Or they'll abandon their treaty with us."

"Will they do that today?" she asked him. "Abandon the treaty?"

He shifted his weight as if he didn't want to answer.

"Doubtful," he admitted. "But with each hour that passes without a meeting, it'll take that much more handholding to reassure them that we're still in the game."

"I'm more than willing to meet them," she said. "But they have to come down here."

"All right," Michel said. "I'll see what I can do."

As he turned to go, a deep bass gong thrummed through the air. Izzy felt its vibration in the bones of her bare feet.

Sequestered in her corner, Sauvage threw her arms around Ruthven and cried, "We're being attacked again!"

Michel closed his eyes, opened them again. He said, "Field agents. And the executive staff. I think they've found something."

"I'll go with you to the door," Izzy told him.

She crossed to her chair and picked up her shoes, stepping into them. The clack of her heels provided a counterpoint to the silent tension in the room.

They went out of the OR and into the monitoring room, where the techs watched the readouts of her mother's life-support machines. Then they went out of that room to the main chamber. The room was dominated by her mother's elaborate gilt bed. Izzy gazed tenderly at her as they passed. She looked like Izzy—an oval face with freckles across the nose, framed with long, black ringlets. In fact, she looked younger. She had only been twenty when she'd fallen into the coma; Jean-Marc had told Izzy that Gifted aged more slowly than Ungifted. He had assumed that now that her powers had awakened, her own aging process would decelerate, and maybe even reverse.

They walked down the center aisle of the chamber. The Femmes Blanches sat in two rows on either side, hands joined, holding Marianne's hands.

Michael opened the chamber door.

A man and a woman in black suits and headsets stood on the other side. The male security agent cradled a two-foot-by-two-foot matte gray container with silver fittings against his chest.

Three other people stood in the hallway, well away from the agents. One was a young, dark-haired woman in a sleek business suit adorned with a flames pin identical to the one Michel wore on his lapel. Two men, one in his midtwenties and one middle-aged, also wore suits and pins.

When they saw Izzy, they bowed. She inclined her head.

"*Oui?*" Michel queried. "Did you find something?"

"*Oui,*" the female agent replied, her eyes bright with excitement. She gestured to the container. "We have some readable fragments of the *bokor* himself."

"Of Esposito?" Michel asked, his voice rising with excitement.

"*Oui,*" she replied proudly. The man holding the container smiled.

"Wonderful work," Michel said.

Izzy parsed the conversation. "Fragments? Are we talking residue?"

"*Oui, madame,*" Michel affirmed, smiling. "Robert and Louise are two of our best. If they say they're readable, that means we can get some useful information off them."

"Readable," she echoed slowly. "As in psychometry?"

"Yes," he said. "And we'll—"

"Psychometry," she continued, "which I'm apparently good at." Her training with Jean-Marc had proven that.

His knit his brows and pursed his lips. "I appreciate your offer to help, but this is new to you, and this will be difficult and grisly work."

"I want to be there," she insisted.

"You are irreplaceable, and this reading could be dangerous. Esposito was working with very powerful spirits. I'm
sure that if Jean-Marc were here—"

"Jean-Marc *is* here," she corrected him. But she wondered
if he knew something that she didn't, if Gifted died differently from other people and he knew Jean-Marc would not
be back.

"Please, madame, how is the regent?" the middle-aged
man asked, stepping forward. "I'm Simon, his assistant. This
is Pierre, Alain's assistant."

"Sophie is my assistant," Michel added, gesturing to the
woman.

"Any news?" Pierre asked.

Izzy said, "The regent is still in surgery. Alain is still
missing. Perhaps we'll learn more from reading the fragments." She gave Michel a look. "So let's get it done."

"You just agreed to a meeting," he argued.

"After."

"Please," Michel pled. "This will be very unpleasant."

She shrugged. "It's like forensics, right? We examine bone
fragments, bits of tissue…and we learn things from their vibrations. Or something."

He blinked. "No, *madame,* it's not like that at all." He
shook his head. "It's…horrible."

Great.

"No problem," she told him. "Let's do it."

Chapter 3

W_{hy} did everything have to be so complicated?

"I repeat, *madame*," Louise said in the hall outside Izzy's mother's chamber, "it would seriously jeopardize both Marianne and the regent to bring Esposito's remains inside the chamber. They're psychically toxic."

So she was back to trusting the doctors and the Femmes Blanches to do no harm.

"We need to take them to the reading chamber, and we need to do it now," Robert said. "They won't keep their integrity long."

She exhaled. "All right. Let's go to the reading chamber, then."

The two security agents looked at Michel. He gave his head a tense little nod, and the quartet walked away. The assistants had not asked to come with them, and appeared to be more than happy to let them leave without them.

Izzy and company used the service stairway. The descent was shadowy and narrow. Izzy's shoulder brushed musty-smelling brickwork; she felt claustrophobic and scared.

Robert, Louise and Michel chanted beneath their breaths; everyone in the party, including Izzy, glowed with white light. Michel's forehead was beaded with sweat as if the effort were costing him dearly.

"This is a protective shield of light, like armor," he told her. "In time, one hopes you will be able to create one for yourself. It's a fairly basic skill for us."

"I'm sure I'll get the hang of it," she replied, wondering if he was trying to insult her or cow her. She stood next in line to rule over them like a queen, and everyone she had met so far was appalled at her ignorance and lack of skills.

After two more flights of stairs, they were in complete darkness. She felt a breeze against her face and heard the squeal of metal on metal. Chains clanked. A chill ran down her spine. Were they going into a dungeon?

Footsteps echoed against what might have been the walls of a cavern, and Izzy could make out the shapes of the two agents and Michel in front of her.

As she followed Michel, a stab of pain cut across the arch of first her right foot and then her left. On the floor, a line glowed with icy white light.

"A ward," Michel informed her. "Very powerful."

A door behind her slammed shut, the sound ricocheting around her. Light flared and flames undulated from the tips of torches set into each point of the white stone walls of an octagonal room. They revealed the mosaic floor beneath her feet, tiled in the familiar design of the head of a short-haired woman surrounded by a halo. Jehanne d'Arc, the patroness.

A figure walked from the shadows. It was six feet tall, dressed in a hooded, satin white robe that concealed its face and body. Its hands were moving inside the hood, and she nearly burst into giddy hysteria when she realized it was taking off a pair of earphones attached to an iPod dangling from its neck.

Her amusement died away when she saw its hands—they were leathery purple claws ending in sharp talons. Devilish, to her Catholic eyes.

"*Bienvenue,*" it said in a hollow, rasping voice.

"May I introduce you to Felix D'Artagnon," Michel said. The creature bowed low. "D'Artagnon is one of a clan of gremlins who has allied himself with our Family, in much the same way as Madame Sange."

"*Madame la Guardienne,*" D'Artagnon intoned.

"I'm Marianne's daughter," Izzy insisted.

Michel continued, "*Gremlin* is a general term for a class of beings that aren't human but also aren't demon. *We* don't deal with demons." His voice tightened. "It's forbidden, and it's punishable by death."

"Got it," Izzy said.

"Monsieur D'Artagnon and his clan are allied with us. They had a falling out with the Malchances about a century ago, and we…assisted them with sorting that out."

D'Artagnon nodded.

"The Malchances. They're not our favorite people," Izzy observed.

"No," Michel replied. "They're not."

D'Artagnon led the way toward a long stone altar in the dead center of the room. Now-familiar objects sat on the altar—a marble vase containing a lily, and a white candle floating in an alabaster bowl before a foot-tall statue of Joan of Arc. The Flames' color was white, the symbol of purity. Above the altar, a chandelier encrusted with opals and moonstones held wax candles that gave off flickering, watery light.

There was no statue of Jean-Marc's patron, the Gray King, nor of anything blue, which was the color of the Devereaux family. Of the three altars she had seen, this was the first without Devereaux symbols. Were they being written off? Seen as no longer relevant by the House of the Flames?

Izzy stood a few feet back with Michel and D'Artagnon while Robert slid the box onto the stone surface of the altar. As he retreated, he stumbled badly.

Louise caught him, grunting, "Hang in, Bob." She said to Michel, "He's had direct contact with the fragments, sir."

"Then get him out of here," Michel said. "Check in with me later."

Izzy said to them, "Thank you for putting yourselves in harm's way for the good of the Family."

"*Merci, Guardienne,*" Robert answered softly.

The two headed for the door. Once it had shut behind them, D'Artagnon moved to a low wooden table at one of the points of the octagonal room. He picked up a cardboard box of Latex gloves identical to the ones Izzy wore on the job in the property room at the Two-Seven.

"*Madame et moi aussi,*" Michel told D'Artagnon, indicating the box.

D'Artagnon used his talons to rip open the box and began pulling out gloves, offering a wad to Michel. As Michel separated them into pairs and held one set out to Izzy, he added, "As you know, we suspect the Malchances are the real forces behind this attack. We do know they've been recruiting disaffected members of our own family."

She waited a beat. "To…?"

"To overthrow the rightful bloodline," he replied, as if it should be obvious. He waggled the gloves at her. "You."

She took the gloves and inserted her fingers into the left one as Michel did the same. Then Michel crossed to the right, standing before the wall, and moved one hand in a circle. A door appeared and opened. Inside, several white robes, shimmering with appliqués of flames, hung from a wooden rod on wooden hangers. They looked similar, but not identical, to D'Artagnon's. Michel snapped his fingers, and two of the robes detached from the rod, floating toward him on their hangers.

He snapped his fingers a second time, and the door, the rod and the hangers disappeared.

The robes magically settled on his and Izzy's bodies. The robe weighed several pounds, and she wondered if it was actually some kind of body armor.

"If you please," Michel said, reaching backward and pulling a hood over his hair.

Izzy did the same. She smelled lavender, and she was very warm.

Michel said to the gremlin, "Let's begin."

Raising their hands like scrubbed-in surgeons, he and D'Artagnon faced the altar. They took deep breaths, centering themselves; Izzy did the same, trying to let go of all the chatter in her brain—her anxiety, her fear. The smell of candle wax overlaid something more odious; she caught a whiff of a terrible stench and figured it was coming from the box. It did nothing to make her feel better.

D'Artagnon said something in French. Michel replied, then translated, "He's worried about your being here. I told him you insisted."

She looked from him to D'Artagnon, whose face was still hidden. He creeped her out. All of this creeped her out. "I'm staying," she said to him.

D'Artagnon inclined his robed head. "*S'il vous plait, Madame la Guardienne.*"

"*D'accord.* Then do as we do, please," Michel said. "Do not depart from our ritual."

He and the gremlin extended their arms and began another chant. Izzy copied them, spreading her arms wide and trying to follow the singsong words, which they repeated in a complex pattern.

The chant seemed to go on endlessly, the stench to increase. A thin layer of something white appeared along the floor.

Michel said, "Don't be alarmed. It's for protection."

It was a mist. It curled around her ankles, cool as whipped cream, smelling of lavender. It billowed up to her knees and grazed her hips, then it rushed all the way up to her chest. As it rose to the level of her chin, she backed out of it, although Michel and D'Artagnon remained inside, breathing deeply.

"It's all right," Michel said. "Come back in, please."

She knew Michel would probably be happy if she bailed. But she stepped back into the fog, closing her eyes, and took an exploratory breath.

Despite the coolness of the vapor, it felt warm as it entered her body; it was soothing, like deep-heat rub on a sore joint. She exhaled and took another breath. The gentle lavender scent filled her nose. With a pang, she thought of the mingled fragrance of roses and oranges that had often accompanied Jean-Marc's soothing spells. Would she ever smell it again?

Michel snapped his fingers, and she started, opening her eyes.

The mist thinned and drifted back toward the floor, condensing into puddles. The atmosphere grew darker, the room, cooler. The shadows themselves seemed braced for whatever came next.

Michael and the gremlin clapped their hands three times, bowed low and knelt on both knees on dry sections of the floor. Izzy's stomach constricted as she knelt, too, and a cold chill washed over her. She trembled, hard.

"You're sure you want to do this," Michel said. "Once we begin, we can't stop."

"Yes." Her voice broke. "I'm sure."

"*Et voilà*," Michel said.

She and Michel began to glow again. On the altar, the lid of the white container popped open like a jack-in-the-box. From the interior, a curl of bruise-colored smoke drifted toward the ceiling. Another followed, roiling, billowing and folding in on itself.

"This is concentrated evil," Michel informed her. "Please keep your distance until we take care of it."

"Not a problem," she muttered.

Enveloped in white light, he got to his feet and pulled an object from inside his robe. It was a golden athame encrusted with opals. Holding it like a switchblade, he cautiously approached the altar, as if the smoke were a wild animal that could spring at any time.

D'Artagnon also pulled an athame from his robe, his made of some sort of ebony material and free of decoration. Whispering another chant, the two arced their arms over their heads—Izzy saw D'Artagnon's long, scaly arm—then whipped them downward and began slicing at the smoke. Wherever their knives connected, the smoke solidified into chunks, which then crashed to the floor. The chunks glowed like embers, then sputtered out.

After a few minutes, no more smoke poured out of the box. The floor was littered with purplish-black briquettes that reeked of decomposition, overpowering the lavender scent.

Panting, both Michel and D'Artagnon lowered their arms to their sides. Michel said to Izzy, "Please come to the altar, but don't touch any of that. It's still very powerful stuff."

I'm glad I put my shoes back on, she thought as she cautiously tiptoed on the balls of her feet to his side.

Michel and D'Artagnon genuflected to the altar. She had seen Jean-Marc do the same at any magical altar he encountered. For the first time since her journey into the world of the Gifted had begun, Izzy did, too.

God forgive me, she prayed, feeling blasphemous.

Holding their athames overhead like flashlights, Michel and D'Artagnon approached the box. After a moment's hesitation, Izzy approached, as well. She didn't have the athame Jean-Marc had made for her, and she had no idea where it was.

Weaponless, she looked inside.

The container was filled with a black, throbbing mass of goolike substance that stank like rotten meat. She covered her mouth and her eyes watered.

This is what's left of Julius Esposito? Had he even been human?

As she watched, the center section of the jelly moved, breaking apart, and in the indentation, a round, human-size eye with a deep-brown iris glared up at her. Her gorge rose and she fought hard not to scream. In that single eye she could see life…and evil.

"Stop looking at it, madame," Michel ordered her.

Sickened, she turned away.

"More than *bokor,*" Michel commented, with the air of a

scientist examining a microscope slide. "What was he messing with?"

The temperature in the room dipped; it was like a meat locker. Izzy shivered, hard. Every instinct for self-preservation was telling her to get the hell out of there. Michel had warned her that this would be unpleasant, but it was horrible. She could barely tolerate the sensation of menace crawling over her.

Then a voice bounced off the stone walls: *"Give me back my soul."* It was a low, terrified howl, and it shook Izzy to her core.

Michel grunted, still peering inside the box. "Malchance magic, I'm sure of it," he murmured. "They're good at soul stealing."

D'Artagnon said, *"Oui."*

"Julius Esposito," Michel said into the box, "I call on you. Who captured your soul?"

"Give me back my soul."

"Tell us who has it, and we'll retrieve it for you," Michel soothed. "We can do that. We're Gifted. We'll help you." Beneath the warmth of his promises, there was an unmistakable edge. He was lying. Izzy wondered if Esposito knew it, too.

"My soul!"

Or perhaps Esposito was beyond caring. He was in agony. She had never heard such terrible despair in her life, and that included her father's pleas to God Himself to bring his beloved wife, Anna Maria, back from the dead.

D'Artagnon murmured something to Michel, who nodded in reply. D'Artagnon extended his athame into the box.

"Stay well back," Michel ordered Izzy.

There was a terrible shriek. The white candle on the altar flickered. The statue of Jehanne shifted.

New mist billowed from the floor, very white, very concentrated, so redolent of lavender that Izzy's eyes watered.
Neither Michel nor D'Artagnon paid it any attention. But the
smell was choking her, making her cough and gag. The mist
hung like a curtain between her and the altar.

A second, more horrible shriek followed.

The candles in the candelabra went out. A cold wind
whistled around the room.

"What are you doing?" Izzy demanded, stumbling
forward. She craned her neck—

A burst of brilliance filled her field of vision.

"Don't look!" Michel cried.

But it was too late.

Where is your gun, Guardienne? *He will take the gun and
he will end the House of the Flames. You have to secure your
gun. You have to do it now.*

*Izzy was running in the nightmare forest, dodging
branches that grabbed at her as the wolves howled in a
ring around her, their hot breath bathing the blood-red
moon. The silver wolf at her side darted ahead, diving into
the cattails at the murky bayou shoreline. Its tail bobbed
like a periscope as the wolf searched frantically, howling
and chuffing.*

*Baying, the other wolves charged in after the silver one,
disappearing into the cattails. Water splashed as they all
jumped in, and Izzy called out, "No! This way!"*

*The bayou was crawling with death. It was all around
them. They had to get out.*

"This way!" she yelled again.

*Sharp rocks sliced her feet as she ran to a trio of cypress trees
jutting from the water. She heard herself sobbing for breath.*

The moon raced across the sky as if hunted like her. Death was coming like a whirlwind.

Pressing her fists against her abdomen as she sucked in air, she glanced up. Her lips parted in terror. Something hung from the center tree...a man...

She saw his shoes, and then his legs...

It was Jean-Marc, gutted, hanging from the tree, his face blackened, worms crawling from his empty eye sockets.

"It didn't happen!" she shouted. "You showed me this before and—"

And he's lying in surgery with his chest cracked open, a voice whispered to her. *He's dying, and he will rot, just like this. And it will be your fault.*

Get your gun.

Chapter 4

I have to get my gun. I have to stop it.

Thrashing, Izzy sat bolt upright. A damp cloth tumbled from her forehead onto her lap, which was swathed in white satin sheets. Beneath the bedclothes, she was wearing an ivory satin nightgown. The rose quartz necklace, the ring and her crucifix still hung around her neck. Andre's gris-gris was missing.

"Shh, *Guardienne*, it's all right. You're safe," a woman's voice murmured. Annette, her mother's nurse, leaned over her.

"What happened?" she said thickly, as she tried to pick up the cloth. Two veiled women were holding her hands. "Where am I?"

"You're in your bedroom in the mansion." Annette took the cloth from Izzy and placed it on a silver tray on a dark wood nightstand beside the bed. She saw gray stone walls, heavy dark furniture and a massive fireplace similar to the one in the safehouse back in New York. In fact, the room was very like the one Jean-Marc had prepared for her in New York. Perhaps it was to make her more comfortable. The truth was, she found both rooms horribly oppressive.

"Reading the *bokor's* corpse was too much for you. It made you very ill. We rushed you in here and took care of you. The doctor left only a few minutes ago to check on the regent and your mother."

She remembered the agents, the box, the gremlin and the eye. And Esposito pleading for his soul. Everything past that was fuzzy.

Annette gestured to the dozen or so veiled women standing around the bed, holding each other's hands. One of them was curled up beside Izzy on the bed.

"The Femmes Blanches linked up with you and shared their magical essence with you. The doctor gave you oxygen and ran some tests. Your electrolytes were severely imbalanced. That's been corrected."

"Thank you," she said, and then, "What did we find out from the reading?"

A figure moved from the darkness and approached the end of Izzy's bed. It was Louise. She said, "I'd like to clear the room before we discuss that."

The Femmes Blanches moved and shifted. Izzy nodded at Annette, who seemed to be in charge. The woman holding her right hand released her. The veiled woman who was seated beside Izzy gave her left hand a squeeze and slid off the bed, joining her sisters as they walked toward the door.

"Please, if you weren't on duty in my mother's chamber, go home," Izzy told them.

The Femmes Blanches had made a vocation of keeping vigil over Izzy's mother. They worked in shifts, took vacations, and some of them even had jobs. They didn't live in the mansion. Some had homes in the garden district, and a few occupied funky bungalows and elegant apartments in the French quarter itself.

Once the women had filed out of the room, Louise said to Annette, "You, too, ma'am."

Annette shifted, unsure.

"It's all right," Izzy told her, although she was equally unsure.

As soon as Annette had closed the door behind herself, Louise said, "First, I want you to know that this is the most heavily warded space in all of Bouvard territory. Nothing gets out, nothing comes in. That's the only reason I'm going to speak so freely."

"Okay," Izzy said.

"Esposito gave up Alain de Devereaux's location. Devereaux is being held in an abandoned convent on Rue de Gasconnes. Michel took Madame Sange and a sizable security team to extract him."

"Michel…*left?*" Izzy asked, her eyes widening. Abandoned her, her mother and Jean-Marc after a direct assault?

Louise's expression was shuttered. Izzy couldn't read her tone of voice, either, as she said, "It was a hard decision, madame. Michel wanted to survey the situation firsthand. If we can prove that the Malchances engineered the attack and the kidnapping, the Grand Covenate will have no choice but to punish them."

Izzy didn't know what to make of that. She had been going on the assumption that most members of the Bouvard family distrusted the Grand Covenate, the governing body of all the Gifted families, clans and tribes. She knew that the last time the Grand Covenate had intervened, Jean-Marc, who was a member of the House of the Shadows, was selected to act as the regent of the House of the Flames. The choice of an outsider from a different family caused a great deal of resentment. The fact that Michel hadn't contacted the Grand Covenate immediately after the attack bolstered her opinion that he would prefer not to deal with them at all.

She asked, "How many people know what happened to me? That I've been unconscious?"

"Very few. Michel ordered strict need-to-know," Louise informed her. She added, before Izzy could ask, "Your mother's condition is unchanged. The regent is out of surgery and the doctor is cautiously optimistic."

Izzy reeled with relief. Oh, thank you, Patroness. *Oh, my dear God, thank you.*

"Is the regent conscious?" Izzy asked. She needed to see him, to touch him, to be sure that it was true. She needed to hear his voice. See those dark eyes flecked with gold.

"No, and we're keeping that under wraps as well," Louise told her. "We've got our best guarding him and your mother both." She lifted her chin. "I've been assigned to you."

"Good," Izzy said. "Thank you." She spied the nightstand beside the bed and, on impulse, slid open the top drawer. Her gris-gris lay coiled inside. Pleased, she draped it over her shoulders. She could feel its enfolding warmth. She decided to take it to Jean-Marc.

Izzy glanced at a large ebony clock on the mantel. It was exactly twelve.

She pointed to the clock. "Is that noon or midnight?"

"Midnight," Louise told her.

Izzy was shocked. She'd been out for an entire day.

She rubbed her forehead as pain blossomed behind her eyes. Then a sudden, sharp image hit her—cattails and cypress trees, the bayou—she saw it all. Remembered it all.

"Madame?" Louise said, instantly on alert.

The pain intensified. Izzy rasped out, "Alain de Devereaux isn't in a building. He's in the bayou. You need to let Michel know. He's searching in the wrong place."

Louise scrutinized Izzy, cocking her head. "Meaning no disrespect, madame, but D'Artagnon assisted with the reading. He's the best we have."

"Have him recheck," Izzy said.

Louise shook her head. "The remains were destroyed during the first reading."

"I *know* he's not there," Izzy insisted. "You have to contact Michel immediately."

Louise shook her head. "His team is on silent running. So are the other search parties. They're so heavily warded we can't even contact them telepathically."

"Then you have to go to Michel," Izzy said. She rethought. That would waste time. "I need to accompany a team into the bayou. I'm the one who can lead them to him."

Louise demurred. "Please, don't even think of that. Michel gave strict orders that you were to rest."

"Michel's not here. He doesn't know what I know. No one does." Izzy threw her legs over the side of the bed and got to her feet.

Izzy said, "I'm in command here. We need to rescue Alain de Devereaux *now*."

Izzy could practically see the wheels turning in the agent's brain. She raised her hand to brush errant tendrils of hair from her forehead, feeling more warmth against her skin as her headache lessened. Her palm was glowing; white heat pulsated in the center of her flame-shaped scar. On impulse, she showed it to Louise.

"Remember, I carry the sign of the House of the Flames," she said. She touched the ring. "And Michel himself handed over the ring. I need to make my orders stick, or there's no point."

Louise appeared to be thinking this over. Ice-water fingers crept down Izzy's backbone as she wondered if she and Louise were facing off. If she was about to find out what her true status was after all.

Louise made her decision, squaring her shoulders and setting her jaw, saying stiffly, "As you wish, *ma Guardienne*. I'll go with you."

I am not the guardienne yet, Izzy wanted to say. But this most definitely was not the time to remind the agent of that.

She said, "Good. First I'll go see Jean—"

Go now, said the voice. *Or it will be too late*.

She paused. Every part of her wanted to check on Jean-Marc first. But she knew she had to listen to the voice.

"What, madame?" Louise asked.

"Never mind. Where's my gun?"

Louise hesitated, then reached inside her jacket and lifted Izzy's Medusa out of her own holster.

"I took possession when you lost consciousness," she said. "You have five .9 mm cartridges left. I'll get you some more ammo."

"Thank you," Izzy said. "Now, we need a plan to rescue Alain without causing more havoc here in the mansion."

"*D'accord*," Louise said. "Let's work one out."

It was a good one, given the short notice. One thing about growing up in the NYPD was that you learned that operations were far messier and more ad hoc than they were characterized in TV and the movies. Improvisation and crossed fingers comprised about fifty percent of a cop's bag of tricks. So they had to leave a lot of holes that they would fill in as their mission got underway. It was the nature of the beast, and Izzy was good with that.

"Okay. Let's go with what we have," Izzy told her.

Louise half opened the door and peered out. "The Femmes Blanches are milling around out there."

Izzy walked to the door and opened it. Veiled faces turned in her direction. Annette, who had been sitting in an ivory brocade chair beside a white marble statue of Jehanne, rose to her feet.

"Thank you for seeing to me," Izzy told them. "I'm very grateful to you, and I'm all better now. Please resume your normal routine."

Annette frowned. "You *are* our normal routine."

"I'm fine," Izzy insisted. "And I need some time by myself. I'll have some guards. I insist," she added, pushing.

Annette acquiesced with a bob of her head. "*Oui, Guardienne.*" She turned to the Femmes Blanches, and Izzy left it to her to disperse them.

From behind her Louise said, "I'll make sure they leave."

"Good," Izzy said. "Meanwhile, I'll get dressed."

"*Oui, Guardienne.* The door will lock behind me. You'll be able to get out, but no one but I will be able to get back in."

With a bow Louise left, shutting the door, which clicked with finality. And Izzy wondered, not for the first time, if she had just become a prisoner.

Opening the armoire opposite the bed, she found all kinds of new clothes in her size. She pulled on black cargo pants and snaked a black turtleneck over her head. Jean-Marc, who had arranged for her wardrobe, had probably assumed she'd be wearing these clothes for training, not an actual mission.

Or had he? He had repeatedly warned her about the chaotic

state of the House of the Flames. He had told her that blood was running in the streets of the French quarter, compliments of Le Fils. What then, had he been training her *for,* if not to get in on the action?

She found black wool socks and slipped them on. As she stepped into a new pair of black leather hiking boots, she glanced again at the antique ebony clock on the fireplace mantel. It was almost 1:00 a.m.

Her busy brain ran through worst-case scenarios. If word got out that she had left the mansion, an assassin might take that as his—or her—cue to kill Jean-Marc and her mother both.

I may be the only thing standing between Jean-Marc, Marianne and their enemies. Maybe I should leave Alain de Devereaux to his fate, no matter how awful it might be.

But what could she do to keep them safe? Her presence was not a guaranteed deterrent against *any* kind of attack on her mother and the regent. She had to play to her strengths: she stood a better chance of protecting them if she had backup she could count on. Allies. Real ones, not just assigned ones, like Michel and Louise. Jean-Marc trusted his cousin. That made saving Alain a priority. And if she could find Andre while she was at it, so much the better.

There was a sharp rap on the door. Louise entered. She was still wearing her suit, and an overstuffed olive-green duffel bag was slung across her shoulders. Sauvage and Ruthven followed her into the room. They had both washed their faces. Izzy had never seen Sauvage without her makeup, and their relative youth and obvious fear gave Izzy pause. Maybe this was not such a good idea....

Sauvage ran over to Izzy, giving her a rib-cracking hug. "One of those chicks with the head scarves said you'd been hurt," she said, gazing up at Izzy with tears in her eyes.

"I'm okay," Izzy said, touched.

Ruthven was bug-eyed and frightened as he slid his hands under his arms and bowed awkwardly.

"Hola, Your Majesty," he said.

"Did Agent Bouvard explain what I want you to do?" Izzy asked Sauvage, dispensing with the formalities.

Sauvage nodded wildly. "Yes, *Guardienne, oui-oui.*" She reached out and grabbed Ruthven's wrist, yanking his hand loose and waggling it. "We're in, right, baby?"

Ruthven swallowed hard. "It won't hurt her, right?"

"Right," Louise replied, stepping forward, taking charge. She said to Sauvage, "You won't feel a thing."

There was another rap on the door. Louise paused, closed her eyes, then crossed and opened it. Another female agent in a black suit briskly stepped into the room. She also carried a duffel bag. She had flaming red hair, and her green eyes reminded Izzy of Pat's. Izzy felt a pang. Would she ever see him again?

"*Madame la Guardienne.*" She greeted Izzy with a curtsy. "My name is Mathilde. It's such an honor."

Mathilde dumped her duffel bag onto the floor, unzipped it and began pulling out black clothing similar to Izzy's. There were two sets of everything.

"I thought we should wait to change in here. I didn't want to rouse suspicion," Louise explained, as she and the redhead took off their suit jackets and began to unbutton their white shirts.

"Yow," Ruthven said, quickly turning his back.

The two agents quickly stripped down to sports bras and underwear. Their bodies were sinewy. At the base of her spine, Louise sported a tattoo identical to the scar on Izzy's palm—the flame icon of the House of the de Bouvards—and Izzy hoped it was a sign that Louise was genuinely on her side. It was going to be a real bitch if they got out into the field and these women turned on Izzy.

As Louise slipped on a pair of black cargo pants, Mathilde said to her, "I made successful contact with the others."

"Good." Louise slipped what looked to be a pair of brass knuckles into a cargo pocket. To Izzy she said, "We'll have two more inside, two outside. So we're six. Plus you, madame."

"That's it?" Izzy asked.

"We're all high-level magic users," Louise assured her. She was grabbing grenades, some piano wire and boxes of ammo to stuff into her pockets. "And there's safety in small numbers. We can travel fast, and hopefully stay under everybody's radar."

Izzy wondered who "everybody" was.

As Mathilde packed her own cargo pants with equipment, Louise reached into her duffel bag with one hand and gestured to Izzy's Medusa on the bed with the other. "I've got that ammo I mentioned."

Hearing that, Ruthven turned back around, as if eager to watch. He and Sauvage put their arms around each other, observing in silence as Louise pushed the flange on the left side of the cylinder, then eased the cylinder out of the frame.

"All you need right now is one more .9mm," Louise said, pressing a lipstick-shaped cartridge into the cylinder. That accomplished, she held it out to Izzy. "Remember, madame, there's no safety."

Mathilde, who was strapping on knee pads, stared at the Medusa and murmured, "Sweet," as Izzy picked it up. Fully loaded, it was much heavier than before. "May I hold it, madame?"

Izzy hesitated, then handed it to her.

Mathilde hefted the Medusa, whistling soundlessly. Her interest bordered on lust, and she exhaled deeply, like a spent lover, when she passed it over to Louise. Izzy kept a lid on her growing anxiety; these women were crack shots, and they were the only two in the room who were armed. She wanted the Medusa back. Now.

"Did Jean-Marc have this made for you?" Louise asked, tracing Izzy's portrait etched in the grip. Izzy was surprised that Louise didn't know that the gun was Marianne's. The picture of Izzy—or Marianne—had magically appeared during their training session in the Cloisters, back in New York.

Izzy picked up her gun belt and wrapped it around her waist, saying, "It's my gun."

She waited a beat. Louise stared back down at the Medusa and said, "If you don't know how to use it, maybe I should keep it. It's extremely powerful."

"I know how to use it," Izzy said steadily, even though that was pretty much a lie. But she wasn't giving up her weapon to anyone.

Louise sighed and handed it over. Then she gathered up her hair and pulled on a black knit cap like Izzy's. Mathilde did the same. They slipped on tight-fitting jackets. Louise handed one to Izzy. When she put it on, static electricity shocks went off like a trail of gunpowder.

Louise and Mathilde reached into their duffels and pulled out heavy-looking, webbed vests. Body armor. As Louise held one out, Mathilde stretched her arms through the armholes. Then she turned around and Louise fanned her fingers. There was a *snick* and Louise said, "You're bolted."

Mathilde did the same for her, down to the "bolting." Then Louise retrieved a third vest for Izzy.

"If you need to get the vest off in a hurry, say this word. I'll spell it for you," Louise said. "*T-e-r-m-i-n-u-s*. Do you speak Latin?"

"Not really," Izzy allowed. "I've heard a little. I'm Catholic," she added.

The two women stopped moving and stared at her. Mathilde paled, while Louise blinked rapidly, her lips parting in shock.

Now what? Izzy wondered. *They must have their own religion. Maybe I'm supposed to be their pope or something.*

The moment passed—or rather, the agents chose to ignore it. Izzy put on knee pads. They checked each other out, running through a verbal checklist as each of them touched their pockets and verified possession of things they described in jargon: *les sploders, wire, poprocks, choses, malfacteus.*

When they were finished, Louise crossed over to Sauvage and said, "It's showtime."

"Oh, my God, I'm so freaked out," Sauvage murmured to Ruthven. Then she kissed her young boyfriend hard on the lips and minced over to the bed in her heeled boots. She sat on the edge of the mattress. "Do I need to take off my clothes?"

"It doesn't matter either way," Louise said.

"Okay," Sauvage whispered as she lay down on the bed. Ruthven backed away. Mathilde and Louise made motions over Sauvage's body. White light poured from their hands and spread over Sauvage like a sheet, throbbing and pulsing all over her body. One moment Sauvage was Sauvage…and the next…

She didn't look exactly like Izzy. She had Izzy's black cloud of hair, her dark eyes and freckles, but she looked more like a close relative than Izzy herself. Still, if the lights were lowered, and she pretended to be asleep, she could probably pass.

Louise ticked her glance to Izzy. "It's not as sophisticated as a Devereaux glamour."

"No one does glamours as well as the Devs," Mathilde said, an envious half smile quirking her face as she bent down beside her duffle and gathered up a fistful of crucifixes.

"Let me see," Sauvage demanded, hopping out of the bed and trotting to the full-length mirror at the foot of the bed. She posed, frowned. "Hey. I don't look that much like you at all."

"Maybe we should go with a fabricant," Louise mused as she crossed her arms and followed Sauvage's gaze into the mirror. "We could probably get a closer match."

Fabricants were magically created beings. Le Fils had sent a fabricant assassin after Izzy in New York. It had seemed terribly real.

"I'd suggest we stick with the glamour," Mathilde said. "We'd have better control." She added, "A fabricant might degrade too fast. We don't know how long we'll be gone."

Then Louise closed her eyes, paused, glanced expectantly at the door and said, "Good. They're here. Mathilde, let them in."

Mathilde crossed to the door, opened it, and let two more women inside. They were also dressed in black suits and white blouses, wearing lapel pins and headsets. Both of them curt-seyed to Izzy, one reaching forward to kiss her bare ring finger.

"Catherine and Laure," Louise said, as the two rose and stood at parade rest. "Top agents. Crack shots, magically and otherwise. We're posting them here to stand guard over Sauvage and Ruthven. They'd rather die than let harm come to the woman lying in that bed."

Both women stared straight ahead, but color rose in their cheeks.

Louise looked at Izzy. "We should mobilize. We're push-ing our luck."

Izzy wanted to ask her if she really believed in luck.

Where did that fit in, exactly, with people who could use magic? Instead, she arranged her gris-gris over the shoulders of her body armor and patted the Medusa in her holster. The weight of the gun, once an unthinkable burden, was now her anchor.

Izzy turned back to Sauvage. "You're being very brave," she told her. "Jean-Marc will be proud of you when he hears how well you handled this." The temptation rose again to go downstairs and see him before they left. She quelled it.

Sauvage's eyes were huge as she raised herself up on her elbows. "Unless he dies," she said mournfully.

"God, Jesse," Ruthven chided her. "Don't say shit like that."

Louise motioned for the others to follow her as she crossed to the stone wall opposite the door. She snapped her fingers. A hand's breadth in front of her, a larger-than-life-size oil portrait of Marianne in her white gown shimmered into view. Her stance was regal, power radiating from every pore. A tiara of white flames glowed from the crown of her dark hair, and she held a clutch of lilies in one veined, muscular hand and an athame in the other. From beneath her gown, a white slipper was planted on top of a skull with glowing red eyes.

Louise looked from the portrait to Izzy and back again, as if measuring the resemblance. Then she pointed her finger and the entire portrait rose into the air, revealing the entrance to a tunnel hewn from the thick marble wall.

"I'll take point," Louise announced.

Mathilde said, "I'll bring up the rear. Stay in the middle, *Guardienne.*"

Izzy looked one last time over her shoulder at Ruthven and Sauvage, huddled together on the bed, gaping at them.

"Be careful," she said. They nodded in silent unison.

Izzy wondered if she would ever see them again.

Chapter 5

Izzy and the two Bouvard agents stepped into the tunnel. A white mist swirled around her ankles and more cascaded from above, tumbling featherlight on her head and shoulders.

Izzy stiffened. Louise said, "It's for protection, *Gardienne*. It won't hurt you."

"I'm okay," Izzy gritted.

As they rose off the ground a lavender scent wafted through the thickening vapor. The fog became so thick she couldn't see her hand before her face. But she did see a white glow below her chin: it was the ring.

They glided forward, or so it seemed. Izzy had no sense of direction.

After a time she said, "What will happen to Esposito's soul?"

"I'm not privy to that," Louise said flatly.

"His body was destroyed," Izzy pressed.

"His remains aren't necessary for the return of his soul. That's only the case when the person whose soul is stolen is still alive," Louise said. It was clear she didn't want to discuss it.

"Alive…" Izzy couldn't even begin to follow that.

"D'Artagnon debriefed Bob and me on the reading," Louise elaborated. "Esposito's soul was taken at the time of death. He probably had a prior arrangement with the Forces of Darkness."

"He…sold his soul to the *Devil?*" Izzy blurted.

"That's one way of putting it, madame. Although so far as we can tell, there is no Devil, per se. The Dark Side is far more loosely structured than the Grand Covenate. They don't even have a governing body, and they don't work together toward any common purpose. They jostle for power among themselves far more than we do."

"But there is a Dark Side," Izzy managed to say. It hadn't even dawned on her to wonder about it; she'd been having enough trouble wrapping her head around the world of the Gifted. "So do they have Houses or…"

"It's a bit more complicated than that," Louise said. "Although a number of us believe the Malchances are in bed with them."

The Malchances again. Who were these people?

"They're the House of the Blood," Izzy said.

"Right. One of the original three, with us and the Devereaux," Louise put in. "We are the House of the Flames. The Devereaux are the House of the Shadows. We were all founded in the 1400s."

"When Joan of Arc tried to unify France," Izzy finished. "And passed her power on to us before she was martyred."

"'Martyred,'" Louise repeated, sounding a bit derisive. "We prefer to say that she was murdered. There is no Catholic connection for us."

"Souls contain mystical energy," Mathilde put in, as if to smooth over the awkward moment. "Absorbing the soul of another can prolong life, enhance Gifts…" She trailed off. "*We* don't do that."

"We Bouvards," Izzy said. The implication being that other Gifted Houses did.

There was the merest hesitation before Louise replied, "*Oui*. We Bouvards."

Louise's hesitation hung in the air. Was it an unconscious admission that she didn't consider Izzy a Bouvard? If that were the case, was this "rescue mission" actually a coup? Was she being hustled offstage to be gotten rid of?

She remembered her NYPD dream, when Esposito had forced her to follow him by taking Sauvage hostage. Was this a mirror of that? Was she being lured out of the mansion supposedly to save Alain…when it was really to take her down?

I'm not liking this, Izzy thought.

As quietly as she could, she eased her Medusa out of its holster and wrapped her right hand around the grip. She felt along the barrel with the fingertips of her left.

They traveled on in silence. Izzy's pulse raced in her neck, her temple. She kept the Medusa close.

A light rose around them, and the mist thinned. The curved interior of the tunnel was covered with symbols. There were reflective triangles, ankhs, crosses and eyes set in the center of hands. Numerals gleamed in white stonework: seven, thirteen, thirty-three, five. In an alcove, a brass brazier burned before a life-size statue of Joan of Arc holding a banner and a sword. Pungent incense permeated the air.

Izzy glanced backward. The entire length of the tunnel was covered with magical charms. It reminded her of the interior of Andre's werewolf van, back in New York.

"All these things are for protection," Mathilde told her. "Most of these charms are centuries old."

Louise raised a hand and said, "We need to perform a ritual before we go any farther."

"It's also for protection," Mathilde said.

The three sank to the tunnel floor in the rapidly evaporating mist.

Mathilde and Louise breathed deeply in, deeply out. Then the two women swayed left, right, leading with their shoulders, exaggerating the movement until they twirled in slow circles, chanting in a lilting, singsong language.

Without any sort of advance warning, all three were outside the tunnel, on the mansion's grounds, shrouded in darkness at the base of a high brick wall. Cool night air tightened Izzy's face.

Louise snapped her fingers, and the wall disappeared. In its place, two black-masked men faced Izzy, Louise and Mathilde, with Uzis drawn and aimed. Solid oaks rose behind them like another wall; above, a bone-white moon stood sentry. Izzy raised her Medusa and pointed it at the taller of the two men.

"Lower your weapons," Louise said. As both men obeyed, she said, "Masks?"

"We're on recon," the taller man replied.

"Take them off," she snapped.

The men yanked the masks off over their heads. They were both dark-eyed and dark-haired, young and in fighting trim.

"Hugues, Bernard," Louise said, addressing each in turn. "Any surprises so far?"

"Got out without incident, patrolled, nothing," the taller one said. Apparently he was Bernard. He looked at Izzy. "Is, this, ah…"

Izzy's Medusa was still aimed at his chest. She said in French, "*Je suis Isabelle de Bouvard, Maison des Flammes.*"

"So it's true," Bernard said, his features softening. "*La fille de la guardienne.*"

Both men sank to one knee.

Izzy considered her next move. Louise had hand picked the security agents surrounding Izzy at this very moment, and Izzy had no idea where their loyalties lay. She concentrated on her gut, trying to feel her way.

Jehanne, guide-moi, je vous en prie.

Go, the wind whispered. *Allez. Vite. Hurry.*

"*Allez vite,*" Izzy commanded them.

They skirted the perimeter of the Bouvard estate. The mansion, magically repaired from the attack, lay beneath a gauzy dome of white beneath the ivory moon. Figures holding Uzis patrolled each of the floors and the roof.

There were more security forces stationed along the wall, within and without, and Louise motioned for the party of five to keep well away as they melted into the bayou just beyond the grounds. It seemed so strange to be hiding from her own bodyguards, but in truth, Izzy had no idea how many of them were "hers."

The moon watched, an enormous eye in the sky, while Izzy and the others picked up the pace and laid tracks between themselves and the compound. As they penetrated the murky rot of the swamp, Izzy was on high alert. She was inside her nightmare; she recognized the landscape—the uneven paths, the skeletal trees—and she was terrified. Her fright-or-flight response was engaged full force.

For ten years I dreamed about this place. Ten long years. And now I'm here.

Bernard was on point, then Louise, then her. Directly behind Izzy was Mathilde, and in the rear, Hugues.

She listened for the Cajun werewolf pack—surely one of them had let loose with the howl she had heard in her mind. She wondered if they were trying to contact her; she hoped so. She realized then that of everyone around her, Andre was the local she trusted most—even more than she trusted Jean-Marc. Andre's agenda was far simpler: he was loyal to Jean-Marc because the regent looked out for the wolf pack, and Jean-Marc had asked Andre to protect Izzy. So he had.

Andre, are you out here? Are you hurt? Tell me where you are, she sent out. *If your people have found you, tell them to let me know.*

The tall marsh grass rustled. Bernard swiveled his weapon. She wondered why they didn't have some kind of night vision goggles to see better in the dappled, thready moonlight. Maybe they naturally possessed better night vision than ordinary human beings, and didn't realize she was having trouble.

I'm not an ordinary human being. I'm a Gifted, too.

But maybe she wasn't a full-blooded Gifted. No one knew who her father was—or at least, that was the party line. Maybe he was just an ordinary person. Or a werewolf. Maybe Andre was her father.

Not old enough. At least, he doesn't look old enough. Jean-Marc said he was older than he looked.

Something fluttered overhead—she hoped it was a bird— and she ducked beneath a ropy vine looped around an overhanging branch. She slipped on slimy mud and shot a hand toward the branch to steady herself.

The vine hissed and sprang at her. She saw nothing but fangs. Snake! Without thinking, she hurled a ball of white light from her palm. It ignited the snake. Encased in fire, it writhed and sizzled, coiling and springing in its death throes, then was still. Smoke and steam rose from the carcass.

Mathilde leaned over her and said, "By the *patronesse,* madame! That was a cottonmouth. Are you all right?" She examined Izzy's hands. She paused, gazing at the flame-shaped brand in the center of Izzy's palm, then added, "Did it bite you?"

"No. I'm fine," Izzy grunted. She planted her boot in the mud and heaved herself up.

"You need to keep alert to your surroundings, madame," Bernard said. "Not meaning any offense. But the bayou is a very dangerous place."

"That's what *we're* supposed to do," Louise snapped. "Let's keep moving." She looked at Izzy. "Which way, madame?"

No clue, Izzy wanted to reply, but that was probably not very wise. She took a moment, waiting for more mystical guidance. A vision had sent her here. Maybe she would have another one and obtain more details.

Just as she was about to give up, something whispered against her left ear, and she turned her head. The others must have read her body language; they stood statue still, as if to let her get a bead on it.

"To the left," she said, pointing toward a thick copse of trees.

"It figures," Bernard drawled, with a lopsided grin. "Swamp's deep there. Lots of gators."

He walked through the dense foliage, pushing aside cattails and rushes. Hugues followed him. Once they stood side by side, they raised arms and murmured an incantation. There was a wild thrashing, like a fierce struggle in the water. After a few moments stillness descended.

"That's gonna cost," Louise muttered. She looked at Izzy and said, "The gators that didn't make it out will probably drown."

Izzy was appalled. "You mean they'll die?" She headed over to the two men. "Stop," she said. "Take it back."

Bernard shook his head. "Please don't ask me to do that. I've already paid. In fact…" He reached over and hoisted her up into his arms, settling her against his chest. "With your permission, madame."

"What?" she cried.

"I'll carry you," he said, shifting her weight in his arms. "There are other things in the water. The gators are just the worst."

"No. Put me down," she said, mortified.

"Carry her," Louise told him

Izzy fumed as the party resumed their trek through the waist-high cattails, then started down a slope. Black water sparkled in the moonlight beneath heavy vines and strange, knobby pieces of wood jutting around the cypress trees.

Louise bent down, picked up a stone and tossed it into the water. The brackish water was shallow there, and Louise said, "Let's go in."

Following behind Louise, Bernard sloshed in. Mathilde was behind her, then Hugues. The water stank. Izzy tried to hold her boots above the surface.

They crossed to a jutting finger of land. Bernard set Izzy down. The ground was soggy, sucking at her feet.

They found a rhythm as they crossed the slippery terrain, Izzy slowing until they hit a patch of drier ground with more traction. The swamp, scene of so many terrible dreams, was a place of unearthly beauty.

"Attack!" Bernard shouted.

Someone tackled Izzy and flung her to the ground. Her nose made a terrible crunching noise as pain shot from the front of her face to the back of her head. She gagged on dirt, fighting for breath as something slammed hard across the back of her head.

She started to pass out until she felt sticklike fingers groping around her waist.

My Medusa!

She drew deep inside herself for reserves, then tossed her head back hard, connecting with the face of her attacker. Something long and sharp dug into her skull. It felt like a knife, or an ice pick, and the pain took the last of her breath away. She began to go fuzzy. She fumbled for the gun, trying to work her spasming muscles to put her hand around it, draw it out and aim it backward.

A tremendous shower of sparks blinded her; a blaze of heat mushroomed against her back. Then a weight fell against her, pushing her onto a mound of mud and rot.

Pinned, she couldn't move her head, but she could open her eyes. The bayou night was as bright as day, as the four Bouvard security agents took out the white-faced, hollow-eyed creatures that were dropping from the trees. They were vampire minions, flying creatures that were all blood-red eyes, fangs and wings, like the ones that had attacked Jean-Marc and her back in New York. Fireballs slammed into them, then submachine gunfire strafed a row of five or six as they bulleted toward Izzy.

"Move, move, move!" Hugues shouted at her as the dead-weight flopped to one side. Izzy crawled forward, but it was all she could do. She couldn't breathe. The world was spinning.

She laid her cheek in the mud and gazed into the evil, red eyes of the thing that had attacked her. It was a minion; its features were ratlike, the color of gristle. As it pulled back its grayish white lips, she saw that one of its fangs had broken off at the gumline. Then she realized that it was imbedded in the back of her head.

Oh, my God, she thought, as its eyes bored into hers. Its mouth clacked.

It lisped, in a low, seductive voice meant only for her ears, "Isabella DeMarco. This is the voice of Le Fils, speaking through my servant. I send you this message—they're playing you. This is not your battle. These are not your people. Go home. I will protect you in New York. I swear it."

Then someone covered her eyes and threw his body across hers as the minion exploded into purple-black light, just like Julius Esposito.

It was Bernard, his face grim as he eased Izzy onto her back. Explosions went off all around them, bathing Bernard in white light. Velcro ripped as he opened various pockets in her cargo pants. He had what looked like a canteen and several glass vials. He broke open the vials and poured the contents into the canteen. He shook it hard, murmuring an incantation, and scooted Izzy up onto her knees, sliding a supporting hand beneath the back of her head and lifting the canteen to her lips.

Izzy couldn't drink. Her throat was filled with dirt. She was suffocating. And her nose...oh, God, her nose...the pain...

Bernard set the canteen down and dug a finger into Izzy's mouth. He pulled out a hunk of dirt. Then he hoisted Izzy up and got behind her, executing a Heimlich with practiced skill.

She hacked up another clot of mud. As she coughed, Bernard bent her forward and pounded on her back, murmuring a spell, easing the raw burning in her throat.

Then he pressed the canteen to her lips and said, "Drink this. It's a healing potion."

A liqueur spread warmth through her veins. Her eyes rolled to the back of her head and she began to lose consciousness. The brandy's warmth kept spreading.

The pain lessened. She tried to raise her hand to her face but Bernard said, "No. Stay still."

He pushed Izzy's mass of hair out of the way of the back of her head and jerked on something, which came free. He showed it to Izzy as Izzy finished off the canteen. It was the vampire's fang.

Oh, my God, I had a vampire tooth imbedded in my head.

There was noise all around them, explosions and gunfire. The shrieking minions.

"Bernard!" Louise barked.

Bernard held out his hand to Izzy. Izzy rose up out of the muck. Suddenly, she felt good. She felt strong. She raced into the melee—a kaleidoscope of fireballs, minions and Bouvards—and dove for the nearest attacker. She leaped onto its back, gripped its jaw with both hands and yanked hard to the side.

Its neck was broken and its head flopped forward. It staggered, flailing at her.

Clenching her jaw against her terror, she put the Medusa to the minion's head and pulled the trigger.

Nothing happened.

She pulled it again as the minion reached its arms back, preparing to grab her.

Still nothing.

Great.

Chapter 6

As the minion reached behind itself and sank its talons into Izzy's sides, Hugues shouted, "I've got it! Get away!"

Izzy grabbed the Medusa with both fists and pounded on the monster's left wrist, then on the top of its head. She kicked and flailed and somehow got it to let go of her. She tumbled off its back, landing hard. As she scooted away, she covered her head.

A gun went off.

There was a moment's delay, and then the minion exploded.

Eyes against her knees, she clasped her hands across the back of her neck in a protective gesture. Smoking fragments thudded to the ground around her head and shoulders. Izzy clutched her malfunctioning gun and breathed hard through her mouth, working to get herself back under control and into the action.

But there was no more shrieking, no more gunfire or explosions. As she sat up, she saw bodies on the ground and fronds and ferns undulating as something raced off. None of the bodies were her people.

Thin moonlight poured down like a weak searchlight.

We're alive. We've all made it.

What the hell is wrong with my gun?

She pulled down the flange on the left side of the barrel and pushed the cylinder open. The cartridges were in the chambers. The mechanism to deliver them must be faulty. Or Louise had done something to it.

"*Guardienne?*" Bernard shouted. He dashed toward her. "*Tu vas bien?*"

"I'm…" she replied, but her voice died away as her focus went past the Medusa to a dark shape slithering next to her right boot.

Another cottonmouth!

"Snake!" she shouted.

"Where? Where?" Bernard yelled, aiming his gun at her feet.

She got to her feet and danced backward. The shape broadened and expanded, filling out into the hazy shadow of a man. It looked like the chalk outline of a murder victim. Then it lifted from the ground and rose into the air like a kite. It hung in the air about two feet from Izzy, assuming a three-dimensional form, devoid of facial detail.

"*Guardienne,*" it rasped. Its voice was a whisper that echoed in her head, in her chest, in her bones.

"Where's the snake?" Bernard asked her.

He and the others and were searching the ground with their weapons pointed down. No one else saw the shadowy figure or heard its voice. Was she having another vision?

"It must have gotten away," Louise observed. "We have to get out of here. They probably weren't alone."

"*Guardienne,*" the voice said again, flat, hollow and almost dead-sounding. "*Vous voyez avant vous le vassal du Roi Gris.*"

Roi Gris. The Gray King. The patron of the Devereauxes. Was this the Gray King? Should she kneel?

"*Je cherche Alain de Devereaux,*" she said aloud, before she even realized what she was doing. *I am looking for Alain de Devereaux.*

"*Moi, aussi,*" the figure said. *Me, also.*

"Madame, what are you seeing?" Louise demanded, her arms extended as she whirled in a circle. Mathilde ripped open one of her cargo pockets, and the two men fanned the perimeter with their machine guns.

"Do you know where he is?" Izzy asked the figure. Her French deserted her, as it usually did after a few spoken words.

The figure rose higher into the air, thinning and streaming like a column of smoke, difficult to see against the black night. Ignoring the questions of the others, Izzy shielded her forehead and squinted hard, straining to separate the figure from the background of trees and darkness.

Her head was throbbing, her chest and throat ached, but she shouted after it, "Where is he?"

"What are you seeing?" Louise yelled at her, circling again. The two men followed her lead, flanking Izzy, placing her inside a circle as they scanned the black bayou with the barrels of their weapons.

The figure became nothing more substantial than a wisp of smoke that arced over the trees and trailed downward.

"What is it?" Louise insisted. "Ms. DeMarco, tell us what is there!"

The two men swiveled in Louise's direction.

Ms. DeMarco? Not *Ma Guardienne?*

In a split-second instant of clarity, Izzy realized that Louise had lied to her: "*Nothing gets in, nothing gets out.*"

Louise had told Izzy that her bedroom was so heavily warded that they didn't need to worry about it being bugged. That Michel was equally warded such that he couldn't be contacted telepathically. Yet, when Catherine and Laure had arrived, she had sensed their presence before they had a chance to knock.

A guilty shadow crossed over Louise's face. Then she said, "Let's hustle!"

"My gun jammed," Izzy said. "You loaded it and it didn't work anymore."

"Give it to me. It should work." Under the guise of reaching for the gun, Louise aimed her palm at Izzy. A burst of light erupted from the center of Louise's hand, shooting straight for her.

"*Non, madame!*" Bernard shouted, rushing Izzy and flinging her to the ground. Crouched in front of her, he formed a palm strike with his left hand. Blue light coalesced into a fireball and slammed into Louise. Louise was thrown backward, her body hurtling through space until she smacked into a cypress tree. Izzy heard the impact. Then she landed on the sharp, jutting sections of cypress root encircling the tree, and fell sideways into the swamp water.

Meanwhile, Mathilde took off at a dead heat. After she'd put in some distance, she wheeled around, reached into her cargo pants, and flung something cylindrical at Bernard.

"Look out!" Izzy yelled, attempting to intercept it with another sphere of energy. But nothing came from her palm.

"Stay down!" Bernard ordered Izzy, as he shot a ball of blue light at the object and it exploded in midair.

Hugues tackled Mathilde, pushing her facedown on the

ground. "Don't move!" he yelled, as Bernard got to his feet and trained his submachine gun on her.

Hugues straddled Mathilde. He wrenched her gun out of her right hand and threw it hard. Then he began patting her down, slapping his hands down her sides and back.

"What else do you have? What do you have?" he shouted at her. "Give it up! Give it all up now or I'll blow your fucking head off!"

"Who are you working for?" The barrel of Bernard's submachine gun jammed against the back of her head. "Talk! *Now!*"

Mathilde didn't move. He nudged her with the barrel. She remained motionless.

Bernard threw down his weapon and yelled, "*Merde!* She's done something. Suicide spell."

"CPR," Hugues said. "Get the armor off her. It's bolted."

Izzy saw the bolt that kept the armor in place. She shouted, "*Terminus!*"

Hugues slid out the bolt and pulled the two halves of the armor apart.

The men fell into French as they stripped her armor off and ripped open her sweater. Bernard pushed down too hard; Mathilde's rib cracked with a terrible wrenching sound.

"*Un, deux, trois,*" Bernard counted as he pushed on Mathilde's chest. Then he waited as Hugues blew into her mouth.

Izzy dropped down beside them, clasping one of Mathilde's hands in both of hers.

"*Hail Mary, full of grace, blessed art Thou among women…*" The Catholic prayer of intercession fell easily from her lips.

Bernard stopped counting and murmured to Hugues. He answered back in French.

"I have a healing Gift," Hugues declared. "Let me join you, madame."

Hugues wrapped his hand over Izzy's. Heat from his flesh scorched her skin, but she didn't flinch, only forced more words of the prayer between her lips.

"*Ne meurs pas, garce,*" Bernard said under his breath. "Don't you die. I will find your soul and I will tear it apart."

Bernard got up and walked to the swamp. He bent down and picked up Louise's body, her arms and legs bent at impossible angles.

"This one is dead, too," he announced.

The back of Izzy's palm began to blister. She bit her lower lip to keep from crying out.

"*Mon Dieu, madame!*" Hugues cried, raising his hand off hers.

Izzy's hand was badly burned. The peeling skin was bright red, the wound, weeping and bloody. Izzy quietly got to her feet and formed a palm strike with her aching hand. But her palm remained cold.

"Too late. She beat us. She's gone," Bernard declared, shaking his head. "Both of them."

Izzy reached down and found Mathilde's gun among the rushes and ferns, and raised it up with both hands. She was in agony. She took a breath, let half of it out and got ready to shoot them dead.

Bernard looked up at her. His eyes widened and he put his hands on his head. "Hugues," he warned.

"*Guardienne,*" Hugues protested, raising his hands where Izzy could see them. "Please, put that down. We're loyal to you. We only want to protect you. We need to get you out of here *now.*"

"You're Louise's men," Izzy said.

A long shriek pierced the shadows. It was terrifyingly close. Izzy had no idea how she kept from jerking the gun. It startled the men, too. Bernard spoke to Hugues in rapid-fire French. Then in place of the dark-haired man, a shaggy blonde with a half-moon scar on his cheek stared steadily back at her. Beside him, Hugues changed as well, to a dark-skinned man in dreadlocks.

"We are members of the House of the Shadows. Devereaux," Bernard said quickly. "I am Maurice, he is Georges. We're on your side. We'll explain, but later. We have to get out of here *now*. It's another attack."

It cost her to lower the weapon, but she did it. The two men immediately leaped to their feet, and Bernard took the submachine gun back from her.

She said, "Okay. Get me out of here."

They each grabbed one of her wrists and held tightly. She felt strength flowing from them into her as they took off at a dead run.

A sphere of light crashed into the nearest tree, lighting up their surroundings.

"*Merde!*" Georges cried.

He spoke to Maurice, then released Izzy's arm and wheeled behind her as Maurice kept her running. More spheres exploded. Maurice pushed her in front of him, cradling her against his body as they rushed through the darkness.

Overhanging trees burst into flame. Explosions shook the ground. Maurice muttered in French as he shielded her, slamming her to the ground and throwing himself on top of her.

Then he dragged her back up to her feet, shouting, "*Vite! Vite!*" She was literally seeing stars, perhaps from the percussion. Her eardrums had shut; she could barely hear him.

They came to another inlet of water. Maurice pushed her

hard, and she tumbled in. Her body armor weighted her down. She flailed, trying to get to the surface, but she was sinking fast. She felt his hand around her forearm; then she broke through the water, gasping.

"Can you swim?" he asked.

As an answer, she tried to progress forward by windmilling her arms, but the armor was too heavy. Seeing her predicament, he propelled her along as he crashed through the water beside her.

Something scaly and sharp bumped against her and the only thing she could do was swim harder, although everything in her wanted to panic. It hit her again and she opened her mouth to scream, but the fetid water filled her mouth and she began to choke and cough.

Maurice shot a blue-tinged fireball over her shoulder. It hissed into the water, and whatever had brushed against her thrashed in response. Izzy had no time to see what it was, no desire to know.

It seemed like hours until Maurice half pulled, half carried her onto land again. All she could do was pant and keep moving. She had both her hands around his wrist and she kept a tight hold.

I'm really glad I didn't shoot this guy.

Maurice murmured words and spread his hands. Blue light issued from his palms, forming a thin veil between them and the place they had just come from. Izzy took the opportunity to catch her breath, planting her unhurt palm on her thigh as she sucked in air.

A vast section of the bayou was on fire. Flames rushed up the trunks in columns and ignited the canopy. Branches fell into the water, making hissing noises. Frantic birds took to the sky. Smoke raced along the water like fog.

"Allons!" Maurice cried, taking her hand.

The smoke raced after them, scrabbling onto the land and grabbing at Izzy's ankles. As she ran with Maurice she looked down. Taloned claws inside the smoke reached for her. A skull face leered up at her as its jaws snapped open and tried to bite her calf.

"Demons!" Maurice shouted. "And zombies, dead ahead!"

About twenty yards before them, the bayou sloped steeply upward to form a rise. White-faced men lined the crest; their eyes were blank. Portions of their faces had rotted away. Their clothes were tattered rags.

They shambled down the embankment, sliding and falling. The next rank walked over them, smashing bones; the hand of a fallen man clasped the ankle of another, and the walker moved on, unaware.

Maurice pressed his hands together and them pulled them apart. A fireball appeared; he flung it, hard. It slammed into a zombie in a decomposed business suit, who kept walking until he fell apart, devoured by the flames.

Maurice hurtled more fireballs. Izzy gazed down at her palm to find it glowing with pure white light. She made a palm strike and aimed it at the closest rank of zombies.

Jehanne, give me power, she prayed.

Flame shot from her palm and sprayed at least half a dozen of the walking dead.

Then more vampire minions divebombed from the trees. She dropped to a crouch and aimed her palm upward. Flying at her, they ignited, shrieking as they went up in flames.

Howls rose above the terrific noise. Rising and falling in crescendos, they were the cries of her vision—the same cries she had heard when Andre leaped off the verandah.

"The wolf pack!" Maurice yelled, pointing. He was jubilant.

The zombies began to fall over like bowling pins as enormous black-and-silver-coated wolves barreled through their ranks. Leaping and snarling, the wolves raced straight for Maurice and Izzy. Izzy was alarmed, but Maurice shouted at them in French, and they gathered around them both. Then half of them—there were maybe ten—turned and faced the oncoming zombies. They snarled and pranced, eager for prey.

The others dove into the smoky fog, attacking the creatures—demons—hiding there. As Izzy looked over her shoulder, a wolf tossed a demon into the air. The demon reminded her of pictures of French gargoyles she had seen—its face distorted, twin horns curling from its forehead, leathery wings flapping and hind legs kicking at nothing as it tried to fly away. Too injured, it fell to earth, and the wolf pounced.

Behind the zombies, a fog boiled up, churning and rolling over itself. It was tinged with blue, and it reminded Izzy of the fog she had seen in her dream, when she had first laid eyes on Jean-Marc.

For a moment she dared to hope that she was about to see him again, magically restored. But as she and Maurice continued to bombard the zombies with fire, the blue fog coalesced into a figure—the same one she had seen before. The color bleached away to gunmetal, and this time the figure spoke aloud.

Izzy couldn't make out the words, but beside her Maurice laughed and said, "We're saved!"

"Good!" she shouted at him, laughing too.

From behind them a gush of blue light arced into the air and hit the line of zombies, all of a piece. The creatures flew into the air, skulls and clavicles and rib cages shattering into hundreds of fragments. They burst apart, raining dust.

The werewolves ran back toward Izzy and Maurice, their

howls like cheers of victory. They flashed through the curtain of zombie dust and approached the hill where they had first appeared.

"Georges!" Maurice yelled, waving.

Izzy spotted him. Georges was slogging onto the shore, his submachine gun slung over his back. He was sopping wet, and his face was slick with blood.

He trotted up to Izzy and Maurice, said, "*Pardon*, madame, but I never thought I would see you again," and kissed Izzy hard. She tasted his blood, but she didn't care. She kissed him back, lustily, rejoicing that he had survived. That all three of them had survived.

Then Maurice slapped him on the back and the two embraced. They spoke in French and roared with laughter.

The enormous gray figure hung in the sky. The trio stumbled up the embankment toward it, kicking up layers of zombie dust.

Now they stood on the hill, Izzy leaning against a tree as she tried to catch her breath. The figure, floating above them like a gray cloud in the field of stars, inclined its head toward them.

Without a sound and without warning, it vanished into nothingness.

Although Izzy cried out in surprise, neither man seemed to be perturbed by the event.

"*Et voilà*," Maurice said, pointing.

Izzy looked down. In the moonlight she could make out several cabins and figures racing around them as the wolves pursued them. A silver wolf leaped onto one figure, throwing it onto its back, and Izzy had to look away. Other figures fled into the trees; the wolves were close behind.

Georges and Maurice began to slid down the steep incline, Maurice saying to Izzy, "Please, wait there."

The hell she would. She pushed off, sliding as best she could after them, but her reserves were spent. Exhaustion made her sloppy; she fell more distance down the hill than she actually slid. She was grateful for her protective clothing.

From her vantage point above them, she watched the men's progress. Preceded by two wolves, they dashed into one of the cabins. They were inside a long time. When they came out again, a man was slung between them. He was wearing a suit. His head drooped forward, and he could barely walk.

When she approached, Maurice looked at her wryly and said, "You're no better at following orders than Jean-Marc."

As he spoke, he and Georges eased the man down onto the wooden porch. He was dark-skinned, like Georges, and deep cuts criss-crossed his cheeks and forehead. His eyes were puffy, nearly swollen shut.

When he saw Izzy, he brightened.

"He did it," he said in heavily accented English, his words slurred. "Jean-Marc got you to New Orleans in one piece."

She guessed he was Alain de Devereaux. He looked nothing like Jean-Marc. "Yes," she replied, "he did it."

Deep within the bayou, Georges and Maurice debriefed Alain. They described Izzy's arrival and her presentation at the elaborate state dinner.

"Then the mansion was attacked," Georges told Alain.

Alain nodded. "*Oui,* I know. My kidnappers were in on it. Followers of Le Fils. They fully expected to take the mansion. When the *bokor,* Esposito, was killed, they were shocked." Alain smiled at Izzy. "You killed him. My congratulations."

"Thank you," she replied, finding no joy in the killing, just grim satisfaction, and the knowledge that it had served only as a reprieve, not an ending.

"Were they Malchances?" Maurice asked Alain. "The ones who kidnapped you? How did it happen?"

Alain wearily shook his head. "I was leaving the mansion to speak to Gelineau about madame's arrival. When I left the compound, I was attacked with heavy mortar fire."

"They got through your wards?" Georges asked, clearly shocked. When Alain nodded, he said, "Did you recognize anyone?"

"*Non*. They were masked. Did you find Matthieu?" Alain asked.

"*Non*," Georges said.

"*Merde*." Alain's face was slack with grief. "Matthieu was my driver," he told Izzy. "He can't have been in on it."

"But the enemy got through the wards," Maurice argued. "*Devereaux* wards. If they had an inside man..." He trailed off, perhaps seeing Alain's despair.

"I'm so sorry," Izzy told Alain. "Maybe he'll be found."

No one replied, and she realized none of them expected to see Matthieu again.

"Gelineau," Georges said, spitting out the name like a curse. "What about him? He knew you were coming to see him. Was *he* in on it?"

"I don't know," Alain said.

"They found some fragments of Esposito," Izzy told him. "I tried to participate in the reading but I got sick or...I don't know. I wound up unconscious. Michel went with a search party to find you at a convent. I had a vision that you were here."

"A powerful vision, for which I thank you." Alain looked to Izzy, cocking his head as he gazed at her with large, sad brown eyes. "I hope it won't alarm you if I tell you that my cousin half hoped he wouldn't find you."

"No," she said. "I'm well past the alarmed stage." She

turned her attention to Maurice and Georges. Maurice was stanching the blood on Georges' forehead with a flow of blue energy from his fingertips.

"Before I go anywhere with any of you, I want to know exactly who you are. And who Louise and Mathilde were."

Georges said, "Our House would never consent to allowing Jean-Marc and Alain to come to New Orleans alone. We're undercover special ops assigned to guard the regent and his cousin."

Maurice took up the thread. "When all this happened yesterday—Alain's disappearance, the attack, Jean-Marc's injuries—we went on high alert. Then Louise handpicked Mathilde, Bernard and Hugues for this mission. We already had cause to believe that Louise was up to something. So we took out Bernard and Hugues—we couldn't get to Mathilde—and used glamours to impersonate them. We don't know the details of the plot, but your trip out of the mansion was intended to be one way."

"Took them out," she repeated.

"Yes." He gazed at her without blinking.

More deaths. The world of the Gifted was filled with them.

"Why didn't Jean-Marc tell me there were other Devereaux nearby?" she asked.

Bernard hesitated. It was Alain who answered. "My cousin Jean-Marc is a very circumspect man. Maybe he thought they would be able to protect you better if they were incognito."

"Then there are Devereauxes guarding him right now," she said. "And guarding my mother?"

"And your mother," Alain assured her. "From a distance. But maybe that should change."

She sighed. If she had known that, she would have done

this whole thing differently. She would have contacted them and conferred with them and ferreted out what to do.

She said, "Why didn't they come to me after Jean-Marc was hurt?"

"He must have told them not to," Alain said.

"Must have? You're the regent's cousin and you don't *know?*"

"*Hélas,*" Alain said, with a shrug that reminded her of Jean-Marc.

That seemed so wrong. She remembered Le Fils's words: *They're playing you. I will protect you in New York.*

And yet, Le Fils's own minions had viciously attacked her and Jean-Marc back in New York.

Maybe it wasn't me they were after. Maybe it was Jean-Marc. Maybe something else is going on that I know nothing about.

Who was telling her the truth?

What *was* the truth?

Chapter 7

Deep in the bayou, the whirr of helicopter rotors startled Izzy. Against the black satin sky, a pair of running lights winked in the darkness, and beyond that pair, the silhouette of a stubby plane whisked across the moon like a black bat.

"They're coming to put out the fire," Alain said. "I hope Mayor Gelineau doesn't find out what really started it. He's this close to dissolving the *politesse* with the Bouvards."

"Michel mentioned he's not very fond of them. Us," she amended.

"No, he's not," he said. "He thinks the Flames are weak and divisive. He needs someone stronger to handle all the supernaturals in New Orleans."

As if the effort of speaking was too much, Alain sucked in his breath. The two operatives put their hands on his shoulders. Indigo blue glowed from their palms.

"What did they do to you, *monsieur?*" Georges asked Alain.

"Not too much. A few blows. They were going to use me as a sacrifice, so they wanted to keep me in one piece," Alain told them, as the muscles in his face relaxed. The Devereaux's ministrations appeared to be taking effect. He shook his head. "Their arrogance was remarkable. They honestly didn't believe you would find me."

The men's answering smiles were hard and angry. "They don't know the Devereauxes," Maurice said. "They're used to the Bouvards."

Then his smile faded as he regarded Izzy. "*Pardonnez-moi, madame.*"

She moved on to more immediate concerns. "A girl came with me from New York. Her name is Sauvage," she said. "Her goth name, anyway. They put a glamour on her so people wouldn't know I'd left the mansion."

The men frowned in disbelief. Alain said, "A Bouvard glamour?"

"Yes," she said. "It wasn't very good."

Georges snorted. "They should have made a fabricant."

"We—they—were worried about what would happen when the fabricant started to wear off," she conceded.

"A Bouvard glamour, a Bouvard fabricant," Alain observed, sounding more than a little tentative. He looked at Izzy. "Your family's magical powers are much weaker than ours, and those of the Malchances. We don't know why. Jean-Marc and I have been investigating it."

"Oh." She didn't know what to say to that. So far, their magic had seemed plenty strong to her.

The plane let loose a shower of some kind of powdery substance. Izzy guessed that it was flame retardant.

"We should get out of here," Alain said. "But of course, first we must give thanks to the vassal."

The three Devereauxes lowered their heads again and soundlessly moved their lips. Then Maurice pulled out his knife and sliced across his palm. Blood welled along the cut and began to drip into the dirt.

He passed the knife to Georges, who did the same, and then to Alain.

The three men clenched their fists, making the blood drip faster. They raised them and spoke in a singsong language.

As the blood splattered on the porch, a wisp of smoke rose from the wooden slats. The men wafted it toward their faces with their hands, inhaling it. Then it disappeared.

The cuts in their hands sealed up. There was no trace of the wounds on any of their hands.

Alain said to Izzy, "The vassal was that figure you saw. He serves our patron, the Gray King. I summoned him, and he came. He showed you where I was." He cocked his head. "It's not often that others of another House can see or hear him. You are a remarkable woman."

"Just lucky that way," she said.

Alain made as if to get up. "It's time to go," he said.

"We can't take her back to the mansion," Georges said.

Georges and Maurice helped Alain to his feet. He winced, rubbing his left shoulder and rolling his neck in a circle.

"I think we need to split up," Maurice ventured. "At least one of us needs to get back to the mansion and reconnoiter with the rest of the ops team."

"Please see if Sauvage is all right," Izzy said. "And her boyfriend."

"We also need to find Michel and his party," Alain said. "I

wonder if he masterminded this whole thing. I swear, he would take the Bouvard ring off my cousin's dead body if he could."

She cleared her throat. "Actually, he did take it. And he gave it me. I've got it around my neck."

Alain raised a brow, and she flushed, feeling unaccountably guilty. As if she had taken something that wasn't hers.

"I wonder if we should bother trying to read Louise and Mathilde's bodies," Georges said. "It doesn't sound as if we can trust D'Artagnon."

"They probably burned up in the fire," Maurice ventured.

"*Oui, monsieur,* they did. And they were tasty," said a silky voice from the shadows.

"Who's there?" Izzy shouted, whirling around.

"Caresse," Alain said, smiling. "She's Andre's mate. And a friend."

"Have you found Andre?" Izzy cried.

Branches bobbed; red eyes glowed from the darkness. They disappeared. A few seconds later a sinewy, naked woman with dark skin, golden eyes and platinum-blond hair sauntered into view.

"*C'est la jolie maîtresse,*" she said. "*Oui,* Isabelle. He was badly hurt, but he's getting better. We have sent for a *bokor* to hurry it up. She's coming to our place."

Her features softened as an idea came to her. "We could shelter madame from all her enemies there. You can leave some bodyguards and make some more magic there, *oui?*" she asked Alain. "Make some healing magic for Andre, too?"

"The thought to take madame to your camp had occurred to me," Alain admitted. "But it could be very dangerous."

"We know it's *dangereuse* in the bayou," Caresse retorted. "It would be so much better if we could shelter her in the mansion. But the Bouvards do not welcome us. *C'est la vie.* They do not welcome her, either."

"You're very clever, Caresse," Alain said. "You give madame a place to stay, which of course must be heavily guarded. And so, your wolf pack is protected from Le Fils and Esposito's henchmen."

She winked at him. "It is clear to me why you are the diplomat."

Izzy took a breath and said, "Did you…did you really eat them?"

Caresse chuckled. "What do you think, *ma belle?*"

I think you didn't answer my question, Izzy thought.

Caresse swung back around and whistled. A half-standing, hunched wolf form padded from the same dark place she had appeared and stared at Izzy. The black fur, the almond-shaped, golden eyes….

"Andre!" she cried, running toward the wolf. She rose on her tiptoes and threw her arms around its neck.

"Not my Andre," Caresse said, amused. "A pack mate. We call him Lucky. When Andre cannot run, he is our alpha."

"Oh." As Izzy took a step backward, the creature's eyes glittered with good humor.

Another darted from the darkness. Then another slunk from around a tree trunk; a fourth appeared behind it. A fifth. These were more like regular wolves. Of all of them, Lucky was the most like Andre—something more than a wolf, something like a monster.

Caresse said, "We should go to our place, us. Now. The swamp is full of Le Fils's vampires and demons. More are on their way." She beckoned Izzy and the three Devereauxes to follow her.

Izzy said, "Shouldn't we perform wards, or—"

"We've been performing wards the entire time we've been with you," Georges said. "We won't stop now."

"As for us, we'll travel strong," Caresse said.

She chuckled low in her throat as she dropped to all fours. Fur sprouted along the ridge on her back. Her ears stretched; her entire head elongated. She was transforming into a wolf before Izzy's eyes, as Andre had.

But where Andre had changed into something else, Caresse became a full wolf. She gazed over her shoulder at Izzy and chuffed like a dog.

Beside Izzy, the three Devereauxes were also changing into wolves.

Glamours? she wondered. Or were they actually werewolves?

Then she looked down at her own body and saw a strange superimposition, like a ghostly reflection, of paws and fur…paws that were padding along the bayou's damp ground. She touched her face with human hands, her own fingertips. But when she looked down, she saw paws, on the ground. A powerful glamour indeed.

And so I'm on the run again, she thought. *I haven't stopped running for over two weeks. And people—or things—have been trying to kill me for over two weeks.*

When will this end? And how?

Dawn was washing the darkness from the sky when Izzy and the others came within sight of the werewolves' compound. The smoke from the bayou fire was dissipating. The whump-whump-whump of the copter rotors had left the sky, as well.

Slowly each wolf transformed back into a human being, and Izzy recognized the pack from New York City. Izzy was startled to realize that Claire, the woman with the cornrows who had served on occasion as Jean-Marc's driver, was the silver wolf that had trotted beside her during the night.

Claire had been one of the werewolves to sneak into the DeMarcos home and corner John Cratty. Rather than allow the wolves to rip him to shreds, Cratty had ended his own life with a bullet from Izzy's Medusa. It had been a horrible, ghoulish undertaking—and yet Izzy was incredibly glad to see Claire. Izzy was cast adrift in a sea of strangers, and Claire was a familiar face.

As she assumed her human shape, Claire grinned at Izzy and said, "*Ça va, jolie?*"

"I've been better," Izzy answered.

Claire made a moue and patted Izzy's shoulder. "We'll treat you well here. Not so much like a queen as like a friend. You saved Jean-Marc's life. That counts big with us."

"Thank you," Izzy said. "But it was really Andre who made it happen."

"Well, he is taking a lot of the credit," Claire replied with a lusty chuckle.

"*Tais-toi,*" Caresse told Claire, but her voice was warm. "He does go on, that man," she said, grinning. "He can't wait to see you, *chére.*"

A tall wooden fence lined with bones and skulls and painted with symbols—swirls, stars, skulls, figures of people—marked the perimeter of the werewolves' compound. Izzy wasn't sure what they were bones and skulls *of,* and she didn't want to know.

The three Devereauxes stopped there. Alain explained that they had placed Devereaux wards around the fence upon first arriving in New Orleans, and they periodically refreshed them. They were going to do that now—and add more, as well.

The werewolves lived in Cajun shacks along the banks of the bayou. Izzy wished she could call them picturesque, but they were ramshackle structures patched together out of mismatched pieces of wood, and topped with corrugated tin roofs. The closest she could get was "functional."

Caresse took Izzy's hand and said, "Let's go see my man, you and me, *chére*."

As they neared a shack hanging over the water, a toddler in a diaper and a T-shirt that said I Love NY appeared in the doorway. He burst into tears when he saw Caresse and held his arms out to her.

"You," she said lovingly as she hoisted him up and settled him against her hip. "All night I'm gone and I'll bet you never cried one time."

"He never stopped crying," said a familiar voice.

The voice issued from the overstuffed depths of a red velvet sofa, incongruous in the extreme in the rustic shack. Andre was lying on it, his wildman hair streaming over his shoulders, a colorful quilt pulled up under his arms. He was wearing several necklaces of small bags, and a pile of small stone hearts painted red were gathered in his lap.

On a chair beside the sofa, surrounded by colorful glasses containing candles, a wizened, dark-skinned woman in a black kerchief sliced through the air with a knife. She was dressed in a shapeless tie-dyed shift decorated with beads and feathers, silver charms of skulls, hands and crosses. The chair was draped with colorful strings of fabric. Incense wafted from a mosaic censor at her feet.

Her gestures were identical to those of Michel and D'Artagnon, when they had cut the evil emanating from the box containing Julius's remains.

Izzy reached around her neck for Andre's gris-gris, walked

over to the sofa, and draped it over Andre's head. Then she leaned down and kissed him on the cheek. The woman completely ignored her as she continued to slice the air.

"Andre, thank God," Izzy breathed, and she knelt down beside him on the floor. "Thank *you*," she amended. "You saved the day."

"*Ma belle*," he said happily. "Heard we won."

She nodded. "But Jean-Marc was badly wounded. He was still unconscious when I left."

"If anyone can pull through, it's Jean-Marc. He's a very strong man," Andre said. "For a while I thought he might be a werewolf. But no such luck."

"Claire was disappointed when she first met him, too," Caresse said with a lilt. "Of course, she was in heat at the time." She was carrying a glass. Izzy realized she was parched, and started to reach for it gratefully. But Caresse handed it to the old woman, her voice low and reverent as she spoke to her in French.

"That one, she's always in heat." Andre chuckled.

The woman gulped the water down noisily. It dribbled down her chin and splashed onto the bodice of her dress. She kept drinking.

"They were attacked in the bayou," Caresse told Andre. "It was Le Fils."

"*Vraiment*," Andre agreed. He looked at Izzy. "The worse shape the House of the Flames is in, the better for that vampire, him. He's attacking tourists now, barely trying to hide his tracks. The voodoo drums are talking. They say he's up to something in that old convent."

"A convent? That's where Michel went to search for Alain," Izzy told them.

"Probably more like Michel went there to join Le Fils,"

Andre said, making a spitting sound. "Don't trust Michel de Bouvard, *chére*. He's a bad man. And that Bouvard mansion is a bad place."

He and Caresse crossed themselves. Izzy did, too.

Caresse said to Andre, "We have to get Jean-Marc out of there, *mon amour*."

"*Oui*," said Andre. "*Chére*," he said to Izzy. "You're their lady. You can tell them that you want—"

The sound of a crashing glass cut him off.

Caresse pointed at the old woman. "'*Dieu!*'" she shouted. "Look at Mamaloi!"

Izzy whirled around on her knees, narrowly missing a chunk of glass that had clattered to the wooden floor. The old woman had dropped the glass. Her back was ramrod straight and her head was tilted slightly back. Her arms were flung to each side, as if she had been crucified.

Her eyes were milky white.

Her mouth dropped open and a low, sinister, very masculine voice rumbled out of it. Her lips didn't move, and yet the voice poured out of her mouth. The words were French.

Caresse said, "The *loa* says, 'Le Fils is the *little* fish. The gator uses him for bait. Once you're in the water, he'll snap you in two!'"

"Who is the gator?" Izzy asked, wondering what a *loa* was.

Caresse spoke in French, directing her questions to the old woman. The voice poured out of the puckered, wizened mouth as if in answer, but the woman's lips still did not move. Though she kept her stiff position, her milky, unfocused eyes seemed to settle on Izzy, and cold fear swept up Izzy's spine. What was looking at her? What was talking to her? And how did it know the answers to her questions?

"'Catch the little fish. He'll take you to the gator,'" Caresse translated.

"But the gator will snap her in two," Andre argued. "She don't want that, Caresse. Make that *loa* explain, him."

"Where is Le Fils?" Izzy asked. "And Michel?"

Caresse spoke again to the old woman.

"Michel is in the French quarter. He is fine."

The voice poured out, and Andre grunted. His face turned gray and a muscle jumped n his cheek. Caresse remained silent and he said, "Tell her, *bébé*. She needs to know."

"Le Fils is killing Matthieu de Bouvard des Flammes," Caresse said. "Alain's chauffeur. Right now. This moment." Her eyes widened as the gravelly voice croaked more words. "*Mon Dieu,* Andre. You hear that? He is torturing him to death. As a sacrifice."

Afraid she was going to be sick, Izzy closed her eyes and pressed her fist over her mouth. "Can we stop it? Can we help him with magic?" she asked. "Alain!" she shouted, rising.

Caresse put a hand on her shoulder and pushed her back down to the floor.

"Don't yell, *chére*. This is Mamaloi's *loa*," Caresse said again. "The voodoo god is speaking through her. It would show disrespect if you left the room. The *loa* might stop speaking altogether."

Alain, venez ici, Izzy thought, slipping into French. *Vite.*

He heard her, and rushed into the room, followed by Maurice. The two stood still, listening. Alain swayed on his feet, blackly silent. Maurice swore under his breath and asked a question in French. Izzy heard the word *Malchances*.

"He is asking Mamaloi's *loa* if the Malchances are working with Le Fils," Andre told Izzy.

There was no answer.

"She's afraid to say," Maurice ventured.

"We don't know that," Caresse countered. "Could be the *loa* doesn't know."

Maurice said to Caresse, "Please, ask her about Esposito. He was a *bokor*, but he was involved in the Dark Arts. Ask her *loa* to explain—"

The deep voice inside Mamaloi rose to a shriek as her entire body convulsed. She flopped in her chair like a dying fish; Izzy reached out to help her, but Andre grabbed her biceps and said, "Stay away, *chére*."

Foam bubbled from her mouth as her body shook and shuddered. Then she collapsed, falling back in her chair. Her head lolled backward, and her breath rattled out of her thin body as if she were dying.

"Mamaloi!" Caresse cried, putting her arms around her. She cradled the old woman's inert body and said, "*Mamaloi, reviens-ici. Mamaloi, tu va bien, eh?*"

There was a moment when everyone held their collective breaths. Then Mamaloi opened her eyes and cleared her throat. Her eyes were back to normal as she blinked at the group staring at her, each in turn. Then she said to Caresse, "*J'ai faim.*"

Caresse smiled at the woman and stroked her cheek. "She says she's hungry," she told Izzy.

"Guess her *loa* didn't want to talk about Esposito," Maurice said, sounding frustrated.

"Or couldn't. Or was afraid to." Alain's voice was strained with despair. "Madame," he said to Mamaloi and continued on in rapid French. The old lady's natural voice was papery soft as she replied.

"She don't remember any of it," Andre told Izzy. "She can't tell us any more."

"Can you do some kind of ritual to call her *loa* back?" Izzy asked Alain.

He shook his head. "We don't do *voudon*," he said in a strangled voice. He was agonized, and she felt for him.

"But if Ungifted can practice it," she argued, "there must be—" she searched for the right word "—instructions, set ways of doing things."

"We're Gifted," Alain said, as if that should satisfy her curiosity. He turned away and went back outside.

It didn't satisfy her curiosity, and she was about to pursue the matter, when Caresse said, "Well, we don't do it, either. And don't bother Mamaloi. She's done, *oui*?"

She patted the old lady's cheek. The woman laid her own hand over Caresse's and said something to her that made Caresse laugh. Then Andre's mate straightened and walked briskly across the cabin to a propane stove.

"Mamaloi is hungry." She reached to a shelf above the stove and retrieved a cast-iron skillet and looked hard at Izzy. "You may not feel like eating, but you had better, *jolie maîtresse*. Ooh-la-la, you had better. You need to feed your blood."

"For the gator?" Izzy asked.

"*Oui*," Caresse answered. She didn't smile.

Chapter 8

The werewolves were hungry.

Caresse put on a pair of jeans, a T-shirt and an Emeril apron, then got down to cooking a Cajun feast—gumbo, crayfish and hush puppies. Claire and a third woman named Felice pitched in.

Izzy began slogging from one moment to the next, with no blood sugar and no energy. Evidently, as a Gifted, she had reserves of energy denied regular human beings. She began to view the ability to collapse as a luxury denied her. She offered halfheartedly to help with the cooking and was relieved when they turned her down.

Instead, Alain enlisted several of the werewolves to pour big plastic buckets of hot water into a cracked porcelain tub sitting on the back porch. Alain explained to Izzy that she needed to wash the magical residue off her body. Unless she got rid of it, she would fall prey to anxiety and probably depression. Jean-Marc had told her the same thing in New York. She had ignored his advice—and paid the price exactly as Alain described it.

The three Devereaux men would make use of a makeshift shower, but Alain wanted Izzy to soak for a while, as a precaution. Hence, the tub.

As he turned to go, Izzy said to Alain, "I'm so sorry about Matthieu. If there's anything I can do…"

He opened his mouth as if to reply. When he remained silent, she asked, "Is there something?"

He shrugged. "You are a de Bouvard. Your House is known for its ability to heal. But this wound for Matthieu…I think I'll carry it awhile, in honor of him."

She dipped her head. She wasn't sure she knew how to heal a wound like that. She reached out and took his hand. "I am so sorry." The words seemed so ineffectual, so superficial.

"It's not so much his death, as how he died," Alain murmured. "From what the *loa* told Mamaloi, they didn't take his soul, so there is at least that comfort." He massaged his temples, then dropped his hands to his sides with a sigh. "I need to shower. Be sure to soak a long time. You're not used to the power of your Gift."

"I will. *Merci,*" she said.

Alain left her, and Claire arrived with a basket of herbs. The young boy who had gone into her house to assist with the killing of the dirty cop, John Cratty, who had been in league with Esposito, sat at her feet playing an accordion while Claire sprinkled the hot water with the herbs. Izzy marveled at the boy's cheerful innocence. In New York, he had witnessed two deaths.

"How old are you?" she asked him, when he stopped playing and smiled up at her, awaiting her approval.

He frowned. Didn't he speak English? She tried again and said, "That was very *jolie*. Thank you."

"He's maybe nine," Claire said, crumbling dried lavender between her fingers. "His parents died when he was just a tit-sucker." She gazed fondly at the boy. "We don't talk about it much, but we think it was Ungifted hunters. Out for sport, didn't know the difference." She sighed as she rubbed her palms together to scatter the last of the herbs on the water.

She found a dried rose petal in her basket and tossed it into the tub. It fluttered like a butterfly as it alighted on the surface. "All that's gone, now that the Devereauxes are here. The Flames never protected us."

"But aren't they…aren't *we* supposed to serve as protectors of the supernaturals and the Ungifted?" Izzy asked, still back at the boy's parents' having been shot by hunters.

Claire snorted. "Show me a Gifted besides Jean-Marc who would protect a werewolf," she said.

"My House should. Don't we protect all the supernaturals and Ungifted around here?"

"That's on a piece of paper," Claire informed her, sniffing. "Never been in real life."

Izzy gave a start as the boy touched the accordion keys and sound blatted out.

"Now Jean-Marc, that one, he loves the *loupes-garoux*." Claire grinned, showing big, white teeth. "He wants to be like us. All them rules, all the pressure. I think it gets to him. He's a wildman in his heart. Wants to run free."

Izzy filed that away. "He's awfully uptight," she said.

Claire raised a brow. "Like you." She flashed her big white teeth at Izzy. "You want to become one of us?"

Izzy's face tingled. "Ah…"

Laughter bubbled out of Claire as she gestured for the boy

to get to his feet. "There's no way to become a werewolf except you have a *maman* or a *papa* who is one already," she said. "Now, vampires, whole other story. If they bite you and suck you dry, you come back." She nodded. Then she reached behind the tub and showed Izzy two big plastic bottles, one clear and one a frosted green. "Shampoo. Conditioner."

"Thank you," Izzy said.

"De rien, chére."

Claire hefted the boy's accordion over her shoulder and put her arm around him, leading him into the shack.

Izzy was so tired that her legs wobbled as she got into the tub. She tilted back her head, drenching her hair. She leaned her head against the edge of the tub and closed her eyes. She began to cry, long and deep and hard, as the magical residue washed off her skin. Each sob contracted her entire body. It was almost orgasmic. She understood it was a release after all the horror, and she let it happen.

Jean-Marc, she sent out. *Are you conscious? Are you safe?*

She shut her eyes tightly, focused and hopeful, listening between sobs. If there could be a sign, any sign—his heartbeat, a single, whispered word. But she heard nothing.

After Izzy dried off, Claire brought her a pair of wool socks, a jeans skirt and a ribbed, olive sweater. No bra, no underwear. As Izzy refastened her crucifix and the rose quartz necklace with the signet ring around her neck, Claire refilled the tub and threw in all Izzy's clothes. She whistled at the body armor and asked her if she might consider outfitting the werewolves with some "for the coming troubles."

"Oh, yes," Alain said, as she conferred after the feast with Andre, the two operatives, and him. Alain had eaten very little; he was still quite subdued. "Troubles are on their way."

They sat on the porch, Andre and Izzy in rickety but serviceable rocking chairs. Alain was seated at their feet on the uneven wooden porch, in a red-and-gray-plaid wool bathrobe. Izzy had tried to give up her chair to him, as he seemed to be in physical as well as emotional pain, but he refused.

The shadows were lengthening as the day stretched toward afternoon. The heavy canopy of trees rustled. Below them, at the water's edge, cattails jittered. There were splashes in the water—animals, birds, reptiles, Andre had assured her. But she had no idea why there couldn't also be *bokors* and demons traveling through the spooky bayou. Though Georges and several of the wolf brothers were escorting Mamaloi back to her own cabin in the swamp, Izzy feared for her. The voodoo woman had given them important information. Would their enemies punish her for it?

Maurice was on his way back to the mansion. After Georges had delivered Mamaloi to her home, he would join him. They were to report back what they found to Alain as soon as possible. Then Alain and Izzy would plan their next move.

Inside the cabin, someone began to play the boy's accordion. The bouncy zydeco provided an ironic backdrop to the heavy conversation on the porch.

"Troubles are *here*," Izzy emphasized, feeling alone and frightened. She wanted to call her men—Pat, Gino and Big Vince. She didn't know how much time had elapsed since she'd last spoken to them. The terrible lie that her life had become tore at her. She wished with all her soul that she *was* at a hotel in Florida, relaxing in the sun, which was what she had told them to explain her sudden absence.

"*Oui*," Alain agreed. "Troubles are here."

"Your assistant is very worried about you," Izzy remembered to tell him.

"Pierre's a good man, for a Bouvard." He gave her a dry smile and didn't bother to apologize for the mild insult. "I told Maurice and Georges to talk to him."

Then he wiped his face with both hands and flattened his palms against his knees. "I've got to get some rest. You should too, madame. When I hear back from our men, we'll decide what to do next."

"All right," she said. She guessed the two Devereaux ops were "her" men, too. "And please, call me Izzy," she said. At his grimace, she said, "Or Isabelle. Your cousin does."

Alain smiled gently as he shook his head. "My cousin is a different breed," he replied, and his smile didn't reach his eyes. "I'd sooner call you…Blanche Neige. That's Snow White in French. Escaping the huntsman in the enchanted forest…" He sighed, unable to continue his joke.

"You're worried about Jean-Marc."

"I am. And you. I'm worried about you." He exhaled, letting the smile go altogether, as if she and he were much too aware of the situation to bother with false optimism. "But we should rest while we can."

Just then, swathed in his quilt in his rocking chair, Andre emitted a long, deep growl. He was snoring. Izzy and Alain both laughed softly. It felt incredibly good to laugh. And so strange.

Detective Pat Kittrell dried off, folded the burnt-orange towel, hung it on the towel rack and padded naked out of the bathroom. He pulled back the bedspread, the blanket and the sheet and lay down. His skin was warm and moist, droplets of water clinging to his chest hairs, the whorl at his navel and the soft blond thatch surrounding his penis and balls.

He was already partially erect, and as his hand wrapped around the shaft, he closed his eyes and whispered, "Iz."

His hand began to move.

So very many thousands of miles away, deeply asleep, Izzy moaned, longing for him. He sensed her, and his back arched slightly off the bed, his pelvis thrusting forward and up, as if to penetrate his invisible bedmate.

"Pat," she whispered, straddling him. He was long, hard, and he filled her completely as she lowered herself on top of him. He molded his hands around her hips, guiding her as they began to move together. She clasped his wrists, feeling his racing pulse as it throbbed against her thumbs. Then it traveled to her rib cage, and beat inside her chest.

His heart was her heart.

"Isabelle," he said, and she looked down at him.

At Jean-Marc, beneath her, filling her, moving his hips inside her open, moist thighs, taking her.

Izzy's eyes flew open in the darkness of the werewolves' cabin.

Oh, my God. I was dreaming about them both.

Then she lifted her head and saw a figure standing at the entrance to the cabin. The door hung open, revealing the stars and the man. She couldn't make out his features, but she knew his silhouette, and now she knew his heartbeat, as its thrusting rhythm picked up inside her own body.

Jean-Marc stood alone in a shimmering aura of blue light. He was wearing battle gear, with a submachine gun slung across his chest. His long, wild hair was caught back in a ponytail. A terrible anger came off him in waves, and she remembered the first rule she had made for herself when she had met him: *Never piss off Jean-Marc.*

But he was here, and he was alive. Joyfully she raised herself off the sofa and got to her feet. She wanted to throw her arms around him and thank God for him. Every part of her body and soul responded to his presence.

She hurried toward him. And yet she didn't put her arms around him as she longed to. She stood inches away from him as he stared at her with his dark eyes, his heart pounding in her chest. In the void between them she could smell his scent. His body heat blazed against her face.

"You can't be here," she managed. "You just had major surgery." She wondered what his chest looked like. She wondered how it had been for him to wake up and find out everything that had happened.

"I'm a Gifted," he said. "I heal fast."

But if you had died, I would never have gotten over it.

"I'm well enough," Jean-Marc replied, and she swallowed, wondering if he had heard her thoughts.

Then he took Izzy's arm and jerked his head toward the front porch.

"Allez vite," he snapped.

As relieved as she was to see him, she was thrown by the way he manhandled her, the way a cop would a recalcitrant suspect.

"Hey," she protested as he moved off the porch and stomped across the dirt courtyard. It was still dark out; she heard frogs and crickets as she padded along beside him in her bare feet.

When they had reached the wooden gate, Jean-Marc released her and whirled on her, stabilizing the Uzi with his right hand.

"Why didn't you listen to me?" he demanded, shaking with fury. "Why didn't you stay in your mother's chamber?"

She remembered that that was the last thing he had said to her before he was wounded. He'd been yelling at her to leave the battle, go to safety. She understood that mentally he was picking up where he had left off.

"A lot has happened," she began.

"I know what's happened. Maurice and Georges briefed me." Then his expression softened as he ticked his gaze from her to his cousin, who was running toward them.

"Thanks be to the Gray King," Alain breathed, clasping Jean-Marc's shoulder, then enfolding him in a sort of hug, made awkward by Jean-Marc's armor and weaponry. Touching him, welcoming him back when Izzy had not.

"*Grâce au Roi Gris*, Alain. Until I was debriefed, I was afraid you were dead."

Alain gestured to Izzy. "Then you know that I owe my life to this brave woman. She led a rescue party to find me."

"I know that she left the mansion in the company of two assassins," Jean-Marc retorted. His voice was harsh, his features sharp. There was no softness for Izzy as he glared at her. "What the *hell* were you thinking?"

"*Mon cousin*," Alain protested, placing a hand on Jean-Marc's shoulder, "she's been through a lot."

"She could have *spared* herself a lot," Jean-Marc said. He rested his hands on the Uzi, waiting for her to account for herself.

Izzy ground her teeth. She was so angry at him…and yet, her body was responding to him as if she hadn't snapped out of her dream.

I was dreaming about Pat. And he…intruded. He is not my lover. Pat is.

And yet, despite every instinct, she was awash with desire for Jean-Marc. Carnal, emotional. She wanted to reach forward and touch his cheek, his jaw, to sink against him and reassure herself that he was here and alive. It was horribly confusing.

Then suddenly, just as she had imagined doing to him, he

reached out, not to touch her, but to grab her. He whipped the Uzi off and laid it on the ground. Then, as she gasped in protest, he fitted her body against his, cupping the back of her head and laying her head against his chest. She heard his heart beating there, as if it had been returned to him, no longer in her care. She felt his erection against her belly, and her body seized.

"It is a natural thing," he said calmly, and she wondered if he was talking about his obvious desire for her.

He pressed the fingertips of his free hand against her forehead. Then she smelled oranges and roses, and felt a soothing warmth spreading throughout her veins. He was calming her with magic. Enchanting her.

In a lower, kinder tone he said, "Let us begin again, eh?"

"I will if you will," she told him. She was literally in no position to argue.

"They said you were having visions. Tell me about them."

As she had in the past, she wondered now if he really cared about her at all. He had already told her that his life was built on the performance of his duty. Had he left his sickbed and raced into the bayou because she mattered to him personally, or because it was his responsibility to deliver her in one piece to the House of the Flames? Was he soothing her now so she would be coherent for her own debriefing?

She took another moment. Misreading her hesitation, Jean-Marc released her, holding her at arm's length as he studied her face.

"Can't you remember them?" he asked, dropping his hands to his sides. "Try. Concentrate. I'll show you how."

Stop pushing, she wanted to tell him. Bereft of his touch, she simply leaned against the fence with its skulls and weird juju paraphernalia and said, "I've had a lot of visions lately.

In one, I actually thought I was back in New York, on the police force. I chased Julius Esposito into the same burning building I saw my father in before you and I left New York."

"It was all jumbled up but very real. And he was using Sauvage as bait."

A muscle jumped in Jean-Marc's cheek. His eyes became hooded, unreadable. He said, "Go on."

She decided not to tell him about Pat. That was private. "That was one vision. Then when I went with Michel and D'Artagnon to read Esposito's...fragments, I had a second vision that Alain was in the bayou." She hesitated, unable to keep from adding, "And some other...things, just before you showed up just now."

He blinked at her. She swore he could read her mind, see the images of Pat, naked. Of himself, making love to her. Her face hot, she looked away. "And...that's it."

There was a moment when no one spoke.

Then he said, "*C'est ma faute,*" lowering his chin against his chest in a gesture of apology. His shoulders rounded, he sighed heavily. "I tried to prepare you, but I didn't have time." He raised his chin, and at her questioning look, he said, "Remember how I told you that magic would be stronger here than in New York?"

"Because New York is neutral territory," she filled in.

"*Oui.* It was the territory of the Borgia Family, but overnight, they disappeared. We don't know why, and it's been declared off-limits to everyone. There is no appreciable energy there anymore.

"But here the emanations are very strong. That's why the de Bouvards originally settled here. New Orleans is a place rich with magical energy. And you are only learning of your powers and how to use them." He turned his attention from her to

Alain and said, "It's a wonder she hasn't gone crazy, *n'est ce pas?*"

"*Oui,*" Alain replied. "*Certainement.*"

Jean-Marc cupped Izzy's chin. "*La pauvre.* Trying to understand what is happening. What is real. Whom to trust. It must be hell for you."

He shook his head, stroking the side of her face with his thumb, an uncommonly gentle gesture for him. It mesmerized her. The dynamic had changed between them; they seemed almost like lovers, no longer mentor and student. Maybe the specter of death had taken off old masks and put on new ones.

In a hoarse whisper he said, "I let you down, Isabelle."

She tried to clear her throat, but her mouth had gone dry. She tried to shake her head to tell him no, he hadn't. He'd gotten hurt. He'd nearly died.

She saw that he was studying the signet ring on her rose quartz necklace and she moved her hands to unfasten it. As she wrapped her hand around the ring, he cocked his head, watching her, and said, "Keep it, Isabelle. It belongs to you."

"It's not mine," she argued.

"Yet," he said. "Not yours yet. But it is more yours than mine."

Michel had said nearly the same thing. "You're still the regent," she insisted. She added, more tentatively, "Aren't you?" *You're not abandoning me, are you?*

"I am still the regent." He molded his hand over hers and gave it a squeeze, tightening her grip around the ring. "And the regent says that you should keep it."

Wordlessly Jean-Marc reached his fingers around her neck and refastened her necklace. Then he took a step away, putting some distance between them.

But the spell was not broken.

"What now?" she asked. Then she forced her mind to the business at hand. "What's happening back at the mansion?"

Judging by his face, the news was bad.

"The two women guarding Sauvage left your bedroom shortly after you did and haven't been seen since. The masquerade of the glamour fell apart, and the Bouvards assume you used the ruse to leave. Most of them think you have abandoned them."

"Oh. There's an idea," she said brightly.

He smiled grimly as if to say, Wait, there's more. "The others think that we Devereauxes have kidnapped you."

She parsed that. "Have you?"

"There's an idea," he deadpanned. "After I fly to New York and risk my life to find you, and bring you back to New Orleans, *then* I'll kidnap you."

"It's so typical of the Flames," Alain said, shaking his head in disgust. "They always look outside for someone to blame for their situation."

"Which situation is that?" Izzy asked, taking in both the Devereaux cousins with one gaze. "The one where Marianne, their *guardienne*, gets pregnant, takes off, has a baby who goes missing for twenty-six years and winds up in a coma?"

"The one where they have not prospered the way the House of the Shadows and the House of the Blood have," Jean-Marc replied.

"The House of the Blood. The bad guys," she said.

"*Oui*. The bad guys. Their magic and ours—the Devereaux, House of the Shadows—is far stronger than yours," Jean-Marc elaborated. "I haven't been able to figure out why. But the de Bouvards who can bring themselves to admit the truth believe it is the result of enemy magic."

"Blanche Neige and I discussed that," Alain said.

Jean-Marc quirked a brow. "'Blanche Neige'? It suits her."

Izzy colored. "Tell me the rest. How is Sauvage?"

"Gone," he said evenly. "I sent her and her boyfriend away. They're Ungifted and it's too dangerous for them here."

She was relieved yet saddened. She would miss that crazy girl. She nodded at him and said, "You were right to do it. But I wish I could have said goodbye."

"Maybe you can contact her later, when things calm down." After another beat, Jean-Marc added, "I've made a few other changes."

"Go on," she said warily.

"It would be easier just to show you. Come with me," he ordered her.

He took her hand, wrapping his fingers around hers. She didn't argue because she wanted to see what he was being so mysterious about. At least, that was what she told herself. It felt good to hold his large, warm hand. It gave her comfort and strength.

Equally curious, Alain trailed behind.

Jean-Marc made motions in front of the broad wooden gate with its bones and painted charms. It clicked open and swung outward with a squeaky creak.

"Abracadabra," Jean-Marc said.

Izzy gaped. Her knees buckled and Jean-Marc smoothly grasped her forearm to keep her upright.

"Oh, my God," she said. "Is this for real?"

Jean-Marc's answer was a smile.

"*Bienvenue,*" he said. "Welcome."

Chapter 9

"Nicely done," Alain told his cousin, as he, Jean-Marc and Izzy walked out of the werewolves' camp, toward Jean-Marc's magical creation. Beneath the silvery moonlight, a small but stately plantation-style mansion rose from among the cypresses and live oaks. It was a miniature of the Flames' family seat—built of brick, it had two stories, fronted with three graceful stone columns. Traditional New Orleans-style iron scrollwork in a flame motif formed the balconies on both verandahs. The exquisite edifice was surrounded by flowering rose bushes and orange trees, and trellises dripping with bougainvillea and wisteria.

"For you," Jean-Marc said to Izzy.

At least a dozen muscular men and women in dark blue body armor, blue pants, black boots and sunglasses stood at attention on the ground-floor verandah of the mansion with

Uzis slung across their chests. Another dozen operatives similarly dressed all in black ringed the second-story balcony.

"Your personal guards," Jean-Marc said. "Devereaux in blue, Bouvard in black."

"*La guardienne!*" one of the men in black bellowed.

Both sets of guards presented arms, slamming the barrels of their machine guns into their palms. Then they knelt on one knee and lowered their heads.

"*Vive!*" they yelled.

"Not yet," Izzy murmured, conscious that she was braless and barefoot, hadn't brushed her teeth and was really not ready to be anyone's commander in chief. But she held out her hands and said, "*Merci, mes gendarmes.*" She had no idea what she had just said.

"*C'est bien,* Isabelle," Jean-Marc murmured approvingly as the troops rose and snapped back to attention. "These are the best. Except for Georges and Maurice. I left them at the de Bouvard mansion for the time being." He looked at Alain. "I had our people break their cover. Michel is *fou.*"

"How naive," Alain drawled. "Did he honestly think you and I had come to New Orleans alone?"

"So it appears, by his reaction." He rolled his eyes and shook his head. "He's an amateur." Then he said to Izzy, "Your mother is inside. I transported her here as well."

"Transported."

"Brought her. I'm not *that* Gifted."

Before she could ask, he added, "Her condition is unchanged. Although she is still alive, she will never wake up."

"And the Femmes Blanches?" Izzy queried. "Are some women caring for her?"

"I asked for volunteers," Jean-Marc answered. "There are

fifty women in there, dedicated to helping you and your mother. Annette is one of them."

She was moved. It must have been a difficult choice, to leave the relative safety of de Bouvard headquarters in favor of a location selected by the Devereaux regent.

"This is *fantastique*," Alain crowed. "Finally we're free of the Bouvards."

That gave Izzy pause. Wasn't the whole point of bringing her to New Orleans so she could lead the Bouvards?

With a dry chuckle, Jean-Marc said, "Michel threatened to go to the Grand Covenate. I told him I would accompany him to the Convening Chamber myself."

"And? It's time, don't you think?" Alain asked.

"Of course he backed down," Jean-Marc replied. "He trusts them even less than he trusts us." He grew more serious. "I want to stabilize the situation and make sure Isabelle is safe. And then we'll contact the Grand Covenate with or without Michel's cooperation. They need to know what's going on down here."

As they walked down the brick path that led into the front door, Izzy looked up at him and said, "Why did you do this?"

"It's not safe for you at the mansion," he told her. "I'm still investigating the assassination attempt. I haven't yet located all the guilty parties." He clenched his jaw, forming dark hollows beneath his high cheekbones. "But when I do, they'll be punished."

She wanted to ask him how. She wondered what kind of authority he had when it came to punishment. Julius Esposito's howls of despair keened through her memory and she took a breath, wondering if Jean-Marc was capable of doing such a thing to another human being.

He glanced down at her; she kept her gaze averted. That was not a conversation she wanted to have right now.

"I'm going to continue your training," he said. "You and your mother will stay here until I'm sure we've cleaned out the dangers inside your headquarters."

"What about the dangers here?" Andre said, coming up behind them. "Did you hear about the vampire minions, the zombies and the demons that Le Fils sent after *la jolie* and your cousin?" He gestured to the trees, the swamp, the moon. "This is the bayou, Jean-Marc. A deadly place." He crossed himself and kissed his thumb.

Jean-Marc raised a brow. *"Bon soir, mon copain.* Tell me, could you see this château from your front porch?"

"I'm glad to see you on your feet, *mon vieux*." Andre shook his head. "All I saw were the trees. It wasn't until I walked out of our compound that I saw it."

"Because it's warded," Jean-Marc said. He waved a hand, revealing a dome of sparkling blue surrounding the house like a snow globe. "The terms of my regency prevented my warding your headquarters with Devereaux magic," he explained to Izzy. "There's no such edict here. And I have very strong magic at my disposal."

"They wouldn't let you use your magic to protect my mother?" she asked, taken aback.

He shook his head. "A foolish point of pride. You'll be safe here, at least for now. And I'll help you with your Gifts. You'll learn to defend yourself. And hopefully you'll be able to sort out the messages in your visions."

In my visions, I've seen you dead and hanging from a tree, she wanted to tell him. *Twice.*

"I promised *la jolie maîtresse* a *fais-dodo*," Andre said. "Maybe we could hold it tonight, inside her new place?" He looked at Izzy. "I'm talking about having a party, *chére*." He playfully gestured to Jean-Marc's ponytail. "Let down our hair. Celebrate life."

Jean-Marc stroked his chin, bemused. He seemed so serious; Izzy had trouble imagining him at a party.

Alain looked at him, and Jean-Marc gazed back. Izzy had the sense that they were communicating with each other telepathically. Alain lowered his head and sighed.

"We have nothing more on Alain's chauffeur than what that *loa* told you," Jean-Marc told Izzy.

She opened her mouth to say she was sorry again, but it was just too banal. She nodded sadly, twisting her hands together.

"*Merci*, Blanche Neige," Alain murmured. He waved a hand. "*Eh, bien*. Andre is right. Madame should have a chance to relax."

"No, not when you're in mourning," she insisted. She said to Andre, "We'll have the *fais-dodo* another time."

"*C'est bien*." Andre scratched his chest through his long johns, acquiescing. "Just say the word and we'll cook up some gumbo and bring the fiddles over."

Jean-Marc said, "I want to get you inside, Isabelle. You should rest. You've had an ordeal." He looked at his cousin. "You, as well."

The two nodded. Izzy was exhausted, and sore from their trek through the bayou. Back in New York, she ran to stay in shape, jogging at least three or four times a week. It had been nearly three weeks since she'd exercised, and she could tell— her quads and hamstrings were bunched and strained.

As if he had read her thoughts, Jean-Marc moved his fingers in a circle. Her aches and pains vanished. She licked her lips, feeling both grateful and intruded upon, and said nothing.

Andre said, "I'm going back to bed."

Izzy turned to say goodbye, and both she and Andre

spotted the second protective blue dome Jean-Marc had created, this one shielding the werewolves' camp. He grinned broadly and said to Jean-Marc, *"Merci bien, mon vieux."* Then he loped back through the wooden gateway.

Alain scrutinized his cousin. "Do you have the energy for that?" he queried gently.

Jean-Marc's answer was a Frenchman's no-big-deal shrug as he led Izzy and Alain into Izzy's new house. It was decorated in white and blue—the colors of the Bouvards and the Devereauxes. The floor was a checkerboard of squares of pure white and blue-veined marble, dancing with colorful light from towering stained-glass windows repeating the image of a white dove flying above a trio of flames. She knew a dove figured prominently in the Devereaux coat of arms—a gauntlet extending from a castle tower, either releasing or capturing the bird of peace, and grace.

A waterfall splashed from the cathedral ceiling into a pool brimming with scarlet koi. In the center of the pool stood a white-marble statue of Jehanne in battle gear, her sword drawn and held in front of her face. Her features were Izzy's features. Her mother's features.

Izzy heard gentle harp music and smelled roses and oranges as Jean-Marc snapped his fingers and mist surrounded their feet. It buoyed them up to the second story, depositing them in front of a wide, ornately carved wooden door. The door was covered with wooden roses and flames twined together, overlaid with the initials *B* and *D*. Bouvard and Devereaux.

Two helmeted medieval knights in full suits of armor materialized and clanked to attention. They were identical to the ones that had guarded Marianne's chamber in the other mansion.

"Je suis Isabelle Celestina DeMarco de Bouvard, Maison des Flammes," Izzy told the knights.

The two knights presented arms—in their case, enormous battle swords—as the more modern guards outside the house had done.

The door disappeared, and a chamber stretched out before Izzy. It was very like the one in the other mansion. Two rows of veiled Femmes Blanches were seated on upholstered benches, holding hands. The double chain of women formed a corridor leading to a gilt bed on a dais at the other end of the chamber. It was Marianne's sickbed, surrounded by alabaster pots of lilies. Behind the bed rose banks of medical equipment. Overlooking Marianne's right shoulder, an exquisitely carved statue of Jehanne stood with her sword lowered to her side, her banner draped around her shoulders like a shawl. Her head was lowered slightly and ringed with the halo of a saint.

Light from the platinum chandelier overhead bathed the still form of the *guardienne*. And…she was glowing. Izzy had only seen her glow once, when she herself had placed her palms on her and willed her to wake up.

"*Mon Dieu*, what does this mean?" Alain asked under his breath.

"Back in the mansion, the magical conduit between Marianne and *les Femmes Blanches* was muted," Jean-Marc explained, pantomiming with his fingers. "Like a flame turned down low. Here they can send her more energy."

"How long has that been going on?" Alain asked. "Did they know they weren't as effective as they could be?"

Jean-Marc shook his head. "It's as much a surprise to them as it was to me. I'm wondering if there is something wrong with the other mansion. With the atmosphere." He turned to Izzy. "Do you remember that I kept you out of your bedroom back in Brooklyn?"

"Yes. You said it was toxic," she replied.

"Perhaps the Bouvard mansion is likewise toxic," Jean-Marc continued. "It would help to explain why they're weaker than us."

"Or perhaps being inside a space warded with Devereaux magic has enhanced their powers. Given their healing Gift a boost," Alain suggested.

"That is another possibility," Jean-Marc concurred. "In either case, it's good news."

Izzy licked her lips, framing the question she wanted so badly to ask that she was afraid to do so. She was afraid of Jean-Marc's answer. "Can they heal her now? Will she wake up?" *Will I meet my mother, and will I be off the hook?*

Her mind filled with the image of Pat. If she wasn't needed here, she could return home. God, she wished for that.

So, apparently, did Le Fils.

"The Femmes Blanches don't know how to interpret the glowing. Medically, her condition hasn't changed," Jean-Marc replied cautiously.

Yet, Izzy thought. *She has to get better. The glowing must mean that her power has increased.* It seemed so obvious to her.

She said to Jean-Marc, "Whatever happens, thank you. As usual, you've served the de Bouvards well." She sounded so formal, so reserved. But it was hard for her to find her way with him now. He had acted in an official capacity when he had located her and brought her here. No doubt he was still acting in an official capacity.

And yet, when she locked gazes with him, she felt the low-level connection that was always present between them. It was an undercurrent of such intensity that for an instant, it crowded out her thoughts.

"*De rien, Isabelle,*" he said, as if with some difficulty.

Then she gestured for Alain and him to remain at the entrance to the chamber, while she walked down the center alone. As she passed the seated women, they rose, inclining their veiled heads.

Bienvenue, chére.

Vive, fille de Marianne.

We're loyal to you, Isabelle.

We'll help you.

She heard their loving thoughts and pressed her hands against her chest, deeply moved. She was grateful to them, and to Jean-Marc, for making all this happen.

Then she reached her mother's bedside and moved to the right side of her bed, trying not to crowd the healing woman who sat silent and veiled in a white satin upholstered chair beside the bed. The woman was holding Marianne's right hand. Behind the bed, medical monitoring equipment was stacked on a table, as it had been in the de Bouvard mansion. The readout windows were covered over with pieces of white paper, as if to shield onlookers from the tragic news: Marianne de Bouvard was still flatline.

Izzy murmured, "*Pardon, merci,*" to the veiled woman, who inclined her head.

Then Izzy placed her hand on Marianne's cheek. The *guardienne*'s skin was dry and cool, her eyes closed, her mouth slack and partly open. Her riot of hair was spread across her satin pillows.

Izzy leaned forward and kissed her forehead. A gentle warmth blossomed against her lips. Then Izzy's entire body began to tingle. She heard gasps around the room as she lifted her mouth and gazed down at her mother.

Her mother was still glowing with white light. And now

Izzy was, too. She raised her arm to see a radiant layer of magical energy emanating from her skin. It was about an inch high, and she could see it pulsing and vibrating.

She examined her other arm, then her torso, raising the jeans skirt so she could see her legs. She was glowing all over—was it from her own Gift? Something Marianne had done? Or the Femmes Blanches, or Jean-Marc?

A louder gasp echoed around the room. Some of the women stood up. Izzy blinked back at them; then the veiled woman behind her tugged on her hand with her own free hand and said, "*Attends, madame!*"

Izzy's attention shifted to the figure in the bed. Her heart leaped.

Marianne was *smiling*.

"By the *patronesse!*" another woman cried. It was Marianne's doctor, Dr. de Bouvard, who rushed from a side door on the right wall of the chamber with Annette at her side. They approached the bed, and Izzy took a step away to give them room to examine her mother.

"Keep touching her," the doctor exhorted Izzy as she un-clicked a penlight from the pocket of her white coat, opened Marianne's right eye and shone the light inside it. "Yes, I have activity," she reported to Annette. She did the same with the left eye. "Left pupil responding as well!"

The door opened again and a man in white scrubs poked his head around it. "We have an EEG reading!" he announced.

The Femmes Blanches began to stir and whisper among themselves. The woman holding Marianne's right hand leaned her head forward and kissed the back of Izzy's hand through her veils. She murmured, "*Merci, Isabelle, Fille des Flammes.*" Daughter of the Flames.

"She's coming back," Annette said to Izzy. She threw her arms around her. "You did it!"

The room erupted into cheers and joyful weeping as the women, still holding hands, began to chant.

"*Isabelle! Marianne! Les Femmes des Flammes!*"

They were cheering for the Women of the Flames—Izzy DeMarco, formerly from Brooklyn, and her mother. Marianne, an enigma who had been unconscious for over a quarter of a century.

Against Jean-Marc's wishes—he wanted her in her own bedroom, safe and sequestered—Izzy put on her white satin gown, which he had brought from the de Bouvard mansion; brushed her teeth and said a quick prayer to the Virgin Mary; and then another, fleetingly and fervently, in thanks to St. Joan of Arc; crawled into bed with her mother and settled in with her arms curled around Marianne. The veiled women kept vigil throughout the day, occasionally giving up their seats for a replacement. Izzy heard their quiet movements, and their occasional good wishes, aimed her way:

Merci, chére. Take care of her.

Make her well again, jolie *Isabelle.*

Marianne, je vous en prie. *Wake up. We have waited so long for you.*

Then she drifted and dreamed, and she saw Marianne towering above her. She was a little girl, a toddler, really, and her mother was smiling down on her. Isabelle was holding out a pure white lily, and her mother was singing an old French lullaby:

Sûr le pont d'Avignon,
on y dansait, on y dansait...

Her voice was beautiful. It was the voice of a saint, of an angel.

Izzy saw her own chubby arms reaching toward Marianne, heard her own voice say in French, *"Maman, je t'aime! Tu est belle!"*

Then the image faded, to be replaced by a glowing white figure at the end of a long, scintillating tunnel, robed and veiled like the Femmes Blanches. Clear, bell-like soprano voices filled the air as it removed the veil from its face and held out its arms. It was glowing so brightly that Izzy had to shield her eyes—and she saw that she was an adult again.

"We did not have a life together," the figure said. *"But I always loved you. I dreamed of you. Hold me now, my daughter."*

"We can still have a life together," Izzy replied in a whisper, curling around her mother in the gilt bed.

And then she fell into a deep, dreamless sleep.

Chapter 10

In the morning, she woke to Jean-Marc and the doctor standing over her. Jean-Marc was wearing a black sweater and jeans, his hair loose. An earring in his left ear—a tiny gold dove—glittered as he moved his head. His eyes were hooded, his expression grim.

Did something happen to Marianne in the night?

Izzy saw that she herself was still glowing. Anxiously she gazed at her mother's face. She was still smiling gently, and *she* was still glowing as well. The veiled women in the room appeared calm. The vibration in the room was still buoyant with hope.

Jean-Marc spoke first. "*Bonjour,*" he said. Annette came up beside him, holding a large tray full of covered dishes. "We'll eat. Then we'll train."

"Train?" She stared at him as if he were speaking a foreign

language. "I'm not going anywhere. I'm staying with my mother." She held Marianne tightly.

Jean-Marc gave the doctor a pointed look. Flushing, the woman cleared her throat and said, "The regent and I have discussed the situation. We've agreed that we'll conduct an experiment. You'll...train, and while you're separated from your mother, we'll see if her condition reverts."

"*Reverts?*" Izzy couldn't believe what she was hearing. "And what will that prove? That I shouldn't have left her side?"

"Isabelle," Jean-Marc said harshly, and she knew then that something was up. She looked at him, hard. He returned her gaze and said nothing more. He was holding out on her, forcing her to get out of the bed before he would talk to her.

"Damn it," she said.

And then she heard the voice: *C'est bien. Go with him.*

He moved to help her; she shrugged him off, kissing Marianne's lips. She held her breath, waiting for a response and getting none. Disappointed and a bit anxious, she rose, stood, and smoothed out her hair.

"Clean up and dress," he said. "In these." He handed her some workout clothes. "And these," he added, bending down and retrieving a pair of black boots and socks.

"I have boots at the cabin," she informed him.

He gave her a look. "They're filthy and stiff with swamp water. You're an heiress, Isabelle. You can afford them."

"All right," she said. "I'll shower in my suite."

"Please wait for the food," he said to Annette. "We need some time." He looked back at Izzy. "Shower long and well. Get the residue off your body."

Aye-aye, sir, she thought. His lip curled and she realized that he'd heard her.

Saying nothing more—aloud or in her mind—she went through the wooden door just off her mother's chamber, where Jean-Marc had created a bedroom suite for her. It was done in white and blue, like the rest of the mansion—in velvets and silks, her walnut four-poster sinking into the luxurious, thick pile of the rich white wool carpet. He had also installed a landline so she could call New York—her father and Pat—and Pennsylvania—her brother, Gino. He had explained that when she dialed, the number that would show on the receiver's caller ID would be the fake number in Florida. When a caller dialed the same number, it would be forwarded to her landline. If she didn't pick up, the "hotel's" message system recorded the calls. It wasn't very magical—it was simple Ungifted technology—but it certainly was effective.

Izzy quickly showered in her immense white-marble bathroom and examined the pile of clothes Jean-Marc had thrust at her. There was a pair of black sweats, a silky black thong, a black sports bra and a black T-shirt. She paused at the thong. Her only alternate pair of underwear was back in Andre's cabin, also filthy and stinky with swamp water. She might as well go with the thong.

She put it on, feeling uncommonly wanton. She took a peek at herself in the freestanding full-view mirror beside the bed. She was topless, and she rather liked the look of the tiny strip of shiny black slung low on her hips.

Then she remembered that back in New York, Jean-Marc had maintained surveillance of her bedroom—for security reasons—by means of a crystal called a scrying stone. It was the magical equivalent of a button cam—a miniaturized video sending unit. As Jean-Marc himself had said, the lines between technology and magic were blurring every day.

Whatever the case, she didn't want him to see her prancing

around like this, so she covered her breasts and quickly dressed.

Next she tried to do something with her hair. She didn't have any hair elastics or barrettes, so she had to settle for letting it run riot, tumbling over her shoulders. She rarely wore makeup, so she didn't mourn the loss. But she did think that if they were going to be staying out here for any appreciable amount of time, she'd need to make a list of things she needed.

She went back through the wooden door of her suite into her mother's chamber. Jean-Marc was standing over her mother's bed. She crossed over to him, and they looked down on Marianne together. She was still glowing, her lips still curved in a smile.

He turned and saw her, and his eyes widened slightly in masculine appreciation. Discomforting as it was coming from Jean-Marc, she enjoyed it. Before Pat, she'd usually been one of the guys down at the station house—she played pool and drank beer with the alpha-male cops, who then sought her advice about their relationships with softer, more datable women.

Pat had changed all that, made her feel beautiful and sensual. It was still new to her.

The veiled heads of the Femmes Blanches shifted slightly as she and Jean-Marc walked past them. She could feel their alertness, their uncertainty about what was happening in the strange new mansion. Their readiness to help her, if she needed it

Jean-Marc propelled her through the ornate wooden door, to the landing flanked by the two knights. Lavender mist swirled around their feet, lowering them to the ground floor.

Jean-Marc walked her past the waterfall and outside, down the brick path to a small clearing between the mansion and the werewolves' camp. It was a grassy, flat square about thirty feet a side, devoid of cypresses and live oaks and their capes of Spanish moss. She was certain it hadn't been there yesterday.

Several white leather bags were grouped around a bulbous plastic form, a head-size sphere perched atop an elongated oval, set into a generous, round base. It was vaguely human-shaped, and there were Xs painted on it in strategic areas—the face, the heart, the midsection, the groin. A submachine gun leaned against it like a man taking a cigarette break.

Training, she thought, not sure how she felt. He had told her he would train her in New Orleans, and she had nearly died in New York for lack of it. But with her mother's condition improved—or at least, changed—she wondered if it should take top priority.

Jean-Marc walked to one of the white bags, unzipped it and pulled out her Medusa. Dangling it by his thumb, he said, "You left this unprotected when you took your bath. You lost track of it. That was very sloppy."

As she reddened, she heard the dream voice:

Secure your gun. Or he will take it. And he will end your House.

The voice didn't mean Jean-Marc, did it? She got quiet, and listened to her intuition. There was nothing more. Ever since she had met Jean-Marc, she had wavered between trusting him and fearing that everything he told her was a lie to entrap her. She was certain of so little. Except for the connection between them. That was real.

Hey, just because he turns me on, doesn't mean he's not evil, she thought. She gazed at the mansion with a different perspective. Was it a sanctuary, or had she just waltzed right into a prison?

"I am waiting," he told her, his dark eyes penetrating the silence.

She walked up to him and grabbed the gun. With a practiced air, she whipped it open. The cartridges had been removed. He had rendered it safe.

"There was something wrong with it," she said, clicking it shut. "I think Louise jimmied it so it wouldn't work."

"I have search parties combing the bayou for her remains," he said. "We may still be able to read something off them."

"Don't they degrade rapidly?" she asked.

He cocked his head. "Who told you that?"

"I think it was Louise." She thought a moment. "It might have been Michel. That was why we had to hurry once they retrieved Esposito's…residue." She frowned. "Why? Isn't that true? Didn't we have to hurry?"

"*Peut-être,*" he replied. "Maybe."

"Are you being deliberately obtuse?" she challenged him.

"Why would I do that?" Raising a brow, Jean-Marc took the Medusa back from her, completely surprising her. He walked backward, moving his lips as he began to speak in what sounded like Latin. Then he turned sideways and raised his arm, sighting down the barrel at a spot parallel to where Izzy stood. Izzy felt herself turning to ice. All he had to do was whip that gun to the left and—

It's not loaded, she reminded herself.

He kept chanting in Latin as he walked over to the equipment bags and leaned over, giving her a view of his rock-hard ass in his tight jeans. With his left hand, he unzipped the closest bag and sorted through it. He brought out a green cardboard box and pulled open the top with his finger. Ammo. She couldn't tell what caliber it was from where she stood. He plucked out a cartridge and opened the cylinder. He loaded the single cartridge into the Medusa and snapped it shut.

His voice rose. Sparkling swirls formed in the rosy

morning air, spinning near the ground and kicking up leaves and twigs. The wind moved faster, blurring into long bands, flattening and expanding. It was taking on a shape. A human shape. The silhouette of a man.

There was a sharp crack, and the air around the silhouette appeared to solidify and drop to the ground in chunks. She thought of how Michel and D'Artagnon had cut the evil in the chamber into briquettes where they had read Esposito's remains. Then the shape took on form and finer definition.

Izzy recoiled. Her heart beat out of rhythm and she felt a sheen of perspiration bead on her forehead and her upper lip. Her hands shook. The dark coat, the scar across its face—it was the assassin that had come after her in New York.

Jean-Marc said to Izzy, "Don't forget. It's a fabricant."

Not a man, she filled in. She remembered how overwhelmed she had been when she thought she had killed a human being in New York. But it had been a magically created being, just like this one.

"*Venez ici,*" Jean-Marc said. When she didn't move, he said, "Please, come here."

She didn't want to come anywhere near that thing. Which was his point, she supposed. He was going to resume her "training."

He said, "If you come to me, I will order it to approach us together. Otherwise…" He trailed off meaningfully.

"I liked you better when you were unconscious," she muttered.

She walked slowly toward him, one eye on the fabricant and one on the Medusa in his fist. Her stomach was churning, her senses on alert.

"*Magnifique,*" he said to her. "Look at yourself."

She glanced down to discover that the thin layer of white

light surrounding her body had thickened. Without losing her focus, she waved her hand in front of her eyes, curious why she didn't view her surroundings through a gauzy glow of white.

"We have many bodies," Jean-Marc said to her. "When you feel threatened, your physical body manufactures more adrenaline, *oui?* Your senses become more acute. You prepare to flee or fight.

"It's the same with our magical bodies. As you feel the need for more power, it increases." His eyes swept down her body, then back up. She felt naked. She felt as if he could see the thong through her sweats. "This is very good."

"So...you're going to scare me and that will make my power grow," she said.

"Muscles are muscles," he said. "Pain is the cornerstone of growth."

She huffed and walked over to him, boldly sweeping her eyes up and down *his* body. "Then why aren't *you* glowing?"

"I am. You just don't see it." He clicked his fingers. Immediately, his body was bathed in thick layers of indigo.

"Very impressive," she said, meaning it.

"Years of training," he replied. Then the glow vanished.

"Okay, you win. I get it. Bring it on. Stress me out."

He handed her the Medusa. She aimed it at the fabricant, who did not seem to be aware of her or Jean-Marc. Maybe he hadn't activated it yet, done whatever it was that he had to do to make it attack her.

"You know that the .9 mm's stop the heart of your target," he said, as he leaned his head toward her, refining her aim with his hand over hers. "Unless there's a demonic component. Then they're likely to explode. Like Esposito."

Izzy licked her lips, struggling not to tremble beneath his touch. "Right."

"The .380 auto rounds erase memories. Sometimes permanently, sometimes not. It depends on your target. If it's a Gifted, it's usually temporary. The .38 Colts diffuse magical energy. So, say you've got someone flinging fireballs at you. If you hit them with one of these, you could decrease their range."

"Or the speed and temperature of the fireball," she ventured, her gaze on the fabricant.

"*Oui. Vraiment.* Excellent, Isabelle." He sounded pleased.

"Why not just stop their hearts? In all cases?" Izzy asked. But she knew the answer. It was the same as in police work. The key words were *stop* and *apprehend*, not *kill*.

"The Bouvards are on record as protectors," Jean-Marc said. "They are supposed to serve a function very much like the Ungifted law enforcement agencies. There are supernaturals who prey on the Ungifted—and sometimes even the Gifted—but others who just want to live in peace."

"But we don't police Gifted from other Houses?" Izzy asked.

"There aren't supposed to be any Gifted from other Houses in your territory," Jean-Marc replied. "The Grand Covenate exists because we divided up the geographical world into territories. We enter the territory of another House by invitation only."

And the Devereaux cousins were not invited, Izzy thought. *The Covenate sent them here.*

"So we…keep the peace between the supernaturals and the Ungifted for the Ungifted government," Izzy said, moving on.

"That is your manifesto." She heard the dryness in his voice. "But we're not doing it."

"No. You're not. Mayor Gelineau has good cause to be irritated with your House. Your presence is disruptive and your leadership is not very helpful."

"I see," she said, not really seeing.

"The .357 Magnums are for demons," he continued, sighting down the gun again. "But if you use one on a nondemon, it's got the power of a standard-issue .357."

Before he could say anything else, she squeezed the trigger. The .9 mm screamed toward the fabricant and slammed into its heart. Or rather, the place where it would have a heart. She had no idea if it did or not. It collapsed to the ground, its eyes open and vacant, to all external appearances, a dead man.

"Hey, it works," Izzy said. "You must have fixed it."

"I didn't tell you to fire," he said, frowning.

"No, you didn't." She lowered the Medusa to her side.

He crossed his arms over his chest. "It took a lot of effort to create that."

"Muscles are muscles," she replied flippantly, although she was sorry—Not that she had shot the fabricant, but that he had gone to all that effort for essentially nothing. The truth was, she couldn't bear the idea of that thing coming at her again. It would be like standing in front of a wall of fire and allowing it to sweep over her.

She turned to apologize and found him gesturing to Annette, who was standing on the first floor verandah with the breakfast tray in her arms. When Izzy turned back, she discovered a white wrought-iron table and three chairs behind her. It hadn't been there two seconds before.

Alain came out of the mansion's front door, saw Annette and took the tray from her. He paused politely, while she walked down the path in front of him.

Jean-Marc pulled a chair out for Izzy. As she sat down, he gritted, "*Tu as raison.* We shouldn't start training until we've eaten. I...pushed. As I do. On occasion."

On occasion? she thought. *How about all the time?*

"Thank you." She hesitated. "I'm sorry I shot your assassin before he could try to assassinate me."

Jean-Marc smiled a lazy grin as he pulled out his own chair. "Shooting first is a valid method of self-defense." His grin grew as he added, "Thank God I only put one cartridge in the gun."

She smiled back at him. "Yes, thank God." She wondered if he believed in God. The patron of his house was the Gray King. Did that leave room for God?

She asked, "What did Louise do to it?"

He shrugged. "A malfunctioning spell. It broke when she died."

So a spell stops working when the person who cast it dies? Izzy thought. She tucked that bit of information away.

Empty-handed, Annette approached the table. She said to Izzy, "The doctor wanted me to tell you that your mother is still the same. She's very pleased."

"Thank you," Izzy said, genuinely grateful. She took a breath as she frowned apologetically at Annette. "I'm sorry I had to trick you like that. With the glamour. I'm sorry that I left you at the mansion without telling you. I didn't know what else to do. I—" She glanced at Jean-Marc.

The man took that as his cue to move away, signaling for Alain to keep his distance as well. The two men walked apart, giving Izzy and Annette some space.

"*Guardienne,*" Annette said, her voice husky and choked with emotion. "It is we who should apologize to you. I know you don't want this. So many other Bouvards have just…left."

Annette lowered her voice, as if she wanted to make sure that Jean-Marc couldn't hear her. "And I wonder myself, why do we continue? What is our purpose? Maybe it's time for our House to fall."

Izzy put her hand on Annette's shoulder, and saw that she was no longer glowing. Beneath the weight of Izzy's fingertips, the other woman trembled.

Izzy said, "My understanding is that we were meant to be protectors. It seems that because of our…situation, we've fallen down on the job. Back in my other life, my dream was to become a cop. A protector. I'll do what I can to keep you safe. And once we're back on our feet, we'll keep other people safe, too."

Why the hell did I just say that? she thought as Annette bobbed her head in agreement. It implied promises she wasn't ready to make.

Annette bobbed a curtsey. "*Merci bien,*" she said. A shadow crossed her face. "*Madame,*" she continued, then fell silent as Jean-Marc and Alain returned. Izzy wondered what she had wanted to say, and she was a little frustrated with Jean-Marc for interrupting.

Annette averted her gaze from the two men and said to Izzy, "I'll be inside."

She left. Alain set the tray on the table and snapped his fingers. The silver covers on the dishes disappeared; there were croissants, and strawberries in white cream; soft-boiled eggs in little silver egg cups and large white cups decorated with flames, containing strong, fragrant coffee.

Alain served the three of them, pouring heaps of sugar and cream into all three cups without asking Izzy how she took her coffee. She usually drank it black, like her father. Like most cops. But as she raised the cup to her lips and took a sip, she found it uncommonly rich and delicious. Pleasurable.

Jean-Marc and Alain lowered their heads for a moment. Izzy wondered if they were praying, and if so, to whom.

Then Jean-Marc picked up his coffee and said, "Did you hear the voodoo drums last night?"

She shook her head.

"Really?" Alain asked, blinking at her. "I barely slept at all."

"They were talking all through the bayou," Jean-Marc went on. "About Le Fils. He is coming after you, Isabelle. Again."

A fistful of fear grabbed her lower back and shook it, hard. "I beat him last time," she said, but her voice cracked.

"You shot Julius Esposito. You didn't touch Le Fils. He simply left."

"Retreated," she argued, but even she could see that that was too fine a point to put on it.

"I told him what Mamaloi's *loa* revealed," Alain told her. He held his hand in the air and a large, white cloth napkin appeared. He laid it across his lap. Then he gestured toward Izzy's lap, and a napkin appeared there, too. "About the little fish and the gator."

"I'm guessing that's why you marched me out here to train first thing," Izzy said to Jean-Marc. "No gator bait for breakfast. Or vice versa."

She was trying to lighten the mood. It didn't work.

Jean-Marc nodded somberly.

"I am trying to save your life," he said.

After Jean-Marc's comment, Izzy could take no pleasure in their breakfast. She ate quietly while Jean-Marc and Alain talked in English, French and occasionally telepathically. When it came time to clear the dishes, Jean-Marc gathered them together himself and carried them into the house. She'd half expected one of the Devereaux cousins to snap his fingers to make them conveniently disappear.

Under a cloud, Izzy watched him go. During their training

session, he hadn't praised her one time, nor given her any feedback except impatient criticism and thinly veiled despair that she had so far to go. Maybe it was childish to need some strokes, but she needed them. And she wasn't going to get them, at least not from Jean-Marc de Devereaux. Not during their workouts, and not during the conversations that followed them, apparently.

Alain turned to Izzy and said, "He is trying, Blanche Neige. This has been a terrible strain on him." He took a breath as if he were considering his next words very carefully. "He...has come to care for you very much. It is making him crazy that you're so vulnerable. Everything in him wants to take you to Montreal, where we live." He smiled sadly. "Where we *used* to live."

"You've been here for three years," she said, her attention back at his caring for her very much. How much? Did he know how attracted to him she was?

Did he know that she cared very deeply about Pat? That she thought she might be in love with the detective back in New York?

"Three long years," he concurred. "And may I say that aside from you, I don't care if I ever meet another Bouvard again. Please don't be offended."

"I'm not," she assured him. "I don't feel very much like a Bouvard."

"Yet," Alain replied.

She was about to ask him what he meant by that when Jean-Marc came back to the table. He wiped his face like someone who was unutterably weary.

Dropping his hands to his sides, he said, "*Bon*. Let's resume."

Preparing for battle was an ugly business. Izzy's stomach lurched as she mimicked pulling the pin on a grenade for

Jean-Marc's inspection. Alain was assisting, mostly by arranging the vast store of supplies Jean-Marc had assembled for Izzy's training. Since Le Fils was a vampire, Jean-Marc's emphasis was on antivampire material. The grenade contained a payload of holy water, although it would still have to be detonated like a standard grenade. He showed her Baggies full of peeled garlic, and handfuls of green-tinted plastic crosses attached to summer-camp-style lanyards.

"Scatter the crucifixes along your escape route," he said. "They're glow-in-the-dark, so you'll be able to trace your path. Vampires won't be able to step on or over them, and it'll slow them down." He dangled one at her. "The plastic strings don't tangle."

Wooden stakes were not part of the gear. Vampires had to be beheaded or set on fire to die the True Death.

"You can also make their heads explode like melons," Izzy added helpfully as Jean-Marc clicked the barrel of her Medusa back into place.

"I've reloaded your gun with the right ammo to do just that," he informed her, as he handed her the Medusa. He watched her slide it into the gun belt he had brought for her. "And I need to remind you that not all those who come against you will be vampires or fabricants."

Her chest tightened. "I've already killed more people than my father in his entire career as a police officer." In case he didn't understand, she said, "One. Esposito."

"It depends on your definition of *people*," Alain said, juggling a couple of grenades in his hands. "A man who trades his soul for power, is he a man?"

"A twelve-year-old boy who sells heroin for food money, is he a drug dealer?" Izzy replied.

"Let's go through the Uzi." Jean-Marc held up a submachine gun and looped the sling around her neck. Her skin crawled. She had processed dozens, if not hundreds, of submachine guns in the prop cage, but this was the first time she had ever gotten close to firing one.

If Jean-Marc noticed her gun phobia, he didn't comment on it.

"The most important thing is that it's not like TV. Don't shoot in long, continuous bursts or the kick will have you pointing at the moon. Three bursts and a rest. *Bam-bam-bam,* pause."

"Got it."

"If you shoot a vampire, it will slow it down so one of us can decapitate it or set it on fire."

She nodded. "Got it.

"*Bon.*" He stood back. "T'll create some fabricants for you to shoot. Once you're proficient, we'll move on to flamethrowers."

"What about rocket launchers?" She was still trying to find that moment of levity.

"After the flamethrowers," he replied, without a trace of irony. "Before we go hand-to-hand. Martial arts, brass knuckles, garrottes, that sort of thing."

That sort of thing.

No levity today.

Chapter 11

During the next week, in addition to working with Izzy, Jean-Marc resumed his full roster of duties as regent for the House of the Flames. He met with Michel de Bouvard, Sange, Mayor Gelineau, Governor Jackson and the superintendent of the New Orleans Police, Broussard. Izzy didn't know exactly what he said to them about the situation, and he kept the information from her. She knew they had wanted to meet her, but Jean-Marc kept her under wraps. He told her to concentrate on her training, and that when it was time to bring her back into the loop of Bouvard leadership, he would do so.

Every day she went across the clearing to visit the werewolves. The women gave her clothes—jeans, T-shirts, slinky tank tops and gypsy skirts. She invited them to her mansion as well. The scents of chicory and wine mingled with the oranges and roses Izzy had come to associate with safety and tranquility, making a new fragrance to soothe her jangled nerves.

They had their *fais do-do,* playing crazy zydeco that echoed down the halls and through the rooms. The werewolves threw back their heads and howled as they played fiddles and accordions and danced with wild abandon. The off-duty Femmes Blanches joined in. So, too, Alain.

Jean-Marc attended, but he didn't dance and he didn't clap along with the music. His smiles, when they came, bordered on polite distance. Izzy didn't want to be part of a situation that engendered more brooding looks on his face and the way he got up out of his chair and walked to the windows, pacing and staring out at the night.

Looking for trouble.

She didn't want there to be any trouble, anywhere, for him to find.

The air of tension around him was palpable. Izzy found herself visiting the werewolves more and more often. They were very different from Jean-Marc—alert but not wary. Careful but not paranoid.

· "He's wound too tight, him," Andre said one day, as he and Izzy leaned against the gate separating the two encampments and watched Jean-Marc and Alain performing tai chi exercises together. Dressed in black sweats and white 'beaters, the two moved in perfect unison, and their slow ballet of forms stirred her deeply. Lust tickled her lower abdomen, and her eyes roamed his body.

Almost as her own form of discipline, she forced her thoughts immediately to Pat. She had spoken to him that morning, weaving all kinds of lies about her nonexistent vacation in Florida.

The little boy whose parents had most likely been shot by

hunters somberly walked up to Izzy and held out a velvety black kitten.

He murmured, "He is Bijou." They were the first words he had spoken to Izzy, ever. She was moved. "For you, lady."

"Oh, I can't take your kitty," Izzy said gently to the small face and enormous eyes that were tilted up to gaze at her. "That's so sweet, though."

"We have a lot more," Andre drawled, putting his hand on the boy's shoulder. "The *maman* of Bijou is a little tart." He showed his teeth. "A real animal."

The cat batted at Izzy's chin and mewed at her. His eyes were enormous.

"Cats are traditional pets among the Gifted," Andre said. "You know the stories about witches and their familiars." He pointed at Bijou. "Take him over there. It'll make that grumpy Jean Marc smile."

Izzy gave the kitten a dubious frown. The kitten mewed again in response. The little boy persisted, holding him out at arm's length, and the kitten's hind legs pawed at the air. Izzy gathered up the little ball of fur in both her hands and tucked his head under her chin. Bijou licked her with his warm, sandpapery tongue, and she smiled, rubbing her nose against the round, furry head.

But Bijou would be another tendril tying her to this world, she realized. Determined to say no, she gave the kitten a little kiss and prepared to give him back. But the little boy turned on his heel and darted away.

"No," she said, with no small amount of desperation.

Andre chuckled. "Take him over there. You can always bring him back."

The cat nuzzled her cheek. She sighed, surrendering. She settled the kitten in crook of her arm, and he began to purr.

"See? He's in love," Andre assured her.

* * *

During the next week, Izzy and Bijou slept nearly every night with her mother; but some nights Izzy was restless. Afraid she would disturb Marianne, she would carry the kitten into her own room and toss and turn in her own bed. Sometimes she would stand on the balcony that looked out over the enchanted grounds, watching the moon play on the cypresses and glimmer on the bayou. She didn't see the blue light of the protective dome, but Jean-Marc assured her it was there. She was safe. Or so he said.

One night, when she was especially restless, she left Bijou in her room and went on a run through the hedge maze Jean-Marc had also created on the grounds. He didn't like her to go outside at night, but she placated him by taking two body-guards with her, as well as her Medusa. Dressed in black sweats and a T-shirt, she jogged through the twists and turns of the ivy-covered privet hedges until she reached the fountain in the center, which contained a statue of Jehanne surrounded by roses and lilies. There were statues of her everywhere. She appreciated Jean-Marc's reverence for the *patronesse*.

She had seen his bedroom only once, during her initial tour of the house, and she knew there was an altar in an alcove to the Gray King. In Alain's room, too, she surmised, although she hadn't inspected his private quarters. Jean-Marc's bedroom was heavy, dark and masculine—ebony furniture and indigo upholstery. She found his personal decorating style as oppressive as her stone bedroom back in the de Bouvard headquarters, and wondered if he had had help decorating the rest of the mansion—it was much airier and filled with light.

After the run, she showered in her private bathroom, luxuriating in the rose-scented soap and lotion that had been provided for her, when the phone rang. Wrapping herself in her oversize bath towel, she stretched across her bed to reach it. Bijou, curled in a fist-size ball on one of her satin pillows, slept through the maneuver.

"Hey, you," Pat said. "Is this too late for you?"

"No," she replied, flopping over on her back, drinking in the sound of his voice. She closed her eyes and could almost feel him in the room with her.

"How's Florida? All sun and fun?"

She flushed, hating to keep up the lie. "Yes. I really needed the break. I'm glad I took it. But I…miss you."

"But you're…okay." He sounded tentative.

"Yeah, fine. I'll be home soon." She winced. She didn't want to make more promises she couldn't keep.

"That's good. That's great."

"Yeah. How's my father?"

He chuckled. "Well, I hope this doesn't put you in therapy, but I think your dad's going out on a date with Captain Clancy tonight."

Or maybe she's just keeping an eye on him, Izzy thought. Maybe Jean-Marc told her something new is going on down here.

"Okay, isn't that fraternizing?" she said, trying to sound amused.

"Maybe not so much," he said. "With all the shit that's coming to light, Clancy's job is on the line."

"It's not her fault," Izzy said.

"Bunch of us went up the chain of command to point that out. But HQ is saying she's the boss, and cops are stealing dope on her watch."

"That is so sad," she murmured. *God knows what's been going on on my watch.*

"Esposito's still at large," he added.

No, he's not. I shot him, she wanted to say. "He must have fled the scene by now."

"That's what I'm thinking. Why stick around? Clancy asked after you, asked how you were," he went on. "Which makes me realize she knows we've got something going on."

"Do you mind? There's no rule against it. You're not my boss."

"I'm kinda proud, actually."

She smiled wistfully, missing him. "How about you? Are you working this evening?"

"Nope. I'm in for the night. I have a good book and a great beer. And if all else fails, ESPN."

"So you can stay on for a while." She wanted to have a good, long conversation.

"I can stay on for hours," he drawled. "How about you? Can you stay on, darlin'?"

Was he asking her to have phone sex? She was intrigued. She'd never done it before.

"Yeah, I can. For hours. And I'm in bed," she told him experimentally.

"Oh?" His voice dropped an octave, low and sexy, deep in his throat.

"I'm in bed, and I've had a couple of dreams about you." She rolled over on her back and flopped open her towel. Her nipples were hard. Her legs splayed open on the soft, satiny bedspread.

"Dreams? You don't know the half of it, Iz." He sounded lusty. "The dreams I've been having about you…I can feel you. And you feel…oh, Iz…"

She let her hand trail down between her legs.

"What are you wearing?" she asked him.

"Bathrobe," he replied.

"And…nothing else?"

"Nothing else."

She licked her lips. "Well, then."

Scrying stone, she thought. She muttered, "Damn it."

"Iz?"

Then suddenly Bijou jerked up on her pillow and let out a shriek. His fur stiffened and his tail went rigid; a second later, her bedroom blared with the sound of thundering drums and the shrill howls of wolves. Their keening rose and fell like sirens; the drums pounded in wild rhythms.

The noise was so loud she couldn't hear herself as she hastily said, "Pat, sorry, something's going on."

She cupped her hand around the phone and could make out Pat's voice as he said, "Are those *sirens?*"

"I'd better see what's up," she told him. "I'll call you back."

She hung up and wrapped the towel around herself. Bijou batted at her ankles and she picked him up. She opened the door to the balcony and stepped out onto the rectangle of waist-high wrought iron. The howls were deafening. The cypresses and live oaks were practically shaking with them.

Then she realized that the trees really were shaking. As she watched, plucking Bijou's tiny claws from her chest as he grabbed on in fright, half a dozen silvery wolves dashed among them, their heads thrown back as they howled. It was the werewolf pack. Were they chasing something down? A vampire? A demon?

She put her free hand on the balcony and leaned forward, scrutinizing the scene. For a moment they were hidden from her view as they shot into a copse of live oaks. Then a

hulking wolflike creature emerged. It was the pack alpha—
Andre or Lucky.

Then she saw Jean-Marc.

Dressed in a black skintight catsuit that clung to his pecs,
biceps and quads, he jogged behind the alpha with an Uzi
slung around his neck. She thought he might be wearing
body armor. His hair was tied back, and although she couldn't
read his expression from where she stood, she could read his
body language. Like the wolves, he was on the hunt.

Still carrying Bijou, Izzy ran to the bathroom and grabbed
her white floor-length bathrobe. Barefoot, she raced into her
mother's chamber and ran to Marianne's bed. Her doctor was
there, examining her. Wolf howls and drumbeats echoed
through the room. The Femmes Blanches sat in their accus-
tomed seats, hands tightly held.

Then Alain dashed into the room, in a midnight-blue robe
covered with silver doves. His hair was tousled and his eyes
were puffy; he had just awakened.

He rushed up to Izzy and said, "Good. You're all right."
He looked at the doctor.

"Marianne is fine," she reported.

"What's happening?" Izzy demanded, absently stroking
Bijou.

"Attack," Alain said. "Jean-Marc and the Cajuns are on it."
He sounded as if he were trying to reassure himself as well
as her. "We'll stay here."

They stood beside the bed, listening to the wolves and the
drums. It seemed to go on for hours. Izzy remained beside
her mother, but she felt a nearly undeniable urge to race out
of the mansion and join the fray. Her muscles contracted; her
blood roared. She felt like a warrior.

She had a sudden, clear vision:

France, the Village of Arc

Young Jehanne knelt beside the Stone of Sainte-Marie, said to be where the Virgin once appeared to some shepherds. Her head was bowed and she was praying her rosary over and over, telling the simple wooden beads with her eyes tightly shut.

"Hail Mary, full of grace," she said aloud, and desperately. Tears rolled down her cheeks. She was terrified.

"Jehanne, allez, vite," a voice whispered inside her head. "Rise up, Warrior of the True King. You must go and fight for France. You must deliver her from the enemy."

"Hail, Mary," Jehanne murmured, giving her head a shake, as if she could force the voice from her mind.

"This is not the time for prayer. This is the time for action," *said the voice.* "Go. Fight. It is your destiny."

"Blanche Neige?" Alain queried.

She blinked. He was staring at her. The doctor was staring at her. The heads of the veiled women had shifted in her direction.

"I'm all right," she said. Her free hand was empty. She had forgotten her Medusa again.

As if he had sussed out her thoughts, Alain said, "You need to stay here."

She nodded, but if anything, the urge was getting stronger. She began to sweat. She looked down at herself and saw that she was blazing with white energy.

Alain saw it, too. He made motions in the air and murmured some words. The white light dimmed, and with it, some of her adrenaline rush. She understood that he'd put a spell on her, and she both resented it and was grateful.

"I had a vision," she finally told him. "When Jehanne was first called to fight for France."

"Jean-Marc warned you the magical field here is very powerful," he said. The drums pounded faster. The howls spiked shriller. "Remember that Jean-Marc is a very powerful magic user, and he is out in the bayou, which amplifes magic as well." He touched her arm. Bijou growled and batted at him. "He'll be all right."

Shortly thereafter, the drums stopped. And then the howling. There was utter stillness.

The veiled women held their collective breath. So did Izzy.

Alain said, "You see? It's over." But he looked worried, as if he had no idea about the battle or the outcome.

I saw Jean-Marc dead and gutted, she thought sickly. *I shouldn't have let him talk me into staying here. I should have gone into the bayou to help him.*

The door to the chamber burst open. Jean-Marc appeared on the threshold, one muscular arm gripping the jamb as he heaved and panted. There was blood on his face and a diagonal gash crossing his heart. Blood dripped from the wound to the marble floor.

Alain swore in French as Izzy raced toward him. Jean-Marc waved her off, but she slid her arm around his waist, steadying him. His bulk surprised her—he was wiry and long-limbed, like a dancer, but his body mass was all muscle, and he was deceptively heavy. She said, "My God, what happened?"

"It's all right," he said. "We took care of it."

"Of what?" she asked, looking from him to Alain as Alain and the doctor joined them.

The doctor sounded worried as she examined his wound and said, "*Monsieur,* this was too soon after your surgery. You've ripped open your sutures."

"*Hélas,*" Jean-Marc replied, very devil-may-care. He turned to Izzy. "I'm fine. Le Fils initiated another attack. We stopped him, pushed him back. Your headquarters is fine. Everything is taken care of. Go to your room."

"What the hell?" she said angrily. "If you think—"

"Blanche Neige, please," Alain cut in softly. "Please, go."

Izzy shook her head. "There's no way I'm leaving until I've been debriefed and I know Jean-Marc's okay."

"If I promise to debrief you, will you give me some peace?" Jean-Marc flung at her. He was shaking with anger. "*I am wounded.*"

She was stung. He didn't want her there. She was in his way. She thought of how frightened she had been when he'd been injured the first time. How she had kept vigil, praying for his recovery. It had been a selfish act in part—she had wanted him back.

And yet, even as he glared at her, she felt the strong, unbroken connection sizzling between them. Even if she left the room, she would be linked with him. Why? If he didn't want her to be with him, why was it there?

"Because it is my duty to protect you," he said. She realized he'd heard her thoughts. He had told her that he couldn't read her mind per se, but since she was new to her powers, she often unwittingly broadcast her thoughts. He couldn't help but pick them up, any more than he couldn't help but hear her when she spoke aloud.

He said more gently, "Allow me the dignity of receiving care in privacy."

She still didn't completely understand, but she did grasp that his need to have her gone was not about her. It was about him.

Then he looked down at her bathrobe. Loosely belted, it had fallen open, and her breasts were almost fully visible.

He said, "Never go anywhere without your gun. And the ring." Then his eyes fluttered and he said something in French to Alain.

"Please, go," Alain murmured to Izzy.

"*D'accord,*" she replied. "All right."

She returned to her bedroom and shut the door behind herself. Bijou pushed out of her embrace and hopped to the floor, scampering toward his litter box. Weary and upset, Izzy crossed to the bed and saw the blinking light on her landline phone base, indicating that she had a message. It had to be Pat, wanting to know what the sirens had been for.

She called him immediately, not checking the message first. As Pat's home phone rang, she pressed the handset against her shoulder with her head while she gathered up her rose quartz necklace from its coil on her nightstand and slid it around her neck. She fastened the clasp.

"Hello. This is Kittrell. I'm unavailable. Leave a message. Thanks."

Maybe he was in the bathroom. Or on the line; maybe he was even calling her back, to see what was up. She said quickly, "Pat, it's me. It's okay. It was a false fire alarm." That sounded so lame. "Well, actually, it was a fire, but it's all right now." She shut her eyes. That was even worse. She wasn't thinking on her feet very well.

She hung up and dialed into her message system, fully expecting to hear Pat's voice.

Instead, she got her father.

"Princess, listen to me. Brace yourself."

She went numb. In a cop's world, words like that could mean only one thing.

"Pat's been shot, Iz. Doesn't look good."

Numb, Izzy sank down onto the bed. *No.* Her hands shook so hard she could barely hold on to the handset. *Not Pat. No way.*

"I'm thinking that if you care about this guy, you might want to catch the next plane," he continued. "I can meet you at the airport. Call me, baby."

That was it.

She sat frozen, trying to remember her own phone number, when another message began to play.

"This is Dr. Annie Jones. I'm attending a patient, Patrick Kittrell. He asked me to call you. He's in surgery for a gunshot wound and I have to tell you that you might want to hurry."

Dr. Jones gave the particulars—the hospital, the phone number. Izzy worked to remember them, then realized they were recorded and she would be able to write them down. Her gorge began to rise. She was hyperventilating.

She put the phone down without hanging it up and ran into the bathroom. She threw up, and then she burst into tears.

Calm down, she told herself. *Stay on it.*

She washed out her mouth and left the bathroom. Picked up the phone. Made some calls.

Picked up her gun.

When Alain came for her, she was dressed in Caresse's hand-me-down jeans and a black turtleneck. The jeans were loose on her thin frame. As she had requested, he brought her a shoulder rig for her Medusa.

"He's okay," Alain said, over and over again. "The doctor sutured him back up and he's going to pull through just fine."

She had no idea if he was lying.

He escorted her through her mother's chamber, through the room where the techs sat monitoring medical equipment and into the OR. It gave her pause that Jean-Marc had included an OR in her little mansion. Violence was never far away in this world.

Annette met them in the OR and led the way to another door, where she stopped, turned and faced Izzy square on.

"He's conscious," Annette informed Izzy. "But he's groggy."

"Docile," Izzy murmured.

Making no reaction, Annette pushed the door open.

The room was beautiful, more like another clearing in the bayou than an actual room. Vases burst with a profusion of lilies and roses, and a waterfall trickled down a wall of stone. The Femmes Blanches sat in a circle around a wooden bed on a dais. And in that bed Jean-Marc lay, turning his head at the sound of the open door. His eyes met hers.

Oh, Jean-Marc, Izzy thought in a rush. She had the insane thought that if Jean-Marc had survived, then Pat had died. She knew she was overwrought, and that her thought was crazy, but she began to weep, tears sliding down her face to land on his cheek.

"I know about Pat," he said. "I know it's bad."

She said, "You promised to keep him safe."

"I did. From *magical* harm," Jean-Marc replied. "But he's a police detective. Harm is in love with him."

It was such a bizarre thing to say. She reminded herself that Jean-Marc was medicated, and that English wasn't his native language, but it still troubled her deeply.

Jean-Marc smiled grimly. He said, "Take the jet and go to him. *Vite.*"

She wasn't going to argue. She wasn't going to ask him what would happen back here if she did go.

She said, "Taking a private jet will raise questions."

"Then lie about it," he said. "Say you're catching a puddle

jumper. You'll meet your father at the hospital. Keep it simple, and you'll be fine." He winced, then he said, "Alain is going with you. And the wolf pack." When her lips parted, he said sharply, "Don't argue."

She flared and said, "Damn it, I wasn't going to argue. I was going to thank you."

"Ah." His eyes crinkled. "There you are. I thought we had lost the warrior queen."

You may have, she thought. She felt as if she were escaping prison, and very close to freedom. It dawned on her that she might insist on staying in New York and close the door on this part of her life forever. Wasn't that what Le Fils had promised? She couldn't think about that now. She had other things to think about.

She reached out and grabbed his hand. Sometimes she hated him. Sometimes she feared him. Even now, with him flat on his back and out of commission, she didn't trust him. But the connection between them was still there, and there was nothing she could do about it. It was a fact of her existence now, just as possessing magical powers was part of her life.

He looked at her and said, "I don't want you to go back there without me. But your mother is holding steady."

"Jean-Marc and I performed a ritual to ask the Gray King to protect you," Alain said, stepping forward. "I've asked Annette to lead the Femmes Blanches in a Bouvard ritual as well."

"Then...I'll pray," Izzy announced. "Please, bow your heads."

The veiled women complied. So did Alain and Annette, and in the bed, Jean-Marc closed his eyes. Izzy hesitated, remembering the shock on the faces of Mathilde and Louise when she had told them she *was* a Catholic, but the fact of the matter was, she was a Catholic. So she crossed herself. Then she placed her hands together, sliding her fingers one over the other, clenching them hard.

"I thank you, St. Joan, for your intercession," Izzy prayed, still uncertain how to make her way as a practicing Catholic among these rituals of magic users, and the miracles Joan of Arc could perform. She did know one thing: she was in desperate need of more of those miracles. Many more.

"Protect these people, and restore Jean-Marc. And please, don't let Pat Kittrell die. Please."

"Blessed be," Jean-Marc said, opening his eyes. "Now go." His lids fluttered. "Hurry, Isabelle."

His words frightened her. What did he know that she didn't know?

"Here. You'll need a coat," Annette said, walking to a small cupboard and opening the door. A black wool ankle-length coat hung on a wooden hanger. She took it off the hanger and handed it to Izzy. "Stay warm. And safe."

"You'll take care of Bijou," she said to Annette. When the woman nodded, Izzy tried to smile her thanks, but she couldn't.

Tears welling, she turned.

The Femmes Blanches called to her in farewell.

"We will pray for you, *notre belle fille*."

"It will be all right, *chére petite*."

"Let's go," she ordered Alain.

"*Adieu,* Daughter of the Flames."

Chapter 12

Three hours later, Big Vince met Izzy in the surgical waiting room at the Metropolitan, where they had taken Pat. She had already removed her shoulder holster and hidden it and her gun in a large carryall. It was like shedding a terrible burden. One look at her father's big Italian eyes flashing with a mixture of worry and joy, and she thought, *I'm home*.

"Isabella," he said, patting her back, "he's still in surgery, but I told that doc if he knows what's good for him, he'll use little stitches."

"Damn straight," said Bill Wilson, one of the other detectives on the force. Cops from the Two-Seven were milling around, drinking coffee, talking tough to hide their feelings. Captain Clancy had called to say she'd be in in a while. Officers from Pat's former precinct checked in as well. Pat was clearly well liked and respected.

In all the confusion, Big Vince didn't ask a lot of questions about how Izzy had gotten back to New York so quickly, although by his conversation it was clear that he assumed she'd taken a commercial flight. Alain had put glamours on himself and the five werewolves who had accompanied them so that they appeared like hospital staff, blending into the background where they could guard the Daughter of the Flames and the men she loved.

Izzy learned for the first time that Jean-Marc had arranged for a contingent of seven Femmes Blanches to occupy the safehouse in Manhattan after he and Izzy had fled the city. The seven had kept vigil in the coop for the last couple of weeks, waiting in case any of Izzy's loved ones needed them. Since magic use and magic users were officially banned from New York City, they had maintained a low profile. Izzy was grateful to them, and when they arrived singly and in pairs at the hospital dressed in street clothes—pants, coats, sweaters—she thanked each one with a bob of her head as they entered the surgical waiting room, pretending to be there for someone else in surgery.

Izzy's father gave her the rundown: gutshot. Bad. According to the officer on the scene, Pat had been following someone down an alleyway when he'd been gunned down. He hadn't called in and he hadn't asked for backup. He'd left his apartment in Brooklyn, driven to 108th Street and walked right into the shooter's line of fire. A passerby saw him and called it in, but didn't stick around.

Izzy and Big Vince sat huddled together on one of the plastic couches. An hour after Izzy had arrived, her brother Gino showed up accompanied by Father Raymond, their parish priest. A seminary student, Gino wore civvies—gray turtleneck sweater, black wool pants, fashionable haircut—

looking more like a *GQ* model than some studly young priest-to-be devoted to lifelong celibacy.

Gino gave Iz a kiss on the cheek and held her tightly as he said, "He's going to be okay, Iz." But of course those were just empty words. When she was a little girl, she had believed Father O'Rourke when he had said the same thing about Anna Maria DeMarco. And she had died.

Father Raymond led the DeMarco family in prayer, Big Vince handed Izzy Anna Maria's cherished rosary and Izzy had a visual of her father knocking around alone in their row house while she was "in Florida" and Gino was away at the seminary. She felt a gentle pity for him, and a lot of harsh guilt.

It's all right, chére, the Femmes Blanches told her. *We're here for you.*

Father Raymond asked gently if Pat was a Catholic.

"United Methodist," Izzy answered, although she knew even that was stretching it. Pat wasn't a churchgoer.

"I'll see if they have a Protestant chaplain on staff," Father Raymond said. He gave Izzy's shoulder a squeeze and left the waiting room.

After another minute or so, Izzy said, "I need to use the ladies'."

She got up and looked over at the seven women, three of whom were stretched out on the couches and chairs as if they were dozing. The other four were pretending to read magazines. But she could feel the strength of their magical vibrations continually weaving protective wards around her, her brother and father.

One of them caught her eye and blinked, rising and sauntering out of the room with Izzy. Alain met them in the hall. He wore the glamour of a handsome young Japanese man.

She felt a pang. Jean-Marc had come for her a number of times disguised with Asian features.

He said, "I heard some nurses talking in the break room. He's out of surgery. They're taking him to surgical recovery." He looked at the Femme Blanche. "Odette, get the women and I'll put glamours on you. You can go in as ICU nurses and do some work on him in there."

The woman bowed her head. "*Oui, monsieur,*" she said deferentially.

"What about me?" Izzy asked Alain. "You could put a glamour on me so I could go in, too."

"Too awkward," he said, shaking his head. "You'd be missed." Seeing her agitation, he added, "You have to remain strong, Blanche Neige. You have to." He hesitated. "I have a scrying stone tuned in to what's happening in New Orleans. Everything is peaceful. Jean-Marc's up and about."

He pulled out the stone and held it out to her. It was a small crystal, and the viewing area was about an inch square.

Jean-Marc was in his bedroom, lying in bed, reading stapled pages from what looked to be a stack of reports beside him on the nightstand. The dark-blue sheets hung loose around his waist. His clean-shaven chest was covered with gauze bandages but whorls of black hair surrounded his navel.

Bijou was curled up beside his hip, asleep, and Jean-Marc absently stroked the kitten, stopping as he turned the stapled page of a report. The kitten mewed, and he resumed petting him.

She swallowed hard and handed the crystal back to Alain. He waved a hand at her. "That one is for you," he said, closing her fist around it.

Then he took a breath. "You know my cousin cares a lot for you."

Her cheeks went hot. She nodded, meeting his gaze.

"You need to know something about Gifted. We don't tend to marry outside our own families. That's part of the reason the Bouvards are having a hard time accepting you. Your line is matrilineal, but it is very important to them that your father is a Bouvard, and we haven't been able to establish that."

"Okay," she said slowly, because she had a feeling that they weren't discussing her parentage at the moment. And…it hurt. She knew a door was closing.

"My cousin's the son of our *guardien*," he went on. "And he'll probably become the *guardien* when his father dies. It's not guaranteed, as it is—or is said to be—in your family. But he'll be expected to carry on the line. With a woman who is a Devereaux."

And the door shut.

"Got it," she said tersely.

He looked sad. "I would love to have you in our family," he continued, reaching out a hand.

"*Hélas*," she said flippantly, mimicking his accent to hide her acute disappointment and embarrassment. *I never wanted him in that way,* she told herself. *I'm Pat's.*

Alain cleared his throat. "The other side of this coin is Pat. He's Ungifted. He wouldn't be suitable for the Daughter of the Flames, either."

She blinked at him. Said nothing. Inwardly she was reeling. She hadn't known that. Hadn't realized it was anyone's business but her own.

It's not. This isn't the Middle Ages. I didn't grow up with these rules. They don't apply to me.

"Thank you for telling me," she said, her voice stone cold.

"Blanche Neige," he began, clasping her icy fingers.

She gave her head a quick shake, warning him off, and he released her. Then she returned to the waiting room, pretending that it was news when Pat's surgeon arrived and gave them a rundown of his injuries—two shots to the abdomen, damage to the spleen and a kidney. She pretended not to notice that the Femmes Blanches were no longer in the waiting room. She thanked the doctor, who said Pat couldn't be seen just yet. She read magazines and watched the clock.

Her father had to go to work. She told him to go. Gino stayed with her. He asked her if there was anyone she wanted him to call. Half the force was in the room already, and one of the other detectives announced that Captain Clancy was on her way.

"No, thank you," Izzy said, continuing to stare at the same page of the same magazine that she had stared at for at least half an hour.

"All right," the surgeon said, returning to the room. All heads turned. "He's doing well, and he's asking for Izzy." He looked at her. "I assume that's you."

"Woo-hoo!" Officer Wilson whooped. "Kittrell, you dog!"

Some of the other cops followed suit, until Izzy was rolling her eyes and telling them to shut up. They were far more interested in her now than they ever had been before, as if the fact that there was competition added to her attractiveness.

She eagerly picked up the carryall that contained her magical gun, and went to join Pat.

The Femmes Blanches had grouped around Pat's bed, which was shielded from the bed farther from the door by a light-blue curtain. They were holding hands with each other and with him. Izzy detected a faint white glow around his body. There were so many tubes going into and out of him that the women looked as though they were dancing a Maypole dance.

As she came into the room, he turned his head and smiled at her. His color was good, and his smile was the pot of gold at the end of the rainbow. His green eyes gleamed when Izzy drew near.

"Hey," she said, bending down to brush her lips over his. She closed her eyes against the sudden rush of emotion. He could have died. She had prayed for him all the way from New Orleans to New York. But she had prayed for Anna Maria DeMarco, too, and she had still died.

"Wanna 'nother one," he said, sighing contentedly as she complied, lingering at his mouth. She felt New Orleans sliding away as she cupped his cheek. It had all been a bad dream.

If only.

As she pulled away, he said, "Hey, Iz, how come I have so many nurses?"

The woman nearest Izzy said in a low voice, "The other bed is unoccupied. We gather whenever he's left alone."

"*Merci bien*," Izzy said. She put her hand on Pat's forehead and stroked the faint white lines in the tanned face. He was sweaty. She closed her eyes and willed energy into her palm. But nothing happened. Disappointed, she kept her hand in place, and took the empty plastic-covered seat beside him on the bed. Then she trailed her fingers down his cheek.

Pat said, "Gather for…?"

"It's okay," she said, both to him and the women. "It's kind of…woo-woo Catholic stuff. If you wouldn't mind…"

He raised a brow. "If it makes you happy, it's fine."

And here it was, the difference between Pat and Jean-Marc. Jean-Marc would have been all over her, asking her questions, demanding more substantial answers. Pat took things in stride, while Jean-Marc was perpetually coiled with tension and suspicion.

Stop comparing them. There's no "either-or" here. There's nothing here. Remember what Alain told you.

Nothing in her believed that.

"A nurse is en route," one of the Femmes Blanches told Izzy. "We'll come back later."

They filed out. About a minute later, a nurse arrived to check Pat's vitals. She suggested Izzy step out to give him some privacy, and she did so. Across the way, the Asian doctor nodded at her, and she nodded back. Alain was close by. He was guarding them.

When the nurse was finished, she told Izzy she could go back in. As she sat back down in the chair, Pat looked hard at her and said, "I'm awake now."

"Yes." She leaned forward and brushed her lips against his. He didn't react, and she pulled back slightly.

Pat said, "We need to talk."

"Okay," she said over the pounding of her heart. He knew something. What, and how much? "Go."

"After you hung up last night, I got a call. Guy said he was a friend of yours, and he wanted to talk to me about where you really were. Gave me a location in our part of town. I should have called it in, but it was personal." He grimaced as he shifted his weight in the bed. "I thought he meant you were with someone."

Where she really was? She swallowed down her anxiety. "Who was it?"

"That's what I'm hoping you'll tell me," he said slowly. "I got there, and he was in the shadows. He wouldn't come out where I could see him. So I went into the alley, just like a damn rookie." He gave his head a shake of disgust. Then he shut his eyes and licked his lips.

"Do you need something for the pain?" she asked him.

He opened his eyes and shook his head again. "I told them to hold off until I had a chance to talk to you.

"The guy told me you killed Esposito. Then he said he had a message from someone called Le Fils. That you'd be safe here in New York. That things were going to get hotter in New Orleans. That if you'd come back here, they'd spare you. But if you stayed in New Orleans, they would rip your soul right out of your body."

Her mouth was dry, her throat tight. She had no idea what to say.

"Then I guess he shot me. And I think he called 911 so I'd be around to deliver his message. I'll know if it was him when I listen to the dispatcher's recording."

"Oh, my God," she croaked.

"Iz." He studied her, confusion coming off him in waves. "Talk to me. *Now*."

So she did. Willing him to believe, she shut Pat's door and told him everything—her recurring nightmare, the fabricant assassin who had almost killed her. How Jean-Marc had rescued her and disclosed her legacy, and started to train her. Then they'd gotten out of New York when Le Fils turned up the heat. And she'd been living in the bayou.

"With some werewolves," Pat deadpanned. "And you took Esposito out yourself. In a battle. And you've been in Louisiana all this time, lying to me."

"To protect you," she insisted, withering inside. Whether or not he believed all of it, telling him was a mistake. She didn't want to put him in harm's way. Alain was across the hall. What did the Gifted do to Ungifted who weren't supposed to know about them?

"Protect me," he repeated.

"I know it's a lot to accept. I know it sounds crazy."

"It does." He was quiet for a long time. Then he heaved a long, drawn-out sigh. "Okay."

"Okay?" She could hardly believe it.

"Remember when you had that vision that your father was in the burning building? And I told you I had a funny feeling like that once?"

"Yes." She had hoped back then that he would talk about it, and then she could have told him what was going on. But that hadn't happened.

"It was when my wife died. I knew it was going to happen. I saw it. We fought and she took the car." His voice dropped to a ragged whisper. Izzy had to lean in to hear his next works. "She was pregnant. I yelled at her to come back in the house. Really yelled. I scared her. She took off."

"It wasn't your fault," Izzy promised him, placing both her hands in his.

"It started raining. Hard."

"Pat." She gathered him up in her arms and rested his head against her breasts. Her heart filled with sorrow. She closed her eyes and rested her cheek against the crown of his head.

"I saw the accident. It was as if I were inside the car with her...and our child. I saw her crying. She wasn't paying attention to the road and that damn drunk drifted across the line. She could have swerved, but she was too upset, and *I saw her die*."

"Oh, God, Pat," she whispered. She held him. And at long last, the tough, alpha-male detective shuddered against her, drowning in grief. She sensed he had never fully acknowledged the depth of his shame, and she was serving as his witness now. She honored his trust and held him as he mourned.

"And so," he said finally, when he was spent, "a part of me actually believes you."

She took that in, and she was grateful down to her soul. It was easier than she had expected. But then, from the get-go, Pat was more than she had expected.

"But just part of me." He shook his head. "The rest of me thinks you're plumb crazy."

"Captain Clancy knows. She's coming to see you later," Izzy said. "She can discuss it with you."

"Oh, great. My boss is nuts, too." She saw him struggling, trying to believe, to understand. She remembered her own struggle, and how she had echoed the prayer of Doubting Thomas: "Lord, I believe. Help thou mine unbelief."

Then, as he eased her back down into her chair, he said, "I will never let another woman I love put herself in danger."

His face was rock hard, his jaw clenched. A muscle jumped in his cheek. "Do you understand me? Whatever the reason you were there, what…cause you're fighting for, it's done. You're not going back to New Orleans. I'll kill anyone who tries to take you back there."

"How are we doing?" Alain-as-the-doctor asked cheerfully from the doorway, staring at her. She realized he was trying to speak to her telepathically, and she concentrated, trying to hear him. But she couldn't hear Alain. Not a syllable.

So she said aloud, "He knows."

"*Merde,*" Alain grunted. He ticked his glance to Pat. "So. You understand that she no longer belongs to herself."

"I sure as hell do *not* know that." Pat raised his head, reached for his covers and tried to throw them back. "And if you think you're dragging her back there—"

Alain moved his hands and recited some words in Latin.

Pat's eyes rolled back in his head. He went boneless and his head lolled against his pillow, chin falling to one side. Izzy jumped to her feet, pushing the chair between herself and Alain.

"What did you do to him?" she cried.

"Only made him sleep. I swear it." His false face was etched with sincerity. "I mean him no harm. Nor you. I am trying to stop harm from coming to you."

At a standoff, they stared at each other. Then she *knew*. Her stomach dropped and her blood turned to ice. Whatever it was, it was bad.

"Something has happened."

"*Oui*. Jean-Marc just contacted me. Your mother is deteriorating. We have to go back. Now."

She felt a wave of panic, but she tamped it down. She remained silent.

He repeated, "We must go."

She knew then that something, somewhere, was giving her a choice. It was as if Alain were standing on one end of a bridge, and she on the other. If she took a step toward him—if she said yes, if she left—she was going to cross that bridge. And once she did, it might very well burn behind her. There would be no turning back.

"No," she said, holding on to the back of the chair. "I'm out. I'm staying in New York."

"Isabelle, you *must*. She is dying." He ran a hand over his face, and his true features appeared. "Tell me what happened," he said. "Tell me what changed."

"Le Fils had him shot," she said. "As a warning to me. He said he'll spare me if I stay here. He told me that in the bayou, too, via a minion. But if I go back, he'll rip out my soul." She flushed. It wasn't like that. It wasn't that he would rip out her soul. It was that he might come after Pat again. And her family.

Alain closed his eyes and swore under his breath. "He's lying. He won't stop. The only way to stop is to take him out. And you can't take him out here. He's in New Orleans."

"Not my problem. Pat is my problem. Big Vince is my problem. And Gino," she said. "Jean-Marc promised me they would be safe if I left. But they'll be safer if I stay." She wondered if she could grab her gun faster than he could zap her with magical energy.

"They won't ever be safe again until Le Fils is destroyed," Alain insisted. "He's after the downfall of the House of the Flames. Whether you like it or not, you *are* the House of the Flames. *Alors,* Blanche Neige, look at what's happening." He gestured to the scrying stone in her pocket.

Against her better judgment, she did as he asked, pulling out the stone and staring into it. She saw her mother, gaunt and sunken, like a corpse.

"No," she whispered, trembling, stricken. "*Maman.*"

"I'm leaving all the werewolves here except Andre," he told her. "I'm sending for Devereaux and Bouvard special ops to occupy the city. Now that Kittrell knows, he can cooperate with them fully." He reached into his pocket and pulled out his cell. "We'll call Clancy. We can make a plan with her. Now that Pat is on our side, we have resources that you didn't have before. But you can't stay here. Le Fils won't stop."

She whipped up her head and reached for Pat's limp hand. She wrapped her fingers around it and tried to infuse her magical power into his body. Her palm was still cool.

"Pat is not on our side. He's an innocent bystander. And I nearly got him killed."

Alain gestured at Pat and snapped his fingers. Izzy's

cowboy let out a gentle, peaceful sigh in his sleep. He sounded untroubled, like a man whose body was healing.

"You know that's not true," Alain insisted. "Give him the credit that he deserves. He won't stand by. He's a protector, like you. There is nothing he wouldn't do for you."

Her thoughts whirled. She fought for calm, for the eye of the storm. Sensing her indecision, Alain kept up his persuasive litany. "Pat can protect your father and your brother with our help. We'll give him backup. We'll do all we can. But we have to go. We have to go now." He held the phone out to her. "Make calls. Take action. Make a plan."

"Where was the backup when he got shot?" Izzy shouted. Then she lowered her voice. "How could you let this happen?" she asked brokenly.

"It was negligent,' he confessed, dipping his head. "And I'm sorry. But we have to go back." He shook the phone at her. "Please. Call."

The bridge loomed in front of her, a rickety suspension bridge hanging above a bottomless pit. What if it broke beneath her weight?

Isabelle, said the voice. *This is your battle.*

"Damn you," Izzy said, grabbing the phone. Clenching it against her chest, she narrowed her eyes at Alain and said, "Get out."

"I can't leave here without you."

She looked at the man in the bed. "I'll be there in a minute." Her voice was as hard and cold as she could make it. She glared at him and said, "Close the door. Secure it. Make sure no one comes in."

"What are you going to do?" Alain asked, and then his face softened. "Of course," he said. "*Oui.* You're right to do it."

She flushed, but she didn't have time for niceties like

coyness or modesty. Before Alain had left the room, she
started shucking off her clothes.

Sex magic was the most potent magic of all, Jean-Marc
had told her. He had told her to go to bed with Pat to protect
him. And she had.

Pat was just out of surgery, so she didn't know how far to
take this. But she got completely naked and put her hand around
his penis. It stiffened. She trailed her fingers along his chest,
and then over her own nipples. She willed herself to arousal—
a daunting task, given her fear level. But she was determined
to do all she could to protect Patrick Kittrell from harm.

About ten minutes later she opened the door to the hallway.
She was dressed. The carryall was slung over her shoulder.

She said, "My father's gone to work, but Gino's still in the
waiting room. I want to say goodbye to my brother before I go."

Alain hesitated. He said, "One of les Femmes Blanches is
wearing a glamour. He thinks she's you."

"Call her out," Izzy said. "I'm telling him goodbye."

Alain inclined his head. "*Oui, Guardienne,*" he said, and
went to do as she ordered.

"Not yet," Izzy whispered brokenly, watching him go.

Chapter 13

It was still dark out when Georges, Maurice and a full complement of armored Bouvard and Devereaux ops picked Izzy, Alain and Andre up at the private airstrip in the bayou outside New Orleans. Alain and Izzy climbed into an armor-plated Humvee. Four camouflaged trucks quickly formed a shield around them. Andre was to be driven back to the werewolves' camp in a separate Humvee, guarded just as well.

The plan was for Izzy and Alain to meet Jean-Marc in the convening chamber. He had already taken Marianne there, and scheduled an emergency meeting of the Grand Covenate to witness the anticipated transfer of power from Marianne to her daughter, Isabelle. He wanted all the families, clans and tribes to acknowledge Izzy's status as *guardienne* as soon as it was conferred upon her—by Marianne's death. It was horrible, ghoulish, but on the flight from New York, Izzy had prepared herself for its inevitability, observing her mother's steady deterioration in the scrying stone.

As she had expected, word of her return had spread among the Bouvards. The verandahs of the House of the Flames were packed with people, cheering, screaming, jeering. Bouvard and Devereaux ops were stationed everywhere, submachine guns slung across their chests.

She thought of Joan of Arc, who had been dragged from her prison in a tumbrel to her funeral pyre. The young woman, only nineteen years old, had been found guilty of witchcraft, and sentenced to burn at the stake.

This isn't that dire, Izzy told herself, but the truth was, she was scared to death.

When they got out of the armored vehicle, the hysteria in the mansion reached fever pitch. Izzy found herself obsessed with worrying about Bijou. Displacement, she realized—focusing on something else as a denial of her real source of anxiety.

Surrounded by guards, Alain hustled her through the side entrance. The twin metallic knights blocked their entrance, parting only when she told them her name. They descended many more flights of stairs than when she had gone to read Esposito's corpse.

"Michel is already in there," Alain informed her. "And Mirielle."

Mirielle was the oldest living de Bouvard. Her daughter had been the regent before Jean-Marc, and rumor had it that she had been murdered. She regarded Izzy as an interloper; she had told Izzy so herself when they had first met.

"And Luc de Malchance will be there," she said. The *guardien* of the House of the Blood, and, quite possibly, the Gifted who was backing Le Fils's bid to destroy the House of the Flames.

"*Oui*," Alain said. "*N'ayez pas de peur.* He won't be able to touch you or enchant you. The convening chamber is exactly like a modern-day teleconferencing room." With pride, he added, "Except that we had that technology hundreds of years ago."

Their security contingent pressed in close. Georges was on point, and Maurice took up the rear as the large group descended. Alain held up a glowing crystal, which revealed letters and symbols carved deeply into the stone walls. The carvings gave way to metal charms, such as had been in the tunnel from the bedroom to the exterior of the mansion. The walls and overhanging ceiling glittered with them.

Then the stone walls gave way to outcroppings of rock. The charms on them were jagged and cracked, with pieces missing. The air thickened with the odor of mud and decomposition. The stairs became uneven stone, slippery with moss. The roof lowered, and Izzy felt squeezed and claustrophobic.

"This is the oldest of your sacred places in the New World," Alain said. "The first *guardienne* to come to New Orleans created it. It is very holy to you."

Maurice and the other ops turned a corner. Then he said in a ringing voice, "*Qui est là?*"

Izzy moved forward, craning her neck to see.

At the bottom of the stairs, Sophie, who was Michel de Bouvard's assistant, stood with Superintendent of NOPD Broussard, the rotund Mayor Gelineau, Governor Jackson and Sange the vampire. Sophie held a glowing crystal to see by, and she looked upset. Sange's long white ringlets of hair brushed the waist of a clinging black catsuit. Her mouth was open, and her jeweled fangs glittered in the light.

"*Bon soir, mesdames et messieurs.* Are you here to witness the transfer?" Alain asked them. "You know that you're welcome to stay here. But only Gifted may attend a meeting of the Grand Covenate."

The governor swept a curious gaze up and down Izzy's form. He said, "I was beginning to think something had happened to you. Why haven't you met with us?"

"We're not here for that," Sange interrupted him. She looked expectantly at the mayor.

Gelineau cleared his throat; he regarded the party somberly and said, "Some of Madame Sange's sirelings have pinpointed Le Fils's position. He's in the tunnels beneath that old convent on Rue de Casconnes. We want you to take him out."

Alain nodded. "*D'accord, Monsieur,*" he said. "We have important business here, oui? Once it is concluded, we'll send some ops and—"

Sange nudged the mayor with her elbow.

"We mean *now,*" Gelineau cut in.

Alain paused. Then he said to Sophie, "Did you speak about this to Michel or Jean-Marc?"

"They were already in the chamber when the gentlemen and the lady arrived," Sophie said, looking awkward and afraid. "I tried to enter the convening chamber, but this is as far as I could go. It's warded against anyone's entry except yours and Madame's. And I can't get their attention inside the chamber."

Alain remained calm as he said to her, "As you know, Sophie, we believe that our *guardienne* is about to place the Kiss of Fire on her daughter. Please take our guests upstairs and I will be with you when I can."

"Le Fils du Diable is there *now,*" Sange said, enunciating each word as if Alain was hard of hearing. "Just tell your men to come with us."

"I will be there," Alain bit off, "when I can."

"Damn it, this beats all," Gelineau said. "You get some manpower on this or I'm dissolving the *politesse* right now."

"Sir, please get away from the door," Alain said. Izzy's eyes widened as his palm began to glow with a deep blue tint. Would he actually attack the mayor if he didn't move?

Gelineau's face went purple. He clearly wasn't used to refusals. "That's it. I want this so-called family out of New Orleans in thirty days," Gelineau said.

"Please, get away now," Alain repeated. 'I'll take madame inside, and then I'll come right back out."

"No," Gelineau said.

And Izzy realized with a shock that he might be *trying* to prevent the transfer from taking place. Was he in league with Le Fils?

Alain raised a hand, and en masse, the Bouvard and Devereaux special ops raised their weapons.

Oh, my God, this is awful, Izzy thought, trembling. *What the hell are we going to do, shoot him?*

Then she felt exactly as if someone had hit her with the taser; the world dissolved to gray, and blood roared in her veins. She wobbled on the stair; then she could no longer *see* the stair. She could see nothing, hear nothing. Her body was numb.

And then she fell into a vision:

Jehanne, in her shining armor, dipped her head as she knelt before the priest in his long robes, the cross dangling from his sash. The battlefield was the valley below, and the enemy troops—the English—clanked with armor and weapons as they assembled on the opposite side. Horses chuffed. It would be the first time she led her troops into battle.

And her last.

"Hear my confession and bless me, mon pére," she begged

the priest. She was shaking. She had already vomited all her breakfast behind a bush. She had no idea how she would ride into battle, how she would carry her banner or raise her sword. To do these things was to die. "If you do not, I shall be damned when I am cut down."

The priest, loyal to France, frowned down on her. Jehanne's name was on the lips of every brother in the monastery, every good sister in the nearby convent. The sun made a corona on the crown of her helmet, like the halo of a saint. All of France awaited her miracle.

"Do you believe you will die this day, Jehanne? In your first battle?"

"Oui," she said fervently, pressing her sweating palms together and raising them toward him. "I am only a girl. What can I do against them? It was madness that brought me to this day, and not my voices."

The man of God towered over her. Then he shook his head and crossed his arms over his chest.

"Then I will not bless you, Jehanne. If you die today, you will be damned. Your soul will suffer in hell for all eternity."

"What?" Clutching the cowl of her chain mail, she stared up at him in horror. "What are you saying? If I die—"

"If you die," he said, with emphasis. "So...don't die." He smiled thinly at her. "Come back to me after you have won the day, and I will bless you thirty times thirty. I will say more masses for you than for the Pope. If you survive."

Then she saw herself training with Jean-Marc, saw the thickness of her magical aura increasing as she stared at the fabricant, anticipating its attack. How he had forced her to be stressed so that she would access more of her Gift.

I'm not ready, she thought. *I haven't awakened enough of*

my power for the transfer of power from my mother to me to
work. I have to be tested in battle.

Yes. Exactement, said the voice in her head. *You wanted*
to become a police officer. A protector. Is that not what you
are here for? Take one more step on the bridge, Isabelle de
Bouvard, Maison des Flammes. Take it now.

Oh, God. He said he'd tear my soul from my body.

And he will, unless you kill him first. Do it, Guardienne.
Or he will tear down your House.

She came out of the vision. Saw the raised weapons, the
looks of outrage on the faces of the Ungifted officials. In
Gelineau's case, it was not sincere. Did no one else see that?
Frustration and amusement warred on Sange's features, and
her blood-red eyes watched Izzy.

"Wait," Izzy said aloud.

All eyes shifted to her.

Do it, said the voice.

Izzy raised her head. "*I'll* go, Mayor Gelineau. I'll take
some ops, and I'll kill Le Fils for you."

Disbelieving silence was Gelineau's response.

Then Sange clapped her hands together. "*Et voila. Brava.*"
She pointed at Izzy. "*There* is a *guardienne.*"

"*Est-ce-que vous êtes folle?*" Alain demanded. "I can't
permit this. I won't let you do this."

"It's not up to you," she said. "It's up to me."

Jean-Marc canceled the meeting with the Grand Covenate.
He sealed Marianne in the convening chamber with a sharp-
shooter team, a dozen Femmes Blanches, Annette and her
doctor. Based on her examination, it was the physician's
opinion that the *guardienne* would die soon.

Michel and Mirielle were shut out of the chamber. Jean-Marc warded the door with Devereaux magic, violating the terms of his regency to prevent them from re-entering, and Michel and Mirielle were livid.

"There will be consequences for all of this!" Michel shrieked in utter fury.

"You are taking over our House," Mirielle chimed in, her gray hair flying around her face, giving her the aspect of a demon. "I knew you would do it some day. You lying Devereaux thugs!"

Jean-Marc ignored them, running Izzy to ground in one of the lower levels of the mansion, where special ops conducted their briefings, and weapons and ammo were stowed. Sange was debriefing the operatives about Le Fils's last-known location.

Stomping over to Izzy and grabbing her arm, he whirled her around and clamped down hard. "What are you doing? You mother is dying. You need to be here! And you need to be alive!"

"I had a vision," she said, not resisting his grip. Since having it, a strange calm had overcome her, and she knew she was on a journey that she must finish. She knew she had to do this. Whatever the outcome, she knew this was her next step, and there was surprising peace in surrendering to it. "I'm right, Jean-Marc. I have to take on Le Fils."

His black-brown eyes flashed with anger as he shook her, bending down to gaze directly in her face. "You are completely delusional. That is *not* what your vision meant. You are *not* supposed to go up against Le Fils. Now come back with me to the convening chamber *now*."

She said nothing.

He raked his fingers through his hair and dropped his hands to his sides with a huff. Then he made a fist and slammed it into the nearest wall. Sange and the ops forces glanced over, glanced away. Jean-Marc continued talking.

"Isabelle, *attends-moi*. When I was in surgery, you had an entire vision of a life you never led. You dreamed you were a police officer. And you are not. But it seemed very real to you. Do you remember how mixed up you were?"

Although she had already thought of that, his words nearly shook her conviction. Inside she flailed for a moment, feeling lost, as she had been in so many nightmares. Then she found the path again, and she said, "I'm the Daughter of the Flames. If I'm not ready for the Kiss of Fire, and my mother dies…then what?"

"How can you not be ready, if you're her daughter?" Jean-Marc shouted. Heads turned. He launched into a barrage of French.

Alain crossed over to him and began speaking to him in a placating tone of voice. Jean-Marc was obviously not ready to listen. He was wild.

Sange came up to Izzy, tilting her head and tsk-tsking with disapproval as she crossed her arms over her chest. She said, "I used to argue like that with Le Fils. Isn't love crazy?"

"It's not love," Izzy said flatly as she watched the two cousins arguing. Then Jean-Marc slammed out of the room.

Alain took a step in the direction Jean-Marc had gone. He raised his arms, then let them drop; his shoulders slumped and he dejectedly crossed over to Izzy, saying apologetically, "He has a point. If you die—'"

"I won't," she said. "I can't."

Alain looked almost as frustrated as Jean-Marc.

"My sirelings are ready," Sange informed them. "It will be dawn soon. We should go."

"All right," Izzy said. She thought to call Pat, but she

decided against it. They didn't have much time. Besides, she didn't know what she would say.

In her bedroom, she dressed quickly in her chosen black cargo pants, black T-shirt, thin jacket and body armor. They loaded into nondescript but heavily warded cars, she and Alain in the passenger seats of a gray Toyota Camry. Jean-Marc was behind the wheel, and he said nothing to her.

It began to rain, hard. As Izzy stared out the tinted window, white faces blurred like reflections in the shadows at the mouths of alleys, on verandahs, just beyond the glow of the streetlamps.

"Vampires," Alain said. "Sange's. Remember, they're not human. And no matter what pretty stories you've read, they feed on human blood. They don't drink from animals. They're vicious killers."

"And they're our allies."

"*Oui*," Alain said. "So if you have to kill a friendly to get to one of Le Fils's vampires, do it."

"Got it," she replied, feeling the bulky pockets of her cargo pants for her antivampire supplies.

Jean-Marc parked in the lot behind a bed and breakfast near Jackson Square. Other cars pulled up, as well. The occupants got out in ones and twos, staggering their exits through the driving rain and entering the back door of the bed and breakfast with calculated imprecision, as if they were tourists getting out of the rain, or paying customers with room reservations.

Jean-Marc and Alain flanked Izzy. Jean-Marc still hadn't spoken to her, and she wondered when he would.

They made an immediate left into a storage room. Moonlight streamed in through a grimy window, revealing a curled-up carpet and a trapdoor in the floor with the lid thrown open. She peered in, to see one of the ops guys from the cars scaling down a rope ladder.

Alain went down next, leaving Izzy alone with Jean-Marc. For a few moments he was stony. Then, with a sigh, he gazed at her with a tenderness she rarely saw, and laid his hand over hers.

He said, "For the love of your *patronesse,* don't die."

The thought came to her: *I won't die, but he might.*

"I might," he said, having heard her. "But I would prefer it to your own death." He glowered at her. "Remain in a defensive position. You're surrounded by professionally trained soldiers. Let them handle it. Don't take stupid chances."

"I won't die," she said again. "Don't you die, either."

He began to say something, then closed his mouth and gave her a nod.

"All right. I won't. So, we have a truce," he said.

"We do."

Taking a breath, she climbed down carefully. Hands eased her off the ladder and she put her boot down in a couple inches of standing water. She looked around, surprised at the size of the tunnel. It was a New-York size aperture, practically big enough for a subway line.

Jean-Marc came down after her, seeming none the worse for wear despite his recent injuries. He had overdone it before, and he was Type *A* enough to do it again. There was nothing she could do about that.

In addition to the security operatives, Sange and a dozen or so vampires were already below. She had on skintight pants and body armor much like Izzy's. Her long hair was pulled back into a shiny platinum rope.

Sange didn't seem to have minions, only full vampires. Izzy had only encountered vampire minions when engaged in battle with Le Fils, and she wondered if good guys didn't have them.

The other vampires, equally divided between male and female, were dressed like commandos in jackets, black pants, boots and bulletproof vests. Their red eyes made it impossible to read their expressions. With their long, white faces, they reminded Izzy of rats. Sange was far more attractive than any of her followers. Izzy wondered how that worked. A few of them were smoking cigarettes, which fascinated her. She didn't know very much about vampires yet, didn't know if their hearts beat and their lungs held breath.

She wondered why they wanted to take on Le Fils so badly. She gathered there were old wounds and lots of hate, and she supposed that was all there needed to be to wish someone dead.

Sange jabbed a finger into the darkness. "He's about half a mile up the sewer line. They're transporting another load of boxes to the convent."

"How many vampires does he have with him?" Alain asked.

"No more than six," Sange said. "No minions. Whatever he's doing, it's something he doesn't trust his nest with."

Sange regarded the operatives as they locked and loaded, grimacing as they crammed their garlic and crosses into their cargo pockets. They checked each other's body-armor bolts. "What level are they?"

"Some seventh, mostly eighth."

"Good," Sange said. "You'll need them."

They moved out. The vampires clustered in the front and the rear, while Sange walked close to Izzy, violating her personal space all to hell. Jean-Marc and Alain flanked them.

"Half a mile isn't far," the vampire said. "We'll be there in no time. So be ready."

They slogged on, then the party went silent, concentrating, staying alert. Darkness fell over them like a net. Izzy stumbled a few times while the others walked steadily onward, skirting bits of debris and potholes. She was positive they could see in the dark.

I need to see, too, she thought.

Ice water poured over her brain. Then suddenly she saw everyone around her in a sort of green, night-vision aura. Jean-Marc marched, grim and determined, beside her; Sange's red eyes darted as she surveyed her surroundings.

Then another cold chill splashed over Izzy like a bucket of ice. Words formed in her brain:

He is coming.

Look to your gun.

Chapter 14

Izzy pulled out her Medusa as she walked through the shrouded tunnel. Jean-Marc took note and gave her a questioning frown.

Look, said the voice.

On impulse, she turned around and craned her neck to see past the special ops and vampires behind her. About twenty yards in the direction they had just come, a shimmering white figure wearing a shirt of chain mail and a knight's helmet stood in the center of the tunnel. She was holding a sword in her right hand.

It's Jehanne.

Izzy pointed at her. Jean-Marc cocked his head, then looked back at Izzy, and shrugged.

He doesn't see her.

Jehanne lifted her sword and waved it slowly, like a

pennant. She was moving in slow motion, as if in a dream. Distant and subtle, armor clanked. Horses chuffed. Tack jingled.

"We have to turn around," Izzy whispered.

"*Mais non,*" Jean-Marc whispered back. "Sange's recon puts him up ahead. We're just meters from contact."

"Sange is wrong," she insisted.

Jean-Marc pursed his lips and looked over his shoulder again. Jehanne was still there. He shook his head, seeing nothing.

Alain leaned in to see what was going on, and she repeated what she had just told Jean-Marc.

"Blanche Neige's instincts were right when we went to search for Michel," Alain reminded Jean-Marc. "And she saw the vassal."

"I have full confidence in my recon," Sange insisted. "Let's *go.*"

"In a *minute,*" Jean-Marc snapped. "Isabelle, are you certain?"

Izzy watched the figure. It slowly faded.

No!

"Yes," she managed. But suddenly, she *wasn't* sure. Where was Jehanne? Why had she disappeared?

Sange glided silently toward her sirelings, who were gathered together in a huddle. While they conferred, Maurice rounded up the ops forces and pointed to the place where Izzy had seen Jehanne.

Sange returned to Izzy's side, saying, "I'm sending half of my sirelings on the original route. Give me some operatives to accompany them. Just in case."

Stiff-lipped and terse, Jean-Marc reconfigured the detail. Sange and six vampires joined Izzy's party, and the party rapidly retraced their steps. This time she was far more sure-footed. She kept her eyes trained on the center of the tunnel, but Jehanne did not reappear. Maybe the *patronesse* was satisfied that Izzy had understood.

Maybe Izzy's ability to see her had been tapped out.

Maybe I made a mistake.

She wouldn't think like that. She couldn't afford the luxury of doubting herself.

Izzy wasn't sure how long they crept along, but they were well past their starting point. This part of the tunnel was filled with the stinking rubble and junk Sange had told them about—several castoff refrigerators, even a rusted car. Lots of barriers to hide behind. It looked like a war zone. It smelled like rotten meat.

There had been no sign of Le Fils nor of Jehanne and the irritation and impatience of the others was palpable. Izzy knew they were blaming her for taking them in the wrong direction.

After a few more steps she felt the sickening sensation of cold, wet cloth sliding across the nape of her neck. Someone was searching for her. May have found her.

Jean-Marc, she sent out mentally. *Do you feel it, too?*

He didn't answer. She didn't know if he had heard her. She reached upward to tap his shoulder. Before she could touch him, he nodded.

"Party time," he whispered, reaching down to his thigh to rip open his cargo pocket, making it easier to grab his supplies.

On Izzy's other side, Alain did the same. He signaled to Sange, who was walking on his right. Sange nodded and turned to her band. She made gestures that they seemed to understand and they gestured back. It was an elaborate code.

Of course. For when they hunt. Izzy was completely creeped out.

She took another step.

Above you! the voice bellowed in her mind. *They're going to pounce!*

Izzy shouted, "Overhead!" whipping out her Medusa and firing straight up.

Shrieks split the air and something crashed to the ground. It was a vampire in street clothes, one of the enemy. His hair was ablaze; the fire raced over his face and then up his arms as Izzy aimed her machine gun at him and fired three quick bursts at him. He wouldn't be able to move, and the fire would consume him.

He is not a person. He is not a human being.

"*Hostie,* Isabelle," Jean-Marc shouted, clearly astonished, as he aimed his submachine gun upward and blasted the ceiling. He let the gun flop against his chest as he created twin fireballs and flung them hard.

Enemy vampires dropped like aerial bombs, their dead weight crushing at least two of Izzy's team against the floor. As she watched, Maurice rolled from underneath a fallen adversary, pulled an enormous, wicked knife from a sheath on his calf and hacked at the vampire's neck.

"Go, go, go!" Maurice shouted, as Jean-Marc grabbed Izzy by the forearm and threw her behind himself. Then he spread his legs wide and fired his weapon.

Sange and her vampires surged forward, meeting the enemy with Uzi spray as the enemy vampires found their footing and rushed them. A swarm of minions drove straight down, twelve o'clock high, and Izzy concentrated on her shooting: *bam-bam-bam,* rest; *bam-bam-bam.*

Izzy grabbed a grenade out of her pocket, grabbed the pin

with her teeth, and lobbed it as hard as she could at the fleet of minions hurtling toward her. The grenade detonated, showering them with holy water.

Sange's vampires shrieked in protest and darted out of the way.

Izzy continued to spray the ceiling as she stepped foot-over-foot toward the large piles of junk. A vampire leaped up from behind a turned-over refrigerator and flung a knife at her. Izzy fell to a crouch and the knife spun on over her head like a top. She cried out, "Jean-Marc, Alain, duck!"

Bam-bam-bam, rest.

Jean-Marc and Alain foxholed on either side of her. The Devereaux cousins' palms spewed fire; the vampire ignited with a shriek.

More vampires appeared among the junk piles, white faces glaring, weapons blazing. Jean-Marc stood in front of Izzy. Alain shielded her from behind.

Up and to the left, Maurice lobbed a holy water grenade over a turned-over refrigerator. It exploded, and screaming vampires popped up, clawing at their blistering faces.

Bam-bam-bam, rest. Adrenaline surged through her body, igniting her reflexes. Power and energy shot like a powder trail up her spine. She looked down at herself. The white light surrounding her was at least a foot wide, and it was gleaming like fiery platinum. The fire-shaped scar on her palm blazed. Tucked between her breasts with her crucifix, the ring of the Bouvards burned into her flesh. She knew it was branding her, and she let it happen.

I was right, she thought fiercely, enduring the pain. *I had to do this.*

Jean-Marc grabbed her shoulder and shouted in her ear, "Let's go!"

He meant that he wanted her to retreat. She shrugged him off and said, "No!" She needed more.

Before he could stop her, she joined a mixed force of operatives and vampires dashing toward the burned-out car. She felt a little crazy, as if she were on some kind of drug. Her hair streamed behind her like a banner and she held her Medusa up like a sword.

Everything sped up—her body, her reflexes—and she kept up handily with Maurice, who was leading the assault.

A vampire charged her; she stopped, planted her legs, set her elbows into a tripod and shot its head off.

Jean-Marc caught up with her again, yelling, "Back off! Back off! *Vas-toi!*" In the heat of battle, his English fractured into French.

She just looked at him and ran ahead with Maurice, Georges, and some others. Le Fils's vampires were swarming, heading for them.

The two sides clashed, going hand-to-hand. Maurice slashed at his opponent with his knife as Georges lobbed a fireball. The vampire shrieked and fell back. Maurice pursued it.

With her own light and the light from the fires and explosions, Izzy could see perfectly. A quick survey, and she knew Le Fils was not among the attackers.

She spotted an immense haystack-shaped pile of rubble pushed up against the tunnel wall. She took it like a hill in a battle, racing up the side and giving a rebel yell.

Her brilliant aura grew to two feet, then three. Jean-Marc spared one astonished look at her before they both got down to business, fending off four enemy vampires as they crested the trash heap. Izzy knew that the shots from her machine gun were not fatal, but killing was not her objective. Finding Le Fils was.

Then a barrage of ammo rained down from the ceiling. Izzy ducked the bullets; she didn't know how she managed to come out of the encounter unscathed. Jean-Marc grabbed her and tried to force her back down the way she had come while Sange's vampires and Bouvard ops flew past them.

"Let me go!" she shouted. "I'm doing fine!"

He clasped his hand around her forearm and started dragging her down. "This is not a game!" he shouted at her. "We are not playing war. You can really die."

"Look at me!" she yelled back, batting at him. "Look at my Gift!"

"You can still die!"

She saw ops staring openmouthed at her as they passed. Vampire friendlies grinned and whooped.

Then a triumphant cry rose up on the other side of the junk heap. Izzy jerked her arm; Jean-Marc let her go, and they both turned around and headed back in the opposite direction.

From their vantage point, they saw Le Fils facedown on the ground, spread-eagle, his long white hair coated with filth and blood. He raised his head and stared straight at Izzy with his deep-red eyes.

She felt a chill down to the tips of her toes.

The special ops formed a circle, digging into their pockets and flinging crosses and garlic at the king vampire, who heaved and clawed the concrete floor of the tunnel, leaving trails of blood from his fingers. Alain trained his submachine gun on Le Fils as he roared in agony.

As she sauntered toward the circle, Sange said, "You'll have to pick those things back up, if you would, so I can saw his head off with my nail file."

At the sound of her voice, Le Fils looked up at her. His red eyes widened, as if he couldn't believe his predicament.

Sange walked the perimeter of the security circle, her arms folded, as she said to Le Fils, "What are you up to now, you *bâtard?* Tell us, or I'll send your soul straight to hell!"

Two Devereaux ops were lugging a wooden box, which they set down in front of Izzy and Jean-Marc. Izzy's white light faded, but she still felt as strong and powerful; she wondered if it was simply invisible. She saw that the box was loaded with large, leather-bound books.

Joining them, Alain plucked the topmost volume from the box. "*Voudon and the Other Dimensions,*" he read aloud. "*Portals and Doors. The Conduit.*"

"Get these things off of me," Le Fils snapped at Izzy, as he strained to get away from the crucifixes and garlic. "I can't think straight."

"Who are you serving?" Jean-Marc demanded. "Tell me now or your corpse will tell me when your mouth is packed with garlic." He pulled a Baggie full of garlic cloves from the cargo pocket on his thigh.

Le Fils's face was gray and blotchy. Blood beaded on his forehead.

There was a long silence. Then Izzy stepped forward and bent down on one knee, gathering up some of the crosses and plucking garlic off the bleeding vampire. The skin on his face and hands had broken out in horrible sores.

"Tell me," she whispered to him. "I will make them save your soul."

She didn't know if she was lying.

With shaking fingers, she picked more pieces of garlic off his damaged body. She said to Le Fils, in the same insinuating tone Michel had used on Esposito, "Just tell us, and the pain will stop."

"*Bon,*" he said finally, his voice so soft that Izzy had to turn her head to hear him. "I have a master. These books are for him."

Sange scoffed. "The day you have a master is the day I walk in the sunlight."

Le Fils looked at Sange full-on, his face a mixture of loathing, hatred and intense pride. He raised his chin. His blood-red eyes blazed. "My master is Aristide, lord of all vampires."

Sange gasped and covered her mouth with both her hands. The vampires gathered behind her, cowering as if from the very name. "He's a myth," Sange whispered. "He doesn't exist."

Jean-Marc planted his feet wide apart and took aim. "Now is not the time for games," he said. "Tell us the real name, or I'll blow off your head."

Le Fils chuckled, low, deep, evil. "That's all I will say. It's enough."

"It's not," Jean-Marc said. He stepped forward and scooped up a handful of garlic. Then he crouched behind Le Fils, grabbed his upper jaw, and began cramming garlic into his mouth.

Blood flowed freely out of his mouth as Le Fils shrieked and struggled, pooling on the dirty concrete. Revolted, Izzy forced herself not to turn away. She was complicit, and her silence was her approval of Jean-Marc's interrogation technique.

"This is stupid. You are stupid, Le Fils du Diable," Sange said. "This is a ghost story you've made up to frighten us and take the blame off yourself. There is no such thing as Aristide."

"Oh, there is, *mon amour,*" Le Fils gurgled through the blood. "And I've told him all about you. He can't wait to meet you."

Sange rushed up and began kicking the suffering vampire. "You're a liar! You liar!" she shrieked. "He's not real!"

"Yes, he is," Le Fils said. Heaving in pain, he closed his eyes. After a succession of convulsions, he became deathly still, like a cobra.

Sange shouted, "He's contacting him!"

She grabbed Izzy's Medusa out of her hand, aimed, and shot Le Fils in the head.

She kept shooting.

"Aristide is a Gifted vampire," Jean-Marc explained as he drove Izzy back to the mansion in a sleek black Jag. She didn't know where it had come from, and she didn't ask. They had taken off their body armor and stowed it in the trunk. Her muscles were trembling with exhaustion, and emotionally she was manic: euphoric, shot through with a sizzling livewire of fear. They had killed the little fish.

She knew now that Aristide was the gator.

The shark-shaped vehicle swam through the rain. In lieu of holding on to the steering wheel, Jean-Marc moved his hands to guide the car. Streetlights and the pastel rainbows of neon signs played over his sharp features, and she watched him for signs of a relapse. He had fought hard, again, after rising from his sickbed, again.

"How can he be both?" she asked. "I thought there were Gifted, like us, and supernaturals, like vampires. Two different things altogether."

Jean-Marc said, "I'll tell you the legend, although I must also tell you, I considered Aristide to be a myth, as well."

"Okay." She settled in to listen.

"In the fourteenth century, there was a nobleman in the French countryside, not far from Domremy, where your *patronesse*, Jehanne, was born. He was Le Baron Samson de Aristide, *Maison des Mortes*. That means of the House of the

Dead. One story goes that the Baron was a leper, hence the name. But back then, rivals said such things to discount their enemies."

"Someone gave him some bad press, in other words," Izzy said.

"*Oui*. Or perhaps it was true. It was also asserted that he consorted with demons, and that he knowingly married a vampire. On their wedding night, she changed him.

"When he awoke to his undead life, he continued his work in the Black Arts. After thirteen years of performing rites and rituals to a demon of hell, he acquired his Gift, and that was when the real trouble began. His patron demanded sacrifices—living human sacrifices—and Aristide gave him hundreds. His reign of terror was unparalleled."

"The Hitler of his times," she said. "What is the name of his patron?"

"I don't know. And if I did, I probably wouldn't speak it aloud. Such names have terrible power."

He motioned and the car downshifted, darting around a corner as the tires gripped the wet tarmac. Rain smacked the window with gray fists.

"The vampire baron transformed into a demon. He became a great lord of hell, promising his minions that he would give them this world in return for their loyalty. To that end, he created a conduit that would bring them through.

"Some say that our own Houses embraced magic in order to fight him. The House of the Flames, the Blood and the Shadows. I don't know about that. It was during the French Civil War, and your House, the Bouvards, was clearly fighting on the side of Joan of Arc. Some say that Jehanne was the commander of us all. The story goes that there was another tremendous battle, our united Houses on one side and Aristide on the other, and the conduit was shattered. Aristide's followers were trapped in hell, and he remained on earth alone. We vanquished his patron, and Aristide went underground, into hiding."

"Those books Le Fils had were about portals and conduits," Izzy said.

"*Oui*," Jean-Marc replied. "Le Fils must have been helping Aristide rebuild the conduit. Assuming such a one exists."

"In the convent?"

"One assumes." Anxiety creased his forehead and etched deep lines around his mouth. "If I had known this, I wouldn't have insisted you come back from New York. I am afraid. For you, and for all of us."

"Thank you," she said, and she meant it. She was afraid, too. But her Gift sang in her blood. "But I'm sure we're both thinking the same thing. If he wanted me to stay away, it's because I pose a threat. That means I have power against him. And if I have power against him, then maybe I have it against his master."

He looked upset. "Everything in me wants to deny that. I…" He pressed a hand against his forehead as he kept his eyes on the road. "If I hadn't found you, Le Fils would have killed you. But I'm sorry I brought you into this."

"You didn't." Moved, she extended her hand. "I can't see my aura. Can you?"

He nodded, sliding a glance at her. "I can. It's blazing as never before. You were right about the battle. It triggered a massive change in you." He regarded her with great respect. "You're definitely more powerful and more confident. More like a true *guardienne*." He sounded sad.

It is not enough, said the voice.

The car sped along, guided by but not precisely driven by

him. She was like the car now, moving under its own speed, with the occasional bit of guidance.

The rain pattered on the windshield. Neon slid across the glass. Lacy balconies floated in the darkness. She saw an illuminated sign for a voodoo shop, another for a ghost tour. Tourists were looking for dark excitement. She was living it. But like them, she was only scratching the surface. To survive, she would have to go deeper. Fully embrace the shadows.

"I need more power. To be able to receive my legacy, and to defeat Aristide." She took a deep breath. "And you can give it to me."

He understood.

"Yes. I can," he said. His voice grew husky as he reached for her hand and squeezed it, then laid it over his large, hard erection. "And I will."

Chapter 15

Jean-Marc and Izzy held hands for the rest of the trip back to the mansion. She could feel his energy sizzling inside her hand, shooting through her blood like an electric shock to jolt her nervous system. Her heartbeat picked up and she tingled everywhere—her lips, the nape of her neck, her collarbone. Her lower abdomen. And then her breasts, her nipples and her sex. She was highly aroused. She assumed he was, too.

He said to her gently, "For Gifted, this is the highest form of magic. We don't share it lightly." He hesitated, as if he was unsure how to proceed with her. "But we do share it. And that is what it means for us, the creation of strong, powerful magic. It's not the same as making love. Do you know what I'm telling you?"

She thought of the things men and women sometimes said

to each other before they went to bed—*no commitment, just physical*—and she swallowed hard. Could she do this?

"It won't be a betrayal of Pat," he continued. "Be clear on that. There's nothing to feel guilty about. I know how you feel about him, and I know how you feel about me."

Do you? she thought.

"Yes," he said aloud. "Even if you don't."

Grasping her forefinger, he slid it into his mouth. Sunburst tingles centered in her stomach, and she gasped.

"Just a taste of things to come," he murmured, as he licked her finger and put her hand back down over his erection. Then he spoke to her in French and Latin, weaving spells. She felt as if she were floating out of the seat; she saw herself beneath him in her bed at the mansion, having sex, he stroking her as she rocked against him. In her mind's eye, she was delirious with lust, heaving and panting, clinging to him. She was an animal.

"I'll know what you want," Jean-Marc said beside her. The muscles in his thigh were taut beneath her hand. "I will make it everything I can."

Word had gotten back to the mansion that Le Fils was dead. Despite the rain, every window in the mansion gleamed, and Bouvards lined the drive of live oaks, cheering and waving the banners of the House of the Flames: the face of Joan of Arc encircled by flames. They were tossing lilies onto the road and waving at Izzy as the Jag blew by. Devereaux and Bouvard operatives were out in full force, facing the crowds.

As the Jag glided to a halt, guards surrounded the vehicle.

"Let them see your power," Jean-Marc said, as one of the Bouvard operatives bent down and opened her door. Jean-Marc snapped his fingers, and her aura shimmered like a kaleidoscope around her body. She had pulled the rose quartz necklace out over her black T-shirt and the ring shone with its own white light. The onlookers went wild, their voices welling with excitement and relief. Shielding his eyes, the Bouvard operative took an involuntary step back, then caught himself and presented arms.

"Madame de Bouvard," he announced squinting against her brilliance.

Izzy waved back at the throng as she and Jean-Marc were hustled to the side door, met there by Michel, Mirielle, the three Ungifted officials and the three assistants. Broussard and Jackson broke into applause. Gelineau joined in, somewhat more restrained.

Michel gaped at Izzy, then dropped to his left knee and said, "Forgive me, madame. I lacked faith, and I ask your apology."

"It's all right," she said. She looked from him to Gelineau. "The *politesse,*" she said. "We're staying in New Orleans, yes?"

He looked ashen. *He thought I would fail,* she thought. *He's in this. Who bought him, Le Fils? Does he even know about Aristide? What about the Malchances?*

"Of course you're staying," Gelineau managed, trying to sound jovial. "We can't thank you enough. I can see now that the House of the Flames is going to rise again."

"*Oui,*" Izzy said. "It is."

Jean-Marc took her arm and said, "We'll debrief later, Monsieur Gelineau. Madame needs to be with her mother now."

"I'd really like to hear what happened," Gelineau pushed. "Maybe just a quick meeting?" He looked to Broussard and Jackson for their votes.

"Later," Jean-Marc said firmly, circumventing any shot at

democracy. He looked at Michel. "Perhaps a celebration is in order? Madame will join you when she can."

"Of course." Michel looked relieved to have a job to do. Actually, he looked relieved to have a job. But all of that mattered only peripherally to Izzy. Willingly under Jean-Marc's spell, she was languid and amorous, her body hungry for his.

"Now," Jean-Marc said, gazing at her. She wondered if the others knew what was about to happen.

She expected that they would go to her bedroom, but to her surprise, he ordered a heavy guard to escort them to the covening chamber. She stood aside as he conducted an elaborate ritual to open the stone entry door, which turned to crystal at his touch. In the center of the darkened chamber, her mother lay in her gilt bed, domed in blue light.

Izzy could barely see her profile, but she looked sunken and fragile. "*Ma mére,*" she said, leaning over her, "please wait. I'm almost ready."

Then she kissed Marianne on the lips. They seemed thinner, and Izzy felt a rush of grief, pushing away her sexual excitement. It occurred to her that if she didn't sleep with Jean-Marc, maybe her mother would never die.

But she knew that would be wrong. It was time to take up the banner.

Jean-Marc conferred with the doctor and spoke to Annette. He brought in the ops teams and left them there.

Then Jean-Marc laced his fingers through hers and walked her through the chamber. Never having been inside, she glanced at the shadowed walls, seeing flame decorations there, and large panels of crystal. Her grief was still overpowering her, and she wondered if she would be able to go through with this after all.

Then he motioned with his hand and a door appeared on

the other side of the chamber. It opened and he went through first, pulling her gently across the threshold. The room wafted with lavender-scented mist, and she couldn't see him. She could only see a blaze of blue light beside her.

Her clothes slid to the floor. She was barefoot. The signet ring dangled from the rose quartz necklace around her neck, a circle of warmth between her breasts.

Through the mist he said, "First, we must clean off the magical residue. That's part of the reason you're feeling so much sorrow."

How do you know what I'm feeling? she thought.

"You know how I know," he said aloud. He took her hand and squeezed it hard. "Don't be afraid. Let all the negative emotions go. I promise you pleasure you've never known before."

The mist descended to the floor and trailed away, to reveal a lagoon of crystalline water tumbling from a waterfall. Lazy palms drooped from white sand, shading purple orchids and cawing red and green parrots from the golden sun. The warm sand tickled her toes; the heady fragrance of a hundred tropical flowers filled her senses.

Jean-Marc stood facing her, and he was naked, too. A large white scar zigzagged through the dark hair on his chest, but other than that, he was perfect. He was powerfully built, his chest wide, with six-pack abs and the long, lean arms and legs she had already admired when they trained together. His hips were narrow, and his erect penis bobbed from the nest of curly black hair between his legs.

Without a word, gazing into her eyes, he picked her up, one large, muscular hand looped around her hip, another under her arm, lazily caressing the curve of her breast. He smelled of musk and sweat. Then he turned and walked straight into the water. It caressed his calves and then his knees, up to his thighs and to his chest. He lowered her into the water, bending his knees so that he sank with her. The bottom of the lagoon disappeared; rose-scented water closed over her head, and she felt tremendous relief as the magical residue washed away.

Jean-Marc put his mouth over hers. He slid his tongue inside and wrapped his hands around her body, pulling her against him, hard. Her breasts were flattened against his chest. She heard the heartbeat…hers, his? It was like the rhythm of ocean waves. He breathed inside her, breathed for her.

She clung to him as he propelled them both back up to the surface of the water. Then she opened her eyes to gaze into his…and saw that they had left the water; they were soaring high above the lagoon, across a tropical night sky glittering with stars and heavy with perfume.

His hair had come loose from his ponytail and streamed behind him. He looked like a warrior angel. He turned her around, his hands around her waist and chest, spooning her as they flew. She felt his penis pressing against her ass. His hands covered her breasts, centering her nipples in his palms.

She and he descended a mountaintop bursting with flowers—orchids, plumeria, wisteria and irises. A bower of fragrant blossoms draped tree limbs, opulent masses twining around trunks and spreading over the grassy earth. They landed gently in a soft pile of flower petals. He leaned over to a small woven mat and picked up two wineglasses, and handed one to her. They both drank deeply, she sighing with pleasure. She remembered the first glass of wine he had ever offered her. She had refused it.

And I was right to do it. But now…this cup is mine.

He took her glass away and put his hands beneath her head, cradling her, as he lowered her down onto the petals. With his eyes boring into hers, he kissed her slowly, deeply, completely.

"Ah, Isabelle, *ma belle, ma femme*," he murmured, covering her face with kisses. His warm lips dotted her neck and shoulders, and her breasts and her stomach.

And then he slid into her. She gasped and clasped his biceps, arching to meet him.

They moved together, rhythms meshing, heart to heart. He took her hand and kissed her knuckles, squeezed her fist.

Then, still inside her, he gently rolled her onto her side. She felt her body shifting, changing; she looked down and saw fur, and claws.

She was a lioness.

A leopard.

An eagle.

Morphing and changing, shifting, making love in all the glamours and guises he conjured.

In deserts and jungles and under the ocean and among the stars. For hours—or was it centuries? He, hard inside her, moving and changing as she moved and changed.

Then they left bodies behind and became beings of light. He was a glowing figure of soft blue and she was pure white. She felt his colors and heard unbelievably beautiful music— the symphony of their union.

His climax was a comet; hers, a shower of stars. Tears ran down her cheeks as she collapsed into his arms, his very human arms.

And at the last, as she opened her eyes, Pat's eyes looked back at her. Pat's mouth smiled at her. In Pat's voice, Jean-Marc said steadily, "You have not betrayed me. You have made it possible to save me."

"I know." Another tear ran down her cheek. "But they told me I can't have you."

"Still, I'm yours," Jean-Marc replied.

In his own voice.

His very own.

Hustle it up. You're on point.

The voice murmured against Izzy's earlobe as she stood in the center of the suspension bridge that spanned the bayou. The water below churned with blood. On the side of the bridge that she'd just left, Pat stood beside her father, Big Vince, who was wearing his NYPD uniform, and Gino, who was dressed in the robes of a Catholic priest. Tanned and sexy, boot-cut jeans molded to his quads and ass above low-heeled cowboy boots, and a chambray shirt stretched across his pecs. There was something in his fist; he turned his hand over and fanned his fingers, revealing a diamond engagement ring. Gino and Big Vince beamed at her, and Gino made the sign of the cross over her.

She took a step toward the trio of men she loved more than anything in this world. Low in her belly, she felt the quickening of life. A child. Pat's child.

She took another step toward them.

The scar-faced fabricant that had tried to kill her appeared behind them. Taller even than Pat, it smiled at her and bent its knees slightly, beckoning her to come back, nodding eagerly as she took a third step. It put its arm around Pat like a brother and gave him a squeeze.

Then it reached around Pat's head, one hand on either side, twisted hard, and snapped his neck. As it tossed Pat's body over the side of the bridge, a greenish-brown alligator at least twenty feet long breached the bloody water and snapped open its enormous jaws. Pat's body tumbled in, and the gator slammed its jaws shut and sank beneath the surface.

Izzy screamed, but no sound came out. Her long legs heaved over the side of the bridge and she dove toward the water.

Gino. Big Vince.

At the last possible moment, she grabbed the bottom of knots of the suspension bridge and held on, whipping backward, pulling her knees to her chest.

The gator leaped, clacking its rivers of teeth at her. She felt the compression of air and smelled Pat's death on its fetid breath.

Then in the way of dreams, she was back on the bridge.

But where the fabricant had menaced Gino and Big Vince, Jean-Marc and Alain now stood, wearing dark-blue magician's robes spangled with silver doves. In place of the fabricant, the ghostly figure she had seen with Georges and Maurice wafted into the cypress trees and hung there like a kite.

Heat ruffled her back. The other side of the bridge—the side she had been going to—burned in slow-motion flames that undulated in colors: white, blue, red. The fire crackled and spit; the flames roared like beasts. They were waiting to devour her.

They were the gator.

Above her in the sky, the figure said, Allez. Vite. Or it will all be for nothing. Look to your gun.

In the flames, her Medusa hung like the Holy Grail, twisting and shining.

And without a moment's hesitation, Izzy turned and ran straight into the fire.

With a gasp, Izzy woke.

She lay cradled in Jean-Marc's arms, her head on his shoulder, his other arm wrapped around her. Her stomach muscles hurt and she smelled the yeasty scent of sex mingling with the fragrance of the tropics. Above them, a canopy of stars and palms twinkled and swayed.

Tell him goodbye, said the voice.

Jean-Marc stirred in his sleep. She felt his erection against her thigh. He shifted again, moaning softly without waking up. His arms tightened around her.

He and his cousin have to go. The Kiss of Fire will not happen until you are alone. He must return to his own House. He is not a son of the Flames.

Izzy gave her head a quick shake. There was no way she could do that. Not now.

Twisting in his embrace, she turned to face him, to see his dark eyes open. His mouth was pulled down, and he looked troubled.

"I won't leave you," he said. He turned her onto her side and entered her from behind. Izzy's eyes rolled back in her head as the pleasure carried her along. She climaxed, hard, and he came after her, gasping and clinging to her.

She felt a rush of power. She felt as if she were on fire.

He has to go.

"I hear it," he said. He shook his head. "I won't do it."

"Jean-Marc." She could feel how strong she was now. It was indescribable, energy thrumming through her like the engine of a powerful jet. She and Jean-Marc had created vast power through sex magic. The flame-shaped brand in her palm was pulsing.

The voice was right. She knew in the depths of her soul that he must leave, or the transfer of power wouldn't happen. She didn't know if her mother was deliberately withholding it, or if Jehanne was in control of its disbursement, but the message was clear.

"Aristide," Jean-Marc argued, gritting his teeth. His dark eyes flashed as he scowled, not at her, but at what was being demanded of him. "There is absolutely no way I am abandoning you, with him at large in New Orleans."

Incredibly, he was hard again. He flipped her over on her back and took her. He was dominating her, or trying to. He wanted her to acquiesce, to tell him to stay. She rode the pleasure, amassing the power, and told him goodbye.

When it was over, and they were both spent for the third time, she trailed her fingertips down the side of his face and said, "Jean-Marc, you've always done what you had to do. You served my House as regent even though you were hated, and people tried to kill you. Then you searched for me, and you brought me here, even though you felt sorry for me and you didn't want to do it. And now…you have to let go."

"I…can't," he whispered, wrapping his hand around her fingers. "I won't. I will not." He began to speak in French. She couldn't follow. But she knew the presence of Aristide had crumbled his resolve.

And maybe it had been more than sex magic for him, too.

The tropical paradise disappeared. They were lying naked on the floor in the center of an octagonal room dominated by white-marble rectangles, each topped with the figure of a recumbent woman in full armor, a sword gripped in her gauntleted fists. Effigies, she realized. Sarcophagi. The walls were elaborate mosaics of flames, the floor, as well, dominated by the now-familiar face of Jehanne, which was repeated in the cathedral ceiling overhead. Torches shaped like swords were lit, giving off smoky light.

"This is our crypt," she whispered, getting to her feet. "You made love with me here?"

"It is the holiest place in the New World for your family,"

he said, rising beside her. "I performed sex magic with you. What we did was holy."

What we did was holy, but we did not make love, she reminded herself.

She counted eleven sarcophagi. When her mother died, there would be twelve. If she were laid to rest here, she would be the thirteenth.

He snapped his fingers, and two robes appeared at their feet. One was white, like the one she had put on to read Esposito's remains with D'Artagnon and Michel. One was midnight blue, covered with tiny silver doves. She had seen Jean-Marc wearing it in her dream. She didn't want him to put it on, but she said nothing as he made motions and the two robes rose into the air, then settled over their heads. Soft ballet slippers covered her feet. He put on his hood; she did the same.

"We'll invoke your *patronesse,*" he said, "and ask her to allow the transfer in my presence. I am your regent," he reminded her before she had a chance to speak. "I should be there."

Tell him no.

"We can't. We shouldn't," she told him. "I already know the answer."

He raised his sharp chin. His dark hair grazed his jawline, falling back slightly to reveal the dove earring he wore. The pulse in his neck was fast and angry. He was poised for a fight.

"Then I'll defy her," he said. "This is wrong." He stepped forward and spread his arms open. "*Jehanne,*" he said in a loud, ringing voice, slowly turning his face toward the arched ceiling. "*Je vous pidez. Attendez-moi, Patronesse de la Maison des Flammes. Je voudrais parler avec vous.*"

The room went black. A cold wind whistled through it, penetrating Izzy's robe, and flapping at the hem. A crackle of lightning zigzagged overhead. A second crackled against the floor, revealing the figures on the sarcophagi—standing atop the marble lids with their swords drawn, marble blades pointed at Jean-Marc. A third flash showed them lying flat again, swords beneath peaceful, clasped hands.

"Oh, my God, what's happening?" she cried.

The wind became a gale, threatening to knock her off her feet; she dropped down beside one of the sarcophagi, using it as a wind shield, drawing herself up into a ball and covering her head in a protective gesture.

"Jean-Marc!" she shouted. "Where are you?"

The wind blew harder; the stone coffin she nestled beside actually moved.

Then someone else bellowed, "Jean-Marc!" and the wind and lightning vanished immediately, as if a switch had been thrown. The room was cast in shadow.

"Jean-Marc." It was Alain, standing in the doorway to the crypt, a ball of light glowing above his outstretched palm. He was still wearing his battle gear. His Uzi was around his neck as he rushed into the room.

Jean-Marc was standing on the other side of the room, his face shadowed. His shoulders were slumped, his head slightly bowed.

"I know," he said to Alain. His voice was low, hoarse and defeated. And yet there was a hard edge to it that raised the hair on the back of Izzy's neck. She remembered her first rule: *Never piss off Jean-Marc*.

"I am sorry," Alain replied. "So very sorry."

"What are you talking about? What's happened?" Izzy asked in a shrill voice.

Alain crossed the room and knelt before Jean-Marc. His glowing sphere cast an upward glow on Jean-Marc's face, accentuating the hollows of his cheeks and hiding his eyes, giving him a demonic appearance.

Alain took Jean-Marc's hand in his and inclined his head. "*Mon Guardien,*" he said.

Jean-Marc placed his hand on the crown of Alain's head and growled, "Not yet." Then he gazed at Izzy. "My father just died," he told her. He was shaking. "I have to leave immediately for Montreal."

Did you do it? Izzy asked the blank-faced statue of Jehanne, which had been placed beside Marianne's bed in the convening chamber. *Did you kill Jean-Marc's father to make him leave?*

Beside the gilt bed, Le Fils's cache of stolen books was heaped on a satin Louis XIV chair. A retinue of Femmes Blanches sat on either side of the chamber, keeping vigil as they had for twenty-six years. Their veiled heads followed Izzy as she walked to the doorway.

Jean-Marc stood before her, his black hair wild and free, his elegantly tailored suit stretching across his shoulders. Wan and disbelieving beside him, Alain politely waited.

Jean-Marc gazed at Izzy. She couldn't read his expression, but she knew emotions were at war inside him. He had tamped them down. He was like that. He could do that. When she had first met him, she thought he was unbelievably cold-blooded and emotionless. He had told her that duty ruled his life. What was best for *his* House first, and then what he must do to fulfill his duty to *her* House as regent.

His allegiance had been tested, and he had failed and he had paid.

For her sake.

"Call me," she told him. "Tell me what's happening. Stay in touch with me."

"Don't worry," he said curtly. "I'll be in constant contact." He gestured to the cell phone he'd given her. It was magically boosted to accept a signal from him, no matter where he was. He'd also included Pat's number, as well. As far as she could tell, he felt no jealousy toward Pat. The world of the Gifted was very different. "I'll be back as soon as I can."

"I, as well," Alain said, moving forward and putting his arms around her. "One assumes that the Kiss of Fire will happen soon, Blanche Neige. You will be very powerful. And as soon as we've settled things in Montreal, we'll come. You won't face Aristide alone."

"*Merci bien,*" she said, shutting her eyes tightly as Alain held her. She wanted Jean-Marc to do the same, but he'd removed himself emotionally. She understood that he needed the distance. Maybe she did, too.

Then Alain took a step away from her and said, "Present arms."

The full contingent of Devereaux special ops clacked to attention on the other side of the door. She heard them. She knew Georges and Maurice were going with them.

Jean-Marc locked gazes with her.

This is not the end, he promised. *Je reviens. I will return.*

She swallowed, steeling herself for the moment when he would turn his back and walk out the chamber door.

It came all too soon.

Chapter 16

Less than an hour after Jean-Marc left, Sange dropped a bomb. She was leaving town with her sirelings—removing a potent source of protection from the House of the Flames's needy arsenal.

"You can see why I'm leaving," she said. She wore her hooded cape and strands of diamonds were wrapped around her white neck. Her fangs glittered; everything about her seemed brittle and uncaring.

"I can see that you're afraid," Izzy said. *I am, too.*

"Jean-Marc is gone, and if Aristide is truly in New Orleans…" She moved her shoulders. "My sirelings depend on me for protection, just as the Bouvards depend on…you."

"Jean-Marc will be back soon," Izzy said. "There will be a ceremony to make him *guardien* and then he'll be back."

"He may not be the next *guardien* of the House of the

Shadows," Sange retorted, giving her head a toss. "They vote. The new *guardien* may order him to stay there."

Deep in the back of her mind, Izzy had known that. She just hadn't wanted to admit it.

"If he comes back, I'll consider returning as well," Sange said grandly. "But for now, it's too dangerous. So."

She cupped Izzy's chin with her icy hand. "This is a shitty deal for you. I feel for you, and I wish I could be of more help. But protectors have tough decisions, eh? And my loyalty lies with my own kind."

"Got it," Izzy said tersely.

Sange turned to Izzy's mother. "*Adieu,* Marianne," she said. Then she turned and swept out of the chamber.

I'm truly alone here, Izzy thought, reeling. *There is no one here I can depend on. Except myself.*

The Femmes Blanches stirred in their chairs.

We're here for you, chére.

Call on us.

She allowed one more visitor before she locked herself in with her mother: Andre flew into a rage and began to transform when she told him that Jean-Marc and all the Devereauxes had left, and Sange as well. Not feeling calm at all herself, she managed to soothe him and halted the process, but he paced like an animal in the chamber, furious.

She could also tell that he was frightened.

"We'll watch the mansion, *chére,*" he promised her. "We've called on all our *bokor* friends to give us good mojo. I can't lie to you, *jolie maîtresse*. If it is really Aristide, that is bad news."

After he left, she asked Michel and Mirielle to come into the chamber with her. Annette was there, as well, fidgety and anxious. Izzy let her be. They were on a death watch.

Jean-Marc called to report that they had landed safely. He was in a limo on his way to the family headquarters. When she told him about Sange, he ordered the driver to turn around take them back to the plane. Apparently Alain countermanded his order, and then he took the phone from his cousin.

"We'll be back as soon as we can," Alain promised. "Stay in the mansion. Wait for the Kiss of Fire."

He didn't have to tell her twice.

And then she called Pat's cell phone.

"Yeah." He answered on the first ring.

"Me."

"Jesus," he said, "where the hell have you been? I've been tearing New York apart looking for you."

"I'm sorry," she said.

"You're *sorry?*"

Her easy-going Texan was MIA. A testosterone-rich protector had taken over his body.

"Pat, I'm okay."

"Hell you are. Give me your location. I'm catching a plane."

"No, you can't."

"Not in my vocabulary. Tell me where you are or I will climb through this fucking phone now."

She thought of the vision of the bridge. His ring. His baby. She closed her eyes. The vision was clear: she couldn't have those things, and if she tried to, he would die—just as Jean-Marc's father had died.

"Remember Le Fils. Remember what he said. Stay in New York, Pat. You're my first line of defense for Big Vince and Gino." *And you have to stay safe. You have to.*

"Damn it, Isabella," he bit off. He had never called her by her given name before. "I am not your damn lapdog. Whatever's going on, it's not going to happen without me there."

Then Captain Clancy was on the line. She said, "I don't think I'm going to be able to keep him here."

"Make him stay," Izzy pleaded. "Even if you have to shoot him." She caught her breath. "That's a joke." *A very bad one.*

"Don't go anywhere, unless it's on a plane back here." That was Pat again.

And then the line went dead.

Then there were no more calls. No more visitors. Izzy sat in the chair, watching her mother, worrying about Pat and trying to read one of the books they had captured from Le Fils. It was called *The Conduit*. It talked about certain places in the world where magic vibrations created vortexes, doors to other planes of existence. It was like her warded bedroom door—with the right spells, those doors were shut tight as drums. With other spells, they were opened.

"And those who dwell on other planes of existence will have the ability to enter," she read. "In the case of benign beings, this is much to be desired. But in the case of dark creatures such as devils and demons, it is imperative that such conduits remain sealed for time and all eternity."

Across the chamber, the gray-headed Mirielle was insisting sotto voce, "It's not going to happen. She's not the Daughter of the Flames. The *patronesse* cannot be fooled."

Michel said tiredly, "Have some discretion. This is a solemn occasion."

"This should take place in the great hall, with all the Bouvards present," Mirielle hissed. "Then, if she's the wrong one, the Kiss of Fire will reach the correct one."

"We've already discussed that," Michel whispered. "It's too risky. The chance of an assassination attempt is too great."

"If she can be killed like that, then she must not be the next *guardienne*. The *patronesse* would protect her."

"If she's not the next *guardienne,* surely the *patronesse* will find a way to transfer the power to the proper recipient," Michel shot back, although Izzy knew he believed she was the proper candidate.

"*Exactement,*" Mirielle retorted. "So we should forget this nonsense and go upstairs."

Izzy threw down the book and jumped to her feet. She was quivering with anger. Tears spilled from her eyes as she glared at them both and said, "Do you mind? *My mother is dying.*"

Michel bowed his head. "*M'excusez,*" he said. "Tempers are short. Emotions are high."

"If you two can't stop arguing about where Marianne should die, I'll have you both escorted out of here." Rays of light radiated from her palm and the ring that hung around her neck. Michel saw it, and nodded. But Mirielle huffed and simply shielded her eyes, as if the telltale shining was an everyday nuisance.

Izzy had a feeling this was but a taste of what was to come, once she had assumed command as the head of the household. Factional politics, jealousies, rivalries. Attempts on her life.

Kind of like being a police officer after all.

"It could happen anytime," the doctor told Izzy. She had no idea how long it had already been. She was exhausted. She had tried to read the book, but her gaze kept drifting to her mother.

Hours dragged by. Jean-Marc checked in to tell her that the Devereaux Grand Council had convened to vote on the next *guardien*. His father lay in state in their chapel, soon to be interred in a crypt, he told her, much like that of the Flames.

"I am so sorry," she said, hearing the heaviness in his voice. She had never asked him about his mother, and she decided against it for now.

"And I, too, for you. You never got to know your mother." He paused a moment. "Isabelle, there is something you need to know, and I have never found a good time to tell you. But Annette is in there with you, *oui?*"

"Yes." Now what? What other bombs can he possibly drop?

Izzy ticked her glance over at Annette, who was sitting quietly with the Femmes Blanches, weeping. Feeling Izzy's eyes on her, she looked up and paled.

"She has been keeping a secret, and it's been weighing heavily on her. When you acquire more power, she probably won't be able to conceal it from you any longer. So let me tell you now.

"Sauvage…she wasn't what she seemed. She was part of the plot to assassinate you that night."

"*What?*" Izzy's cheeks stung as if she'd been slapped.

"*Oui.* She went through the motions of the glamour to help Louise get you out of the mansion. I found out. And…I took her out, Isabelle."

Silence froze the moment. Izzy couldn't begin to comprehend what he was saying. Her stomach heaved. The room wobbled. "You…*killed* her?"

"I had to. She allowed me to recruit her so she could work for Le Fils. After you killed Esposito, she was afraid you would find out. So she wanted you dead. She wanted us both dead."

"No," Izzy protested, covering her mouth. Her world was shifting, turning.

Ending.

"It was quick, Isabelle. She didn't even feel a thing. Annette knows. It has been a terrible burden for her, but I demanded that she keep it from you. I didn't want you to hear it from her. I wanted you to hear it from me."

Annette rose and minced toward her. Izzy pressed a shaking hand to her forehead. "No. I can't believe it. Oh, my God." Tears streamed down her face.

"*Je regret*," Jean-Marc told her.

"Ruthven," she rasped out. "*Please.*" She realized she was begging for his life, as if she could go back in time and stop Jean-Marc from killing him. If indeed he had. *Don't let it have happened. Don't.*

Jean-Marc said, "An innocent. I sent him ahead of me to Montreal in my family plane. He's here. He's safe."

He must be terrified, Izzy thought.

"When things are…calmer, he can leave if he wants. But for now, he needs to stay here."

"How is he?"

"Afraid," Jean-Marc replied. "I'm needed here. I'll call again."

As Izzy hung up the phone, Annette knelt before her, looking up at her with puffy eyes. Izzy was crying, too, and she reached out her hands to Annette and pulled her to her feet.

"I wanted so badly to tell you," Annette said. "I almost did, that first morning at the mansion in the bayou."

They wept together, arms around each other. The Gifted world was filled with death—her mother, a young girl, a little boy's parents. Izzy wanted no part of it. She was done.

As the two women cried, the Femmes Blanches snaked their way around them, centering them in a shifting line of Gifted feminine magic. The powerful heart of the House of the Flames descended from mother to daughter—from woman to woman—and these women, bound to the service of the *guardienne* for over a quarter of century, offered their hearts to Izzy.

Words came: *I am a warrior. And I will not turn my back on the battlefield.*

Like the steady drip of water on stone, the tears of Jehanne echoed through the centuries: *Take this from me. Give it to me. Don't make me do this. Allow me to do this. Take this cup. This cup is mine.*

I am a warrior...

Izzy let the vision come:

There was no door to the tunnel. The white light blazed like a supernova as Izzy glided in, unhampered, welcome. Angels sang as the beautiful glowing figure held out her arms and enfolded Izzy in love so deep, so profound, so unlike anything Izzy had known in the darker world. Izzy laid her head on the shimmering chest and drank in the chant of her heartbeat.

The figure said, "You heard this song in my womb, ma belle, ma jeune fille. And now this heart breaks for you, because it's time."

"Non, Maman," Izzy whispered, wrapping her arms around the soul of her mother. "Don't go."

"I can no longer allow you to remain unprotected," Marianne murmured, smoothing the hair away from Izzy's forehead. "The power given to us by Jehanne must flow to you."

Izzy grabbed her hand and laid her cheek against it. Tears spilled fast and hard onto the luminescent skin.

"Non. Come back with me. Come back to us. Your Family

needs you. I need you. Oh, please, don't leave me now. They have all left me."

"You are a warrior, my darling. Strong, and powerful." Marianne held her close and laid her cheek on Izzy's head. *"I am so proud of you, my dearest, sweetest daughter."*

"Maman, please..." Izzy clung to her. *"Please, don't go. Oh, please."*

Then Marianne pulled Izzy away from her and cupped her head. Izzy saw no features. She longed to see her face one last time. Just one.

"Listen to me, Isabelle. There is another one. You must take care. The Other is coming for you."

"The gator?" Izzy asked. *"Aristide?"*

"Oui," Marianne said. *"The gator. But not Aristide. The Other. Which is why I must kiss you one last time. You cannot know how many kisses I showered upon you when you were born. This kiss is my last,* ma petite.*"*

Izzy woke with a scream.

She was on fire. The smoke choked her as the flames danced along her arms and singed away her hair. Every part of her body shrieked in agony; every cell, every nerve, burned.

The Femmes Blanches were screaming, too, gathering around her, holding her, rushing for help—

In the Burning Times, women accused of witchcraft were often burned inside a tower of wood, so that the mob would not see how hideous a death it truly was. But Jehanne they displayed, so that the French would see what happened to those who opposed their new English masters.

Men wept; soldiers wept; the executioner, who lit the

bonfire, sobbed and begged God himself for forgiveness. For who could watch such a young, innocent woman die so horribly, and not burn with shame and horror?

Izzy's body convulsed; her muscles contracted. Her eyes rolled back in her head. She retched. She prayed to die, begged for it. This was unimaginable pain. This was beyond enduring.

"Help me!" she cried. "Someone help me!"

Her hair blazed; her skin singed. Blisters raised along her skin, bubbling. Then her skin burned away to reveal the blood boiling in her veins and her bones charring to ash.

Stop it! she begged. *I'm dying!*

And she was…to her old life. In her mind's eye she was crossing the bridge, dashing headlong into the fire. Straight for it… Pat was shouting her name; her father was screaming; Gino wept.

I'm leaving them behind. I'm leaving my whole world. No, it's too much. It hurts too much.

Directly into the fire as it blazed like a whirlwind around her, the heat blasting her into the sky like a shooting star, like a comet…

Jean-Marc, Jean-Marc help me!

He was there. He wore a magician's robe and a crown over his long hair, and he stepped into the fire with her and protectively moved around her.

"*I'm here. I will always be here,*" he swore.

Then all at once, it was gone. Jean-Marc, and the fire and the pain…all gone.

And so was Marianne. As Izzy lay collapsed over her body, Marianne's lips were full and lush, her dark brown eyes open and unfocused. But she was beautiful again, the lovely young Sleeping Beauty. Her mother.

Her mother.

"She has been kissed!" Annette cried. "The legacy has passed unbroken from mother to daughter!"

Izzy looked down at her own hand. Light strobed from her body, flashing, glistening, glittering. She felt unbelievable. Such energy, such strength…it was indescribable. It was beyond what she could have imagined.

All the Femmes Blanches were on their knees. Mirielle and Michel, the bodyguards and Annette, all bowed their heads. Cries and whispers ricocheted around the room.

"We're here, *jolie guardienne.*"

"*Vive La Guardienne Isabelle!*"

With a sob, Izzy kissed Marianne's cheek. Volts of energy surged through her body…surely she could make her live again.

Maman, adieu. Comme je t'aime. In another life, I will see you again.

Then the chamber blazed with all the colors of the spectrum, blinding Izzy, who flinched and covered her eyes with her hands. She felt heat against her skin and kept her eyes tightly shut, afraid that if she opened them she'd be blinded.

She opened her eyes. The chamber was filled with light. The walls appeared to have been carved out of living rock, and faded pictures were painted on them: a woman with a halo, a sword and a crucifix. A waist-high border of flames decorated the entire room.

"She has been kissed!" Annette cried again.

All at once the walls became crystalline. Pastel light shot up the faces as if they were being lit at floor level. The colors moved and danced, rippling as a strange hum vibrated through Izzy's feet.

Then blurry faces appeared on each of the walls, their

features softened by the light. As if someone had thrown a switch, they snapped into sharp focus.

There were hundreds of them. Round, soft brown faces. A purple-black masculine face striated with ritual scarification and heavy eye makeup. A woman's middle-aged face bearing a red dot on her forehead. No bodies, only faces.

All staring at Izzy DeMarco, lately from Brooklyn, twenty-six, a civilian working for the NYPD in Property…and a magic-wielding dynastic monarch. She felt high, and frightened, triumphant and completely and totally defeated. None of this had been in the five-year plan for her life. In any plan for her life.

And yet…

From the sea of faces, the chocolate-brown features of a beautiful young woman commanded Izzy's attention. She wore cornrows and large hoop earrings. Her generous mouth glistened with scarlet lip gloss, and her heavy eye makeup was turquoise.

Michel said, "*Il faut présenter Isabelle de Bouvard, Maison des Flammes.*" To Izzy, "*Il faut présenter Hasana Zuri, notre dame des affaires.*" He said in English, "Hasana Zuri leads the Grand Covenate."

"I bid you welcome, *Guardienne,*" Hasana Zuri greeted her, in a high, clear voice with a British accent.

Then a low, husky voice said, "*Mes sympathies pour votre perte.*"

Izzy looked at the speaker. She was galvanized.

He was the antithesis of Jean-Marc. His close-cut hair was tawny and shot with gold. His angular face was nearly the same color, although there was a sunset sheen to his cheeks and full mouth; his eyes, a deep sea blue, nearly purple. There was a day's growth of beard on the hollow of his cheeks, reddish brown, that matched his eyebrows.

He looked warm and tantalizing, and Izzy couldn't stop staring at him. He seemed to be having the same trouble, because as he gazed at Izzy, his mouth worked, but no sound came out.

In the depths of Izzy's body, he moved her. She felt as if he were standing in front of her, with his hands on her naked body. She had never felt such a palpable attraction. She was so aroused, so fascinated, she was certain everyone else could tell.

Magic, she told herself. *It has to be.*

"I'm Luc de Malchance, *Maison du Sang,*" he said in a thick French accent, clearing his throat as he spoke. "You are…the missing daughter of Marianne?"

Izzy managed a single nod, reminding herself that Jean-Marc had believed that the Malchances had backed Le Fils…which meant Aristide.

No, her body protested.

Mirielle raised a fist at him. "Malchance! You attacked us!"

Luc de Malchance's glorious face pinched with concern as he shook his head, but his mesmerized gaze did not leave Izzy. Full lips pulled downward in protest of his innocence.

"Not we, madame," he said. "I swear it."

"What is this?" Hasana Zuri asked sharply, looking from Michel to Mirielle to Izzy.

"With your permission, we would like to table that for another time," Michel soothed. He shot a murderous look at Mirielle. Michel hated the Grand Covenate. The last thing he would want to do was air their troubles in front of them.

"This is a serious charge." Hasana Zuri cocked her head at Mirielle. "Would you care to elaborate?"

"Madame, please, this is not the time," Michel said, but Mirielle took a step forward.

Her thin fingers curled into a fist that she shook at Luc.

Her lined face grew taut, taking years off her appearance. "Le Fils attacked us! And you put him up to it!"

"This is a local matter," Michel cut in. "We really prefer not to dwell on it at this sacred time."

"Indeed, if a local vampire has been harassing you, that's your private business," Hasana Zuri said blithely. "Let's move on."

Mirielle opened her mouth in protest.

The woman with the red dot on her forehead spoke up.

"*Madame la Guardienne,* I am Chandra Shankar. I lead a Family called the Children of Shiva. I would be delighted to see you restore order to your Family."

"Thank you," Izzy said. "That's my intention." She was amazed at how calm she felt.

Hasana Zuri spoke again. "We are awaiting word on the decision in Montreal. Have you informed your former regent that you've assumed the guardianship?"

"Not yet," Izzy said. She felt in her pocket for the cell phone.

"Will you be attending his investiture?" Hasana Zuri caught herself and said, "If he does indeed become the guardian?"

Michel said, "We'll be holding a funeral in a week's time, and then madame's own investiture. Due to her peculiar circumstances, I think it unwise for her to venture up to Montreal in the immediate future."

Izzy didn't know how she felt about that. She had too much else to think about. Jean-Marc, a *guardien*. How would that change their relationship? How would it change him?

"We'll make preparations to attend," Hasana Zuri informed him. The other faces in the walls solemnly nodded. Izzy figured that for good news. The mansion would be full of powerful Gifted. If Aristide tried anything while the big boys were in town, he'd be squashed like a bug.

"And I will be there." It was Luc de Malchance, the amber lion. His sea-blue eyes danced and glittered as he gazed at Izzy. When he smiled at her, she felt faint.

"How do you feel?" Luc asked her. "When my own transfer of power occurred, I was in bed for three days."

"Hiding all the evidence," Mirielle muttered under her breath.

"I beg your pardon?" Luc asked with a polite, quizzical smile.

"Nothing. She said nothing," Michel interjected.

Then suddenly Izzy hit the wall. Draining fatigue sapped her strength as if someone had sucked it out of her with a vacuum. Or a spell.

She looked for assistance at Michel, who said, "May I remind the Grand Covenate that the transfer has just occurred. Madame is understandably overwhelmed, and we need to inform our people."

"Of course. If the Grand Covenate can be of assistance with anything, Isabelle, please don't hesitate to call on us."

"Madame thanks you." Michel put an arm around Izzy and led her to the Louis XIV chair.

Call on me, and I will help you, Luc de Malchance told Izzy. *I will do anything I can.*

Then all the screens went dark.

And Izzy collapsed.

In the night:
Now it has begun. The hunt. The chase. The capture.
Look to your gun.
It is the answer.

Chapter 17

Izzy woke in bed to discover that she had slept for three days, just as Luc Malchance had said that he had. Bijou was purring beside her. The Femmes Blanches were seated around her bed as before. Annette was fast asleep, her head on Izzy's bed.

When Michel received word that Izzy had awakened, he came to her bedroom to debrief her. Jean-Marc had been made *guardien* of the *Maison des Ombres,* and sent his greetings. He promised he would be there for the funeral and the investiture. Michel had already launched into preparations, with technical assistance from Mirielle, who seemed to have made peace with the new order of things. As the oldest living Bouvard, she still remembered Marianne's investiture and the funeral of her mother and grandmother.

Sophie took on the protocol and administrative tasks. She

worked on the housing arrangements for all the heads of families, as well as a formal ball to be held in Izzy's honor.

Izzy personally contacted Gelineau, Broussard and Jackson and invited them to the funeral and the ball after her investiture. They would not be allowed at the investiture; it was for Gifted only. Broussard and Jackson prized their invitations—who wouldn't, with all the Gifted in attendance? But Gelineau was far more subdued.

You backed the wrong horse, didn't you? she thought, as he thanked her for the gracious invitation.

Mirielle argued with Izzy when she invited Andre's clan to the funeral, calling the werewolves "nothing but Cajun riffraff," but Izzy prevailed. And when Sange came back to New Orleans, only mildly apologetic, she didn't wait for an invitation. She simply took it for granted that she would be there.

And then…what to do about her family? Gino, Big Vince and Pat?

The Bouvards set to work, wielding their magic, and Izzy wondered if Jean-Marc had been wrong about the supposed toxicity of her family seat. Maybe Marianne's strange half-life had been the cause of their weaker Gifts. Within hours, three duplicates of the sprawling Bouvard mansion had been created on the grounds. Each bedroom in each mansion was exquisitely appointed, befitting a head of state.

Flowers burst into bloom; music played everywhere— lutes, harps, recorders. The air was heavy with scent. It was like a fairy tale after a long curse has been lifted—even the Bouvards themselves had more color, more life.

Incredible quantities of food arrived—from local producers, in private jets, and some that she suspected was magically created. There were fruits she had never heard of, tastes she had never savored before. There was enough wine and champagne to get the entire borough of Brooklyn drunk—all top-of-the-line brands, a single glass of which would be far beyond a cop's salary.

She was fitted for two new white gowns and a white cape with a twenty-foot train. Sophie retrieved the tiara her mother wore in the portrait in her bedroom from an attic room loaded with Bouvard treasures: jewels, the original deed to the mansion, old correspondence, books of spells, and arcana—athames, wands, powders, amulets and crystals. Izzy wanted to spend hours pouring through it all. Perhaps she could solve the mystery of her father's identity.

But she had to backburner that as the Gifted began arriving after dark. Gifted ceremonies took place at night, when the moon was strong. She met Karen of the House of Magnusen, whose territory included the midwestern United States; and Richard Lockloth, the *guardien* of Australia; Mei Huang, of the Yellow River House of Q'in; and Ichiro Kanno, the *Guardien* of Honshu, one of the four main islands of Japan. Hasana Zuri came with an entourage, all outfitted in tribal gowns of green and black.

And…

"Monsieur Luc de Malchance, Guardien, Maison du Sang."

Three hours before the funeral, the two metallic knights at the entrance of the great hall announced Luc's arrival, and he swept through the double doors, golden and warm, dressed in a finely cut black suit with a black mourning band around the upper arm.

He bowed first to Hasana Zuri, who smiled faintly and inclined her head, and then went to Izzy, who had been seated in a chair conferring with Michel.

"Madame," he said, bowing low.

His voice was like a balm on her frazzled, grieving nerves. She knew it could be a spell, but she didn't care. She was tired and overloaded and her head hurt.

He blinked.

Her head stopped hurting.

"Thank you," she said.

He took her hand. "If I might." He pressed his fingertips against her forehead and cupped her other hand beneath his chin.

To her horror she began to cry.

"Let's go see her," he said. He slid her arm around his and walked her out of the great hall. Heads turned as they left. Michel followed at a discreet distance.

They went into Marianne's original chamber, which was hung with black for the funeral. The Femmes Blanches—the White Women—were dressed all in black, their ebony veils over their faces. They kept their places as Luc entered with Izzy, who was still weeping uncontrollably.

Dark pennants decorated with red flames hung from the rafters. The white mosaics were covered over. Candles grouped around a statue of Joan of Arc softly flickered in the background.

He walked her up to her mother's bier. So young-looking, so beloved. Marianne was dressed identically to Izzy, in a white coffin surrounded by lilies and white candles. Her hands were clasped across her heart.

Maman. Ma maman.

Izzy knelt at the side of the coffin and cried, while Luc stood quietly beside her. She gazed down at Marianne and could not let go. And could not let her own life go. But she'd done it already.

She didn't know how long she cried; she was aware that

the chamber door opened and closed several times. Voices whispered.

After a long time she looked over at Luc, and said, "Make me stop crying."

"Not for the world," he replied steadily. "You have held your tears in your entire life. If I am ever to meet the real *guardienne* of the Flames, your tears must shed the outer shell like a cocoon. The false strength, mothering your father, staying in control while your little heart broke."

"I'm drowning in grief," she implored him.

"You are learning to swim," he said softly.

At last, Jean-Marc and Alain arrived. Dressed in a black suit, his hair tied back, Jean-Marc stood framed in the door of the chamber as Izzy sobbed.

Then he strode to the coffin and wrapped his arms around her, murmuring to her in French as he drew her aside, barking at Luc, who responded coolly.

Shielding her from the coffin, he pressed his fingers to her forehead. Oranges and roses filled her nostrils as he whispered to her in Latin, French and English.

"What is he thinking, what was he doing?" he muttered under his breath, as he stroked her forehead. "This is too much for you. You've grieved enough. He wants you to wallow. That's an evil in itself."

"He...I needed to cry," she whispered. She laid her head against his chest. "Oh, God, Jean-Marc. She's dead."

"But you're alive. I feel your power," he said. His arms held her. His lips brushed the crown of her hair. "You've changed."

"You've changed, too," she ventured. He was warmer. Kinder.

"Not as much," he said. "Our transfer of leadership isn't as dramatic as yours."

Then it was time for the funeral. Izzy sat with the Bouvards; Jean-Marc and Alain, with the other guests.

She had thought it would be a kind, loving ceremony. A celebration of her mother's life. But it was violent, and about grief and despair. Banshees' wails shook the platinum chandelier. Brittle white flames shot toward the ceiling, then winked out. The Femmes Blanches, for now the Femmes Noires, sobbed on their knees.

Michel delivered a eulogy that talked about the horrible loss to the House of the Flames. How a lovely light had been extinguished. Izzy thought of the waste—decades asleep, inert and ineffectual.

But she spoke to me before she died. She may have a life...elsewhere. Some other kind of existence.

Izzy hoped so.

After Alain's speech, there was music on harps and flutes and other instruments Izzy had never seen. It was a heart-breaking, despairing dirge. She couldn't stand it. She was bitter and disappointed.

Then, just as she reached the breaking point, there was release.

White mist descended, scented with lavender. The lilting sweet soprano chorus filled the room, and white light— Bouvard light—gleamed from the coffin. The glowing figure of the patroness—St. Joan, Jehanne d'Arc—appeared in full armor, blazing with glory.

Izzy gazed around the room, uncertain if anyone else saw her.

The martyr leaned over Marianne's body, planting a kiss on her lips. When Jehanne straightened, a glowing copy of Marianne lay in her arms. A golden cord extended from the back of the double's head to the corpse in the coffin.

In her gauntleted right hand, Jehanne gathered up the cord.

Her direct gaze fell on Izzy, and it was the first time Izzy had seen her face. She had dark eyes and a lush mouth and freckles across her nose. Her smile was tender and sweet.

She'll ride with me now, so say farewell. Her lips didn't move. Her voice was inside Izzy's heart.

"*Adieu, Maman,*" Izzy said aloud.

Then Jehanne gave the cord a slight tug. It glimmered and blazed, filling the room with golden light that played over the black drapes and the somber clothes and the long faces. It was like a sunrise.

Then saint and warrior vanished in a flash of light. And Izzy, left behind, raised her tear-streaked face and raised her chin.

"*Vive, Guardienne!*" The cry rang around the room. "*Isabelle, Maison des Flammes! Vive!*"

The funeral was followed by a sumptuous buffet of New Orleans culinary specialties, champagne and liquor. Eating nothing, drinking a glass of red wine, she accepted the condolences of scores of people. Gelineau, his wife and his daughters, Desta and Monique, were there; and Broussard and Jackson, both stag. Izzy remembered her vision when she had seen Desta sacrificed to Esposito's dark voodoo gods, and she had a terrible thought. Had Gelineau planned to let Esposito kill his own child? She'd have to table that for now…but it was definitely on her list to look into.

The reception was brief; the Gifted had attended Jean-Marc's House's ceremonies and now those of the Flames, and they were tired, just like regular people. By then, the triumphant notes of the funeral had faded, and Izzy was completely hollowed out by nerves and grief.

Jean-Marc walked with her as her heavy escort took her

to her room. His eyes were hooded, wary, his gait quick and alert.

He said in a low voice, "Watch out for Luc."

She nodded. "I am. I can't deny that I feel a pull."

His face was grim. "Of course you do. He's Gifted."

It's more than that. Beyond the intense physical attraction, she couldn't help liking him.

As they reached her door, his expression became grimmer still. Izzy braced herself for bad news.

"*Attends,* Isabelle. After the investiture, I have to go back to Montreal for a couple more days. There's a faction in my House that's very distressed that I was made *guardien.* A cousin of mine made an end run, pointing out that I was gone for three years. I need to make a presence. Then I'll be back."

No, she protested. *Oh, God, don't leave me in the middle of this.* But she took a deep breath and nodded. "You do what you have to do," she said. "Your duty."

"My duty." He said it as if it were a dirty word. His lip curled in disgust.

"Your duty was to find me. All this other crap is my crap," she said.

"I will be back," he repeated firmly. Then he looked hard at her and a vivid image of them together in bed blossomed in her mind. He was offering her his strength before he left. She'd be a fool to turn him down, but images of Pat superimposed themselves over the erotic visuals of her with Jean-Marc.

"It's not the same as making love," he reminded her. "It is a transfer of magical essence. Power."

But my heart doesn't know that, she thought. *Maybe this is asking too much of it.*

She didn't answer.

* * *

Her investiture.

Izzy sat on a golden throne in an octagonal room that had been magically created on the grounds of the Bouvards' estate for the event. It was enormous, holding all the Bouvards and the visiting Gifted heads of state. Stained-glass windows revealed the brilliant moon.

All around the room, white fire blazed without giving off heat or smoke. White mist enveloped the space, thinned and vanished. The room filled with the joyful singing of the angelic sopranos and the voices of the Bouvard children, sons and daughters of the Flames.

The Bouvards were all dressed in white. The members of the Grand Covenate wore elaborate robes and gowns, some of them like magicians; others, like Egyptian priestess, druids and mages. In turbans, veils, crowns, head-dresses and masks, they each performed a spell to imbue the new *guardienne* with strength, wisdom, courage and intuition. Many of the spells were danced or sung. One involved what looked to Izzy like fireworks sparklers. She had to hide hysterical laughter at how bizarre some of them seemed to her.

She was so tired that her eyes were glazing over. She sat on her throne holding lilies and her athame, and her head ached.

Then Mirielle placed the tiara on Izzy's head. The only thing left was to put on her mother's ring, the symbol of her office. The Femmes Blanches gathered protectively around her as the moment arrived. The soprano voices rose in a chorus of jubilation. The hundreds of Gifted watched.

Izzy handed her lilies and her athame to Mirielle.

She stood.

Wearing the dark-blue spangled robe she had seen in her

vision, Jean-Marc unfastened the necklace and slid off the heavy gold ring of office.

She held out her hand.

"I am Jean-Marc de Devereaux, Maison des Ombres," he said, "the former regent of the House of the Flames." He slipped the ring onto her finger. "With great pleasure, I present to you your lady, your *guardienne*."

The cheers were deafening.

Across the room, the luminous figure of Jehanne sat astride a horse, her helmet down, her banner flying.

You are my warrior, she heard Jehanne proclaim.

Izzy smelled smoke and flame. She felt heat and danger. She did not feel love.

She felt power, expanding out, making her shaky and dizzy and...ready.

Jehanne raised her pennant and disappeared.

Izzy began to glow from head to toe, the brilliant white light blinding the others, who had to turn their heads.

Now I've done it, Izzy thought. *Now I'm in.*

The ball was held in the same room as the investiture. Everyone changed into ball gowns and tuxes. Hasana Zuri held court, and Sange danced with young, handsome Bouvard men. Caresse and Andre showed the string quartet how to play zydeco and soon had everyone stomping their feet and whistling.

Ice sculptures burned with white fire. Food and drink flowed freely. The affair was elegant, joyful but fraught with tension. And there was Jean-Marc, gazing at her with unabashed desire.

Luc, too, drew her like a magnet. His lazy smile and his loose ease reminded her of Pat.

Sexual energy coiled around both men—Gifted men, men who were used to exchanging power through passion.

When she finally left, Luc smiled at her and touched two fingers to his forehead in a salute. He raised his brows as if to say, "Tonight? Me?"

She was pleasant but firm as she gave her head a little shake.

When she got to her room, she found Jean-Marc standing beside the bed in his tux, drinking a flute of champagne. When he saw her, he set it down on the nightstand and watched her walk into the room.

She remembered how life-changing going to bed with Pat had been. Sex with Jean-Marc had been even more incredible. Her body quivered at the memory. But more important, it had imbued her with magical strength. Strength she might need to call on while Jean-Marc was gone.

He held out his hand. "This is important for you. I won't be here to help."

She took a deep breath. "I'm not going to do it, Jean-Marc. I understand what it means in your world. *Our* world. But it's not what it means in…his."

She closed her eyes against her tears as she heard herself. Pat's world was all she had ever wanted.

Jean-Marc sighed. "It's too soon for you. This has happened too fast, and I'm sorry, Isabelle. You know that." He gestured to the bed. "I would almost force you, so you would have the benefit. Part of me is telling me to do just that."

Tears welling, she smiled crookedly and said, "No naked blindfolds."

He smiled back. It was something she had said to him long ago. He picked up his champagne again, toasted her, and took a sip.

"There is fine power in your integrity," he said. "That will help."

* * *

After Jean-Marc left, she called Pat.

"Tell me where you are," he said. "*Now.*"

"I can't," she said. She took a breath, trying to form the words to tell him to stop looking for her. But she didn't have *that* much integrity.

Chapter 18

Pat, holding her, cradling her, kissing her forehead and her cheeks, gazing into her eyes and murmuring, "Hey, you."

Pat, spooning her, nuzzling her, his drowsy sigh against her temple. Whispering, "Honey, you asleep?"

Izzy woke. She wondered if Jean-Marc had given her a nighttime of lovemaking with Pat—for that was what it had been, making love. He had told her that the Devereauxes were master manipulators, and one of their specialties was altering dreams.

She thought of her erotic dream at Andre's cabin, and wondered about that.

A few hours later, at a formal dinner, she thanked all her guests for coming. So many of them had asked for meetings and private audiences in the coming months that she couldn't keep them all straight. She was leaving the scheduling to Michel. For now, everyone was going back to their homes, to give her some time to begin her reign.

In the driveway, as they loaded into a limo, Jean-Marc held her hands in his and reminded her of his promise to return soon.

They shared a long look and then she said, "I'll be okay."

"I know," he said.

She wondered if they were lying.

Alain kissed her on both cheeks, and they left.

She didn't call Pat. The dreams had brought home that what she wanted from him was not what she could have. So she sat for a while with that thought.

And then she cried, long and hard.

She called her father—or the man she had always assumed was her father, until Jean-Marc had located her and told her about her mother. Now she had no idea who her real father was.

"Hey, Big Vince," she began, taking a deep breath. "I have something we need to talk about. The reason I've been gone so long—"

"Yeah, Iz," he said. "Captain Clancy told me all about it."

Izzy pulled in her stomach as if she'd been gut-punched. That hadn't been what she'd expected to hear. She and Clancy had certainly not discussed it.

"Heard you're helping out the Feebs. Esposito's connected, eh? Tough duty, having to hang out in Florida."

She closed her eyes. Whose brilliant idea had it been to tell him she was working with the FBI? It didn't surprise her that he'd bought it. Jean-Marc had explained to her that Gifted could come to Ungifted in dreams and slowly plant whatever information they wanted them to believe. But why hadn't she been consulted? *Now* what was she going to say?

"Gino's bragging to all the other guys that his sister's going to join the FBI. There's a thought, Iz. Not out in the field, but as a data analyst, something like that."

"You're right, Big Vince," she said. "There's a thought. Great thought." She pressed her fingertips against her forehead. "Well, I'll check in again later."

They hung up. The unreality of her real life swept over her again in huge waves—she was going to have to tell him sometime; she had just postponed the inevitable. Clearly Gino hadn't told Big Vince that Izzy had confided in him about her adoption. But then, Gino had thought she was on a vacation and due to come home soon. So the whole mess was all still on her plate

Exasperated and unnerved, she sought solace with a run, jogging the perimeter of the vast grounds with two stalwart Bouvard operatives in tow. Other operatives, locked and loaded, kept watch from the verandahs and rooftop of the original mansion. It was afternoon, the first day of the rest of her life. Muscles and emotions ratcheted up; then her endorphins kicked in and she began to feel slightly less jangled.

When she was finished, the two Bouvards kept their distance as she stretched her calf muscles and popped open a sports bottle of water and toweled off her face and arms. But they were smiling. A lot of people around the mansion were smiling. Her mother's reign had been a strain on everyone.

She said, "Same time tomorrow?" and they both bowed low, smiles becoming grins.

"Of course, *Guardienne*," said the taller of the two.

And then she spotted Luc de Malchance ambling toward her with Michel and Sophie in tow. Charisma rolled off Luc in waves, and Izzy couldn't help her response. She wanted to put herself on her guard. She wanted to mistrust him, the way everyone else in her family did. The way the Devereauxes did. But he seemed like a sunny, happy man with an unfortunately theatrical last name.

For his part, Michel looked like he was choking, and Sophie, as if she would prefer to be anywhere else. The three Bouvard guards walking behind them looked like they had itchy trigger fingers.

"*Guardienne,*" Luc said, hailing her. "I was hoping for a few moments with you before I left."

To give herself time to consider, Izzy tapped the plastic spigot against her tongue for the last few drops. Sophie darted forward to retrieve it from her. She held her hand out for the towel, as well, but Izzy kept it.

"All right. Let's walk," she said to Luc, waiting for him to come to her. He did. Good feelings, good humor emanated off him in waves. After everything she'd heard about the Malchances, she'd expected some kind of deformed villain with a black cape and a handlebar moustache. Appearances could certainly be deceiving, she reminded herself. Hadn't Lucifer been the most beautiful of all the angels?

The rest of the party—Michel, Sophie and the three guards—followed three paces behind. As she strolled beside Luc in the sunshine, Izzy inhaled freshly mown grass, the far-off moldy odor of the swamp. A bird trilled.

"Aristide," he said without preamble. "Here, in New Orleans."

She lifted her brows. The world was full of surprises today.

Sliding a glance his way, she said, "We thought he was a myth."

"We know he's not," Luc replied. "In fact, we've been doing fact-gathering on him for years. We're not surprised he's made a move. We've been wondering when. And where."

"And?" she prompted, although she knew full well where he was going with this.

"We have a lot to offer you. We can help."

"And in return?"

He shrugged, and the gesture reminded her of Jean-Marc. And that reminded her that he wasn't here. She was on her own.

"We want to get rid of him, too. You know that our patron is a demon. Like the Devereauxes. Malfeur doesn't care for Aristide and his ambitions. And we like to keep our patron happy." He crossed his eyes. "Grumpy patron, grumpy House."

"That's very practical," she drawled, amused.

He bent down and plucked a dandelion from the grass. Smiled at it as they walked together. "Plus, we could use the goodwill. Somewhere along the line, we developed bad blood—that's a pun—with the House of the Flames and the House of the Shadows. But we were the original three, founded to defeat Aristide."

"So the legend goes," Izzy said. She forced herself to look away from his face. She couldn't help liking him. Wanting him. "There's a trust issue."

"*Bien sûr.* Exactly what I'm saying." He took a breath and blew on the dandelion. None of the little fibers detached from the puffy sphere, and he smiled. "Maybe if we help you defeat Aristide, you will trust us."

"The Devereauxes have offered," she pointed out.

"I have no problem with that." He held out the dandelion. "This is my olive branch. I'm rather new as *guardien* myself, did you know that? My uncle Etienne was our *guardien* until about five years ago."

He wiggled the dandelion at her. "We're the new generation. Seriously, Isabelle—may I call you Isabelle?" At her nod, he continued. "We have information. We'll give it to you, no strings. If you want more help, you let me know."

"I'll talk to my cabinet," she said. Which she had yet to form.

"*D'accord.* Now, I have a plane to catch," he said. With a deep bow, he wheeled around and left her standing alone. She gave the dandelion a puff, and the little wisps of white scattered.

"You forgot to make a wish," Luc said over his shoulder.

Then he left, simple as that.

Michel approached. "What did he say? What did he do?" he demanded.

Izzy told him.

"We should refuse," Michel said. "Stay as far away from them as we can."

"I'll take that under consideration," Izzy promised, her gaze following Luc as he ambled away.

Later on, she took Bijou with her to Marianne's chamber— now called simply "the" chamber—to work on Bouvard healing magic with the Femmes Blanches. It seemed that aside from an occasional burst, she had no facility for healing other than through sex, which she was not about to discuss with them.

"I must not have been there when they passed out the healing gene," she apologized to one of the women.

"*Oui, madame,*" the woman replied, but it was obvious to Izzy that all the Femmes Blanches were very troubled.

As day was turning into afternoon, she called Michel into her office to ask him about it. Standing in front of her large white desk covered with a calendar blotter imprinted with the Flames logo and, she assumed, Jean-Marc's spare handwriting in the squares of the month—for plans that no longer pertained—he looked just as concerned as the Femmes Blanches.

"Each House has basic Gifts," he said. "The Devereauxes, for example, are excellent at glamours. The Malchances are quick and sharp in battle—be it against supernaturals or in the boardroom. They're very good at summoning demons, which we, of course, do not condone."

Izzy said, "The Devereauxes can also summon demons."

"There is that," Michel said, as if that proved a particularly favorite point of his. Which it did. "I think you have been told that for us, though, it is an act punishable by death."

She picked up a white pen and clicked the point in and out, in and out. Caught herself, and put it down. She was edgy. She needed to shower off the magical residue from working with the Femmes Blanches.

"Yes, understood," she said. "But why?"

"It's our tradition," he replied, again as if that should suffice.

She let it go. She had no plans to raise demons in the near future, anyway.

He paced, as edgy as she, apparently. "It is privately believed by us that the Malchances are also adept at stealing souls. And we are the healers. It is part of who we are."

"Except for me," Izzy said. "Are you're saying that means I'm not a Bouvard?"

Paling, he stopped and waved a hand in front of his face, casting anxious glances left and right, as if someone would overhear, although they were alone. He had assured her that the office was warded, but she wondered if that were really the case. How many scrying stones were tuned in, spying on the new *guardienne* to see how she was working out?

He said in a hushed tone, "You know there are unhappy members of our family who would love to use what you just said against you."

"This room is warded," she reminded him, testing him.

"And yet," he beseeched her.

So I am being spied on.

She tried another tack. "Have you made any headway finding out who my father is?" If lack of a healing Gift indicated that she wasn't fully de Bouvard, what was she?

He shook his head. "So much has been going on."

"*Eh, bon,*" she said. She pushed back from her desk. "Let's keep looking."

He inclined his head. "*Oui, Guardienne.*"

During the next few nights, Izzy stood on the verandah and listened to the voodoo drums rumbling in the bayou. Large bonfires flickered and shimmered; smoke rose into the night sky and caressed the moon.

Against Michel's wishes, she traveled through the bayou, by day, and visited the werewolves' camp. Half the pack had remained in New York to guard Pat, Gino and Big Vince. Andre had arranged for her to meet with Mamaloi, since the old voodoo woman refused to come to the Bouvards' mansion. Izzy took note of Mamaloi's ill will toward the Gifted being charged with protecting all Ungifted and supernaturals within their borders. It still wasn't clear to her why the Flames insisted that *voudon* lay beyond their provenance.

So she ate gumbo and listened to the little boy's accordion and assured him that Bijou was just fine. She took a nice long bath in the cracked porcelain tub while Caresse made *beignets*.

Then Mamaloi communed with her *loa*. Her god had bad news: Aristide was practicing *voudon* to gain more power in his bid to open the conduit.

"You should come to the mansion," Izzy urged Andre.

"We're safer in the bayou," he replied, arranging his gris-gris around her neck. "You would be, too."

Later, Izzy was sitting in bed reading the large dossier on Aristide that Luc had e-mailed her. Le Fils's cache of arcane books sat beside her bed. Steam was practically rising from the top of her head; she'd had a bad fight on the phone with Jean-Marc, who didn't want her to have anything to do with Luc. But she'd pointed out quite reasonably that she, not he, was the one listening to voodoo drums whose message Mamaloi reluctantly translated: they foretold Aristide's victory over "the world."

Jean-Marc was frustrated he couldn't be there. He had serious problems in Montreal. He'd made a lot of enemies. Some of them claimed that his father's death was suspiciously well timed: out of a job in New Orleans, a supposedly power-hungry Jean-Marc was more than ready to clear the way for the mantel of *guardien*.

So while he couldn't come down to help her himself, he wanted her to reject any and all contact with Luc on general principle. Maybe Luc *was* feeding her disinformation. Maybe he *had* already thrown his lot in with Aristide himself. She didn't see the harm in reading a simple download, which had been checked and rechecked for magic spells by her special ops forces and D'Artagnon himself—although she thought his abilities and his loyalties both were questionable.

She turned to a page labeled Known Associates. The names Le Fils and Baron Samedi popped out at her. She had learned from Andre and Mamaloi that Baron Samedi was one of the most powerful *bokors* in all of *voudon,* and that he was Haitian. The Malchance headquarters was in Haiti.

"Samedi last seen in Port-au-Prince. Voodoo ceremony. Six young girls and three men sacrificed."

The date was three months before.

"Le Fils: estranged mate of Sange, Vampire Doyenne of New Orleans. Associates with Julius Esposito, *bokor.*"

Written four months before. If she'd seen this report when it had been written, she would have known that Esposito was working with Le Fils.

"Sauvage, Ungifted goth, infiltrated regent's inner circle, works for Le Fils."

"God," Izzy said aloud. All this could have been so much help.

The voodoo drums played on.

The book *The Conduit* talked about magical confluence and stellar alignments, and Michel set several learned Bouvard scholars to the task of establishing a time window when Aristide's attempt to open a portal to hell might be propitious. Failing that, they looked to coded events: "when the moon bleeds"; "when the daughter burns."

"When the daughter burns—could this mean when you became *guardienne*?" Michel asked during one of their late-night meetings.

She debated about asking Luc. She didn't know if he knew about the books they'd confiscated. He had given her valuable information. All she'd given him in return was hope for a relationship with her House. She figured that given the unequal risk levels, it was a fair trade. But eventually he would want some payback. She wondered if he was withholding data so that she would have to play a little fairer to get it.

The voodoo drums talked about the abandoned convent. It was said to be haunted; Marie Laveau, the voodoo queen of nineteenth-century New Orleans, was said to have kidnapped young postulants—virgins—to use in sacrifices. Some said the vibrations of fear and horror there would aid in the use of the Dark Arts.

But nothing showed up on the scrying stones the Bouvards

had planted all over the tunnel, and in the abandoned convent itself. None of Izzy's armed patrols came up with anything.

Still...tourists went missing. There was a news report about a daylight attack on a woman by a white-faced, fanged creature. Reporters were beginning to ask questions that hit too close to the mark: Could it be that New Orleans actually *was* home to vampires?

Sange was enraged.

"You must do something," she told Izzy as she paced in Izzy's office. "I have a nest in the French Quarter. My sire-lings are terrified that vigilantes will come after them. You have a duty to protect us. We have a treaty with you."

Feeling the pressure, Izzy passed Luc's report and all the books to Michel and better-educated Bouvards who had a shot at understanding them. At a loss, she trained and honed her fighting skills...and worked on her Gift. Nothing came of her attempts to heal.

One night, just as Izzy was getting ready for bed, Pat called.

"Where the hell have you been?" she demanded, aware that she was echoing his outraged question of not so long ago.

He said, "Iz, I've been underground. Things in New York got hot. I want you to know that I'm on my way to New Orleans."

"Hot?"

"It's okay now. Werewolves took care of it. They told me where you are in return. I'll fill you in later."

"Damn it," she said. "Pat, go back. Stay away."

The phone went dead.

She checked the cell, dialed *69 to call him back. There was nothing.

She slipped on a pair of jeans and a white sweater and

asked the guard in the hall to summon Michel. Michel arrived and worked magic to boost the phone's signal. Nothing.

Izzy slid her Medusa into her shoulder holster and grabbed a black jacket out of the armoire.

In Izzy's octagonal office, the walls were covered with photos, daguerreotypes and oils of the unbroken line of *guardiennes*. Their eyes seemed to watch Izzy and Michel as they tried the mansion's bank of phones. Every single line was nonfunctional.

I dreamed this. It was set back in New York, but parts of it were about this.

"I'm feeling very ill," Michel reported.

With a start, Izzy became aware that she was, too. It was a sensation like food poisoning, rolling in her gut and giving her the shakes.

Annette appeared in the office doorway. Her face was gray and she was sweating profusely. She said, "Madame, monsieur, something's wrong with our magical field. No one's spells are working. People are getting sick."

Michael inhaled sharply. "We're under magical attack," he said. "We'll gather everyone in the chamber to organize a defense. I'll alert security."

Within minutes a heavy guard escorted Izzy down the chamber. The Femmes Blanches had already assembled, and one of them explained to Izzy that they were trying to cleanse the mansion.

"It's contaminated," she said, panting. Then she turned and bolted, throwing up in one of the vases of lilies near Izzy's throne.

Mirielle dragged herself forward, pointed to Izzy and said, "It's because something is wrong with her. She's not supposed to be our *guardienne*."

Michel, who was leading a stream of Bouvards, approached Mirielle and put his hands around hers.

"Please, Madame Mirielle, not now, eh? We're in crisis."

"But it *is* because of her," Mirielle insisted. She huffed and turned away. She stomped over to an empty chair and flopped down, hanging her head over her knees. "I am dying," she reported.

Izzy sat on her throne and tried to keep from vomiting as the Bouvards gathered. The crush of people was overwhelming. She was getting sweatier by the second. She leaned her head back as chills ran through her, twisting her joints and muscles. The Femmes Blanches came to her, holding her hands.

"Madame," Alain said, jiggling her shoulder. "Madame, the mayor has arrived."

She jerked to attention. *Why was the mayor here? First Pat, then the mansion is magically altered, now the mayor was calling on them?*

Mayor Gelineau stood in front of her, and his appearance shocked her. The man had aged twenty years since she had last seen him.

"My daughter Desta is missing," he said, running his hands along the sides of his face. "I can't find her anywhere."

Izzy's blood ran cold. Although she had suspected him before of willingly handing his daughter over for sacrifice, his terror appeared to be genuine. The anxiety was flying off him; she could practically see it.

She said to Michel, "Send out search parties. Go everywhere. Comb the French quarter. And the bayou."

"Oh, God, thank you," Gelineau said, grabbing her hand. "Thank you."

"It's okay. We'll find her," she said tersely. She looked down at her jeans. "I'll change." She'd search the bayou herself.

Michel caught her drift immediately. "You can't leave the mansion."

She looked at him hard and said, "I'll change."

"But I like you just like that," Luc said from the entrance to the chamber.

Dressed in black leather, a submachine gun around his neck, he smiled sunnily at her. The enormous contingent of men and women dressed in black body armor behind him did not.

Chapter 19

Izzy signaled for her Bouvards to take Luc, but most of them were doubled over, vomiting and passing out. Shaking hands went for "sploders," Uzis. A few took aim.

Click-click-click. Nothing worked. None of their weapons fired.

Michel croaked, "Dampening field. On our own turf."

An operative tried to physically attack the nearest Malchance op, but he ricocheted off a large dome of red light that flared up around the invasion force.

"How did you do this?" she asked Luc as her legs gave way and she was forced to sit back down. "Where did you get the power?"

"I think you know," he said, striding down the main aisle of the chamber.

"Aristide? Then why pretend to help me?" she asked, wiping her mouth, her forehead. She was deathly ill.

"I didn't give you anything you could actually use," he replied.

He reached her side. Bending down, he said, "I hate to see you suffer so. Don't worry. It won't last. Now, let's move this along, shall we?" He straightened and said over his shoulder, "The chalice, please," he said.

One of the armed men approached Luc with a red velvet box large enough to hold a soccer ball. Luc opened the box with a flourish. He reached in and pulled out an ornate black goblet decorated with red-and-black jeweled skulls.

"This is the chalice of the House of the Blood," he announced, raising it up for all to see. He looked at Izzy. "As we, too, sprang from Catholic roots, surely you grasp the symbolism. But it goes deeper than that."

He handed the box to his Malchance guard. Then he reached into his leather pants pocket and pulled out a beautiful golden athame studded with red stones.

"We are called the House of the Blood because when our patron, Malfeur, agreed to sponsor us in the world of magic, he changed us. We are very different from the rest of you. Genetically. Biologically." He inclined his head. "One may argue that we're superior."

"You are evil incarnate!" Mirielle said, from her chair.

"Please, madame, calm down. Now, watch," he said to Izzy, brimming with inappropriate enthusiasm. He grabbed Mirielle's hand, turned it over, and slashed his knife across her palm.

"No!" Izzy cried. She jerked her hands free and tried to form fireballs, but her palms remained cold.

He raised Mirielle's hand over the chalice and let her blood drip into it. Then he waved a hand at Mirielle's wound and it closed up instantly.

He gestured to the same Malchance guard, who opened a square of white cloth and held it beneath the chalice. Luc tipped it over. Mirielle's droplets of blood dribbled out, spreading across the white.

He held it up.

"Bouvard blood," he said.

"Now. Malchance blood." He slashed his own palm and squeezed it over the chalice. The guard produced a fresh square of cloth. Luc tipped the chalice over as before.

The blood that hit the cloth was a deep reddish black. Izzy had never seen anything like it.

"Malchance blood," he announced, and Izzy could tell by their looks that this was what the Bouvards had expected to see.

"Now." He made a big deal out of wiping his blood out of the chalice. Then one of the other guards brought him a little dish of water, and he washed the chalice out, until the water came out clear.

"No more Malchance blood in the chalice," he said.

Then he reached for Izzy's hand.

And it all became clear.

He's my father.

"Don't be silly. I'm not old enough," he said aloud. "However…"

She didn't feel it as he slashed her hand. She was cold, numb and very scared. She blinked rapidly as her blood dribbled into the chalice, as he turned it over…

…and the resulting stain was almost, but not quite, as dark as Luc's.

The Bouvards gasped. Mirielle glared at Izzy with overwhelming disgust. Michel covered his mouth, his face as white as a vampire's.

"It's a trick," Izzy insisted.

"No trick, and if you search your heart, you know it." He laced his fingers through hers and raised her hand into the air.

"*Mesdames, messieurs,* I present to you the Daughter of the Flames and of the Blood," he said. He smiled at Izzy "My long-lost cousin."

He paused a moment to let them absorb the revelation as he lowered their arms. Then he cocked his head lazily and said to Mirielle, "Isn't she, madame? The Daughter of the Blood?"

Mirielle looked away.

"Come now. It's all out," he prodded. "You no longer have to carry the burden alone."

Mirielle's shoulders sagged. She aged visibly before Izzy's eyes, haggard, care-worn, angry and defeated.

"She loved him," Mirielle said. "I told her it was evil, but he had cast his spell on her."

"You mean my uncle, Etienne. My predecessor," Luc said. "The previous *guardien* of the House of the Blood."

"She ran off to have the child," Mirielle said, her eyes glazed as if from far away. "That young girl Stephanie went with her. Everyone seems to have forgotten *petite* Stephanie. No one mourned *her* or wondered where *she* went."

"I believe she died," Luc said blandly. "At least, that's what my uncle told me."

Loathing consumed Mirielle as she glared at Luc. "You are all monsters."

"No. We're family," he said, giving her a wink.

So, at last I know, Izzy thought sickly as the Bouvards stared at her as if she were the Devil. *I'm one of the bad guys.*

"I know your plan," Mirielle said. "You'll try to take over. You'll tell Hasana Zuri that our two Houses should become one. That's been your plan all along. That was why you were looking for her."

"Of course we were looking for her. She's one of us."

"*Bâtard!*" Mirielle shouted. She lunged at him. Luc pointed a finger at her, and she fell back against her chair, rooted to the spot.

"*Madame,* calm yourself," he said.

Izzy said, "Here's a better idea. Why don't you go to the Grand Covenate and tell them that I've resigned? I'll go away and leave you all to sort this out."

He scrunched up his nose. "Let's think outside the box, Isabelle. We're done with the Grand Covenate. We've moved to the other side."

The Dark Side. The evil side.

"The Grand Covenate will use force against you," she said, although she had no idea if that was true.

"Pfft," he scoffed. Then he reached forward and slid his hand into her jacket. He lifted the Medusa out of the holster. He flipped it open and said to the Malchance who had brought him the chalice, "We've got some .357 caliber, *oui?*"

"*Oui, Monsieur le Guardien,*" the man replied.

"We'll load on the way," he said as he took Izzy's hand and faced the Bouvards. "*Bon,* dear cousins, I apologize for gathering you here in the middle of the night and frightening you. My troops will keep you company."

He clasped Izzy's hand. "Now, where are all those helpful books Le Fils was gathering for our good friend Aristide?"

Michel said, "I'll never tell you."

"Oh. There they are," Luc announced, pointing to two of

his ops at the entrance to the chamber, carrying Le Fils's wooden box between them. *"Bon.* No need to delay any longer."

He pressed Izzy's Medusa against her temple and began dragging her down the main aisle as an inner file of his security team shadowed them, submachine guns trained on the Bouvards. Outer rows of guards remained stationary, some aiming their weapons at the Bouvards, others making the motions of magical spells. Izzy read misery, anguish, repulsion and hatred on the faces that she passed.

Moving into the hall, she was in for another awful surprise: in addition to more Malchance ops, Luc had brought zombies. Dozens of them.

Luc said to Izzy, "Been hearing voodoo drums lately?"

"What are they for?" she asked him.

"Backup. Fodder."

As they progressed through the mansion, the living up front, the walking dead behind, they came upon armed Malchance after armed Malchance, stationed in strategic positions—doorways, stairwells and the chamber.

"Where are we going?" she asked. She assumed their destination was the convent.

"Wait and see," he replied, sounding mischievous and playful, and not at all like an evil slime. "Oh, and by the way?" he said to the nearest operative. "Cuff her."

The bayou.

For ten years Izzy had dreamed of this very path. Her arms wrenched tightly behind her back, she was in the forest of her recurring nightmare, not in a nightgown, nor being chased by faceless monsters. But she was there.

"Allons, vite," Luc said, picking up the pace.

Izzy's foot caught on a root; she stumbled to the right and steadied herself against a live oak tree.

There were four fresh slash marks cut into the bark.

Werewolves? Andre? she thought hopefully. And where was Pat? God, she hoped Ruthven had gotten lost. They'd flown in via private jet. She wouldn't be able to navigate from the commercial New Orleans airport to the mansion.

She looked around, then quickly moved on before any of the Malchances had time to notice the slashes.

They kept going. Though she was beginning to recover from her physical illness, she was cold with the sweat of fear.

Then, through the noisy bayou night, heavy footfalls crushed twigs and fern fronds. A radiophone squawked on. Chatter erupted from the speaker.

Luc signaled everyone to crouch and hide among the cattails. Gazing at Izzy, he put his finger against his lips and held up the Medusa.

As if she needed reminding.

"Hustle it up!" said a male voice into the radiophone. "They're dogging you!"

A chill centered in the small of her back. Those were the exact words from her nightmare. But she had always heard them directed at her.

The ferns shivered as the man with the radiophone charged past. She craned her neck and saw a dark windbreaker, and on the back, NOPD in white letters.

More chatter as he raced away.

They waited a few more seconds. Then Luc smiled and said, "What do you think they're doing out here?"

"Looking for Desta," she said.

"You definitely have your brains from my side of the family," he crowed.

They picked up their pace. Izzy looked for signs of NOPD, saw none, kept going. Her Gifted reserves kicked in, like endorphins, and Luc gave her a look.

He said, "Malchances are known for their stamina. I know you fucked Jean-Marc. Pffft. He's nothing compared to me."

She ignored him.

Jean-Marc, she called, *where are you? I need you. I'm in trouble.* Au secours.

And then she realized that she had completely forgotten to call on the *patronesse.*

Jehanne, ma Patronesse, je vous en prie. *Please, help me. Help us. Help the Bouvards.*

Jehanne must have known what Marianne had done. She must have known that Izzy was half Malchance. And yet she had allowed her Gift to be given to Izzy. To what end? What did she expect her to do with it? Bouvards were supposed to protect the weak. The Malchances were in league with the Devil. How could she reconcile that?

At a signal from Luc, everyone turned left and slid down a sharp incline. A rope bridge was slung from one finger of land to another one about twenty feet away.

She stepped onto the rickety bridge. Luc came right behind, and she could almost feel the Medusa pointed at her head as he said, "Just walk. Nothing funny."

She froze. The gator—was it on the bridge or under it? Where was he taking her?

"Isabelle," he prompted, "do as I say. You're not indispensable."

"I am Marianne's daughter," she reminded him.

"That's right," he said jovially. Then he chuckled as if he had a wonderful secret. His good humor was almost impish, his emotional responses bordering on childish. She began to wonder if he was crazy.

Once off the bridge, Izzy's boots slogged into thick, swampy mud. She walked on, wondering where this would end.

Her answer came soon enough. They reached a spot about thirty feet in diameter, cleared of cypress trees and bushes freshly hacked down and lying on their sides. A bonfire crackled in the center, and Izzy felt a keen sense of despair. If they could burn a fire, they weren't worried about being discovered.

Oh, no. No.

The police officer who had spoken into his radiophone lay gagged and spread-eagle over one of the trunks. His eyes bulged above the gag. Candles and foot-high statues of a hideous, distorted, humanlike shape lined the trunk from one end to the other. There was a gold athame dotted with red stones, and the chalice Luc had used to reveal the secret of her parentage. It was clear to her that Luc was going to sacrifice the man.

I'm going to kill Luc, she thought. Then something rippled through her consciousness—a hot, angry flash of emotion so intense it was almost palpable. She shook, nervous scrambling, gray dots forming as if she'd been hit with a stun gun. A whine keened in her ears.

What the hell was that? she thought as it faded.

Beyond the trunk, a dark-green glow rippled and ebbed like a jellyfish through the trees as a figure stepped from the shadows. It—he, it looked masculine—was at least seven feet tall, and draped in a spangled black-and-silver robe that fell to the floor. His white hair hung around his shoulders. His skin was the color of a bloated corpse. His eyes were completely black, and two sharp, canine fangs jutted from his upper jaw.

In one curved, clawed hand he held an athame; in the other, a goblet. He emanated power and menace. Evil rolled off him in waves. She could feel it, taste it, bitter and lethal.

"Aristide," she rasped.

"*Oui.*" The voice echoed through the swamp as the tall vampire inclined his head, looking pleased that she knew who he was. His voice echoed through the bayou clearing; it sounded electric and unreal.

She closed her eyes and willed energy into her palm, but it was cold.

Another figure stepped from the darkness. It appeared to be a man almost as tall as Aristide. He wore a mask that looked like a human skull—she prayed it was only a mask— and he was dressed in a black robe with copper charms, chicken feet and goats' hooves attached to it. There were bands of copper on his wrists and around his ankles. His feet were bare.

"You brought her," Aristide said to Luc.

"Of course I did. And here are the books." He gestured, and the two guards carrying the chest minced uncertainly toward Aristide, nearly dropping their burden as they presented to him and quickly backed away.

They needed the books. And I'm a big-ticket item, too, Izzy thought. *Luc extracted me specifically to bring me here. To render me harmless or because I'm needed? For what?*

Trying not to dissolve into panic, she glanced left and right as she searched for something to extract her from her predicament.

Drums sounded, though she saw no drummers. The bayou floor vibrated. She realized it was the *bokor's* footfalls as he approached. Practically nose-to-nose, he planted his feet and spread wide his arms. His skull mask leered as he tilted his head left and right, as if to get a better view of her through the eyeholes in the deep, black sockets.

"I am Baron Samedi," he said. "Tonight the stars are weeping and the magic of this place is slave to me. I have subdued the *loa*. I am in command. It is the perfect time to open the door between this world and that of my master, Monseigneur Aristide."

She said nothing. Better to let him talk.

"Demons will pour into this bayou, and then we will march on your house. And get rid of the Bouvards once and for all."

"Not just the Bouvards," she said, finding her voice, though how, she had no idea.

"The Malchances are our friends," Aristide told her.

"Grumpy patron?" Izzy asked Luc without turning her head.

Luc came up beside her, slinging his arm around her, his weight adding discomfort to her restrained arms. "Patron likes Aristide. Patron is in."

There was a lull while Aristide set down the chalice beside the head of the captive police officer and looked through the books, choosing one and then discarding it, choosing another and doing the same. Izzy wondered if they'd collected all of them. An image of the book she'd tried to wade through came into her mind.

"*Merci, cousine.* Try *The Conduit*," Luc told Aristide.
Great.

The high-pitched screams of a young girl pierced the bayou. Luc signaled to his ops to investigate. Three of them peeled off and crashed into the undergrowth.

Izzy called out, "Desta! Run!"

"Good guess," Luc said. He kissed her cheek. "Maybe it's one of the werewolves, though. We'll have to see."

She said, "I'm seriously wondering about your sanity."

He laughed. "We're a little nutty on my side. You ever been to see a shrink?"

She had. For recurring nightmares, which she now understood to be her awakening magical powers. She wondered what Luc's diagnosis would be. Too much inbreeding?

After a few minutes the three ops returned, dragging Desta Gelineau, who had been gagged and bound with glowing bands of scarlet. The petite goth with henna hair was wearing a tulle skirt, jeans jacket and cowboy boots. The man holding the rope—very tall, with black hair and blacker eyes, a scar running vertically from above one eye, across the lid and through the side of his mouth—was with them.

"Oh, there you are," Luc said conversationally. "Glad you could make it."

Desta flailed. Her captor gave her a hard shake and said, "*Tais-toi.*" Whimpering, she grew still.

"No more conversation," Aristide said, looking up from the familiar volume of *The Conduit*. "As my fellow baron observed, it is time." He held the book out to Baron Samedi. "*Monsieur,* here is the incantation." His fangs glistened and gleamed as he smiled at Luc. "Good job."

Taking the book, Samedi studied it for a moment. Then he arched his back shouting in a language she didn't understand. He stomped one foot, and the trees shook. The green light swirled; purplish black light mixed with it, casting the two figures in mottled light that briefly distorted their features. They looked like monsters, with long snouts and reptilian eyes.

They look like gators, she thought, balling her fists to keep herself from screaming.

Baron Samedi shouted again. The water in the bayou thrashed.

Aristide picked up the knife and the chalice. He looked calmly at the captive police officer and moved the knife across the top of his head without cutting so much as a brown hair on his head. The man's terrible shriek nearly jerked her heart out of her chest.

The Gifted vampire dipped the knife into the goblet again. The man screamed and writhed. Aristide swiped the man's head again, and stabbed the goblet again. The resulting scream rattled Izzy's bones.

The purple-green light concentrated behind Aristide wobbled and rotated in a spherical shape. Chanting, Baron Samedi moved toward it, and the light shimmered.

Flashes of lightning crackled against the sky. Clouds gathered, and rain shot down like bullets.

Setting down his athame, Aristide said, *"Barbarus est magnus—"*

Black light blazed around him.

"Cason magnus dux—"

He plunged his claws into the police officer's skull.

The man thrashed and shouted in terror as his head glowed with iridescent black light. His eyes shot open. They were pure white.

He bellowed and writhed in agony. Aristide yanked back his claws. Something white and translucent pulsed and glowed between them. A twinkling gold cord was attached to it. It was attached at the other end of the man's forehead.

"That's his soul," Luc said. "That's the cord. That's what he's going to do to you. *Your* soul is very powerful. Very special."

Aristide picked up the athame and smiled at Izzy, letting

her see the sharpness of the blade, making his intention to cut the cord very clear.

"No! No! No!" she shrieked. "Jehanne, stop them!"

With a single clean motion, he cut the cord.

The police officer began to gibber crazily, panting and groaning. He wasn't dead. From her vantage point, Izzy could see his eyes, spinning and jittering. The lights were blazing, but no one was home.

Aristide placed the glowing white mass into the chalice at his elbow, and carried it to the pulsating green light, tossing the man's soul into it like a man throwing out the garbage.

The green light thickened and took a vaguely oval shape.

"The conduit is forming," Luc said excitedly.

Aristide walked to Izzy and held the glinting tip of the knife inches from her left eye. She felt his icy breath, and her eyes welled with tears of sheer terror.

Jehanne, save me now. Give me power. Free my hands and let me defend myself. Send help.

"I can feel your prayers," Aristide said, chuckling, angling the knife at her. "They won't work. You can't imagine how many people have prayed against me. Even the Pope. For centuries, I've bided my time, waiting for the opportunity to bring my followers into this world. And it's all finally come together."

Laughter burbled out of his mouth. Izzy felt another surge of nearly uncontrollable rage…and again something indefinable deep inside her…grew.

She saw a young woman dressed in battle armor waving a pennant as English soldiers overran the battlefield. They had been informed where Jehanne was heading, and moved swift and sure by the dead of night to cut her off.

The informant was Chevalier Jean-Luc de Malchance, a Frenchman eager to curry favor with those who would soon wear the French crown.

Undaunted, Joan of Arc crossed herself and sang out in ringing tones, "No spawn of the Devil shall take me or my warriors! God and His angels shall deliver us!

But a year later, she had died at the stake, screaming for heaven....

She was betrayed by a Malchance, Izzy thought. *Just like me.*

Her rage grew.

The *thing* inside her grew.

She looked across the clearing, beyond the oval of green. Against the trees, a shadow mushroomed.

Je viens, it said in her mind. I come.

"I'll be quick with the next one," Aristide said, his black, soulless eyes gazing down at Izzy as he approached Desta. Before the girl had a chance to react, six Malchances trained Uzis on her. Athame in his hand, Aristide walked calmly up and cut her throat from ear to ear. Blood gushed from the fatal wound.

As Izzy screamed, one of her guards who had brought Desta leaped at Aristide, reciting an incantation. Aristide lunged at the man, cutting a gash in his arm. The other two operatives fell on him, raining fists down on him, grabbing his arms and smashing pulses of red energy against his body. The wounded man morphed into Alain de Devereaux.

And Desta Gelineau became poor Ruthven, who fell to his knees and collapsed. Izzy knew enough to know that he would bleed out in seconds. If he wasn't dead now, he would be very soon.

While Alain's assailants subdued him, Aristide extracted

Ruthven's soul. He fed it to the green oval, which grew again, until it was approximately six feet in diameter.

"I'm sorry, Blanche Neige," Alain said through broken teeth. Though his legs gave way, the two Malchances held him up, his face cut and already swelling. His nose had been broken.

With great effort, Alain looked over his shoulder and whispered, "Ah, *non*."

Two more operatives dragged Jean-Marc into the clearing. They had beaten so him badly that, like Alain, he could barely stand. He was cuffed and gagged, and when he saw Izzy, his eyes bored hard into her.

Jean-Marc, she sent out in her mind, but she heard nothing from him.

One of the men spat at Jean-Marc. The spittle hit his cheek and hung there. He and the other man laughed derisively. He grabbed Jean-Marc's hand, grabbed a finger, and pulled it backward. Izzy heard the snap from where she stood. Jean-Marc only grunted, clenching his teeth hard as if to keep from crying out.

"Shall we break them all?" the operative asked his companion.

Anger welled inside Izzy, and a hatred so deep she could taste it. It tasted like blood.

It grew. She felt the energy of it, the intensity.

"The Devereauxes are legendary for their amazing arrogance," Luc said into Izzy's ear, shaking his head at Alain and Jean-Marc. He gestured to two of his team and said, "Hold her."

Then he stomped over to the prisoners. He kicked Ruthven, who didn't move, and stood nose-to-nose with Alain. "Did you really think I wouldn't notice that you were using glamours? *Grâce à Malfeur*, I'm the *guardien* of my House!"

He turned to Jean-Marc, opened his fingers and sent ripples of red energy over Jean-Marc's body. He convulsed, baring his teeth.

"Stop!" Izzy shouted, straining against the two men who held her. Jean-Marc slowly straightened and lifted his chin. He could barely see out of his eyes.

"You should be glad he showed up," Luc said. He turned to Aristide, who stood at the makeshift tree-trunk altar. "We can make a substitution, eh? His soul instead of hers? I do like her. And she's Family."

Aristide considered. "Why not both?"

"We don't need both," Luc replied. He beamed at Izzy. "We could always save her. Just in case."

"Ah, *bon,*" Aristide said, sounding indulgent.

"You won't take Jean-Marc's soul," she flung at them.

"Ah. And you will stop us," Luc mocked.

"I will *end* you," she promised.

"Yes, we'll save her," Aristide said drily. "So she can murder you in your sleep."

Luc turned and pointed at her. Crackling red energy shot from his fingers and caught her up in an excruciating net. She jangled and shook.

"She just needs some education," Luc said.

As she fought to pull herself back together, the sky lowered and darkened, and Izzy felt cold down to her soul. A smell filled her nose—death, decay and smoke.

"Let's see how much more we need. Then we'll use the Gifted man next," Aristide said. "The cousin, Alain." He spread his arms wide. Nearly shouting above the drumbeat, he began to chant, "*Sume tibi ferrum inventum ex...*"

He and Luc threw back their heads. Luc whispered along, "...*et fac tibi fieri clauem...*"

The oval stretched and snapped, loosening its rigid form, expanding into a jagged hole. Rays of green and black light shot out from it as if from an exploding cannon.

"It's opening!" Luc cried.

"Not yet," Aristide said. "We need more energy." His gaze swept over Izzy, Alain and Jean-Marc.

"Ah, yes, we do," Luc said. Advancing toward the altar, he reached inside his black leather jacket, pulled out Izzy's Medusa and shot Aristide point-blank in the chest. Then he pulled the trigger, and shot him again.

The Gifted vampire stood stock-still for perhaps one full second. His eyes widened. A horrible roar burst out of him, sending shockwaves through the bayou. He grabbed at his chest with his talons, as if he could dig out the cartridges.

And then he exploded in wild fireworks of purple and black. They arced into the sky and shot outward at Izzy, Luc and his troops. Luc flung Izzy in front of his body to shield himself.

And Jean-Marc took a protective step forward, bellowing, "Duck, darlin'! Get out of there!"

That's not Jean-Marc, she realized as she covered her head with her arms. Incredibly, none of the pieces of the thing that had been Aristide touched her. They fell in hard chunks against the ground, like the concentrated evil that had wafted from Esposito's remains.

The aftershocks of the explosion thrummed through her. She barely had time to recover when her eardrums were pummeled by the beating of a dozen drums.

She dropped her arms and opened her eyes. Where there had been only Luc's operatives, about three dozen dark-skinned men in black-and-red robes lined the perimeter of the clearing, playing wildly on waist-high drums. Voodoo *bokors*. Weaving among them, women in robes danced, holding torches, knives, huge snakes and roosters. Their eyes were completely white. They gyrated and whooped. The snakes hissed, their black tongues tasting the air.

The voodoo *bokor,* Baron Samedi, was gyrating, too. He looked at Luc and laughed, giving him a thumbs-up. They'd been in on the double-cross of Aristide together.

"We never could have done it without your Medusa," Luc told her. "Now the *real* fun will begin." He clapped his hands above his head and gestured to the smoking fragments of Aristide. "*Allez, vite,*" he said.

Half a dozen of his people pulled on blue Latex gloves. From a place beneath the trunk, one of them retrieved some black pails and tongs. He distributed them, and the operatives collected the chunks, and carried them to the oval.

As they worked, Izzy found "Jean-Marc" again. Jean-Marc and Alain must have discovered Pat en route to the mansion, and he had consented to wear the glamour of Jean-Marc. She had to get him out of here. She had to save him.

The special ops tossed the chunks of Aristide into the hole one by one, as if they were stoking a fire.

"*Now* we have plenty of power!" Luc crowed. He gave Izzy a squeeze and trailed the Medusa along the side of her face. "I would never have stolen your soul, *ma belle cousine.* It's so pretty inside your body."

The last chunk was thrown into the hole, and the operatives stood expectantly back.

A roar thundered through the bones in Izzy's feet. Then a dark shape appeared in the hole. It shifted and changed, twisted, grew and stepped out of the hole on long, cloven hooves.

"Malfeur! *Bienvenue!*" Luc cried, bouncing on the balls of his feet. "Isabelle, here is our family patron!"

Izzy screamed. It was an enormous gargoyle. Demon, she corrected. Hunched, black and scaly, it stood at least twelve feet high. It flapped open its wings, which were covered with black skin, the edges ribbed with sharp talons. Its head was like a gargoyle's, with blazing red almond-shaped eyes and a trio of horns protruding from the top. Its mouth was a nightmare of rows and rows of enormous serrated teeth.

It pointed at Izzy and said, in a whisper filled with wicked delight, "*Ma fille.*" My daughter.

"No," she said, clenching her fists. "I am not!"

The creature laughed. "*Tu est ma fille. Je suis Malfeur, ton seigneur.*" I am your lord.

"He is your lord, and the author of your being," Luc said. "Malfeur changed my family back in the 1400s. He made us like him, and you are one of us."

Izzy's stomach rebelled. She leaned forward and dry heaved.

Luc tsk-tsked and held out a hand. "*Ma pauvre cousine.*"

He grabbed her around the neck and kissed her, sliding his tongue into her mouth. Held between the two Malchance guards, Pat-as-Jean-Marc yelled, "No!" like the jealous lover that he was.

Luc ended the kiss, lustily running his tongue over his own mouth. Izzy swayed on her feet, feeling violated and disgusted. Her rage began to build again and she let it; something was happening. The white-hot feeling inside her was creating something…something alive.

The sweet soprano chorus vibrated inside her. She saw with her mind's eye her mother, Marianne, standing beside

Jehanne. They were luminescent, angelic, and they held out their arms toward her.

"Better you should die, than call forth a demon," the pa-tronesse said. "Do not do it, or you will cut yourself off from us forever. It is not our way, my warrior."

Izzy jerked, coming back to herself. *I'm calling a demon?* Then she heard a familiar howl.

It was the cavalry, dear God. *Oh, thank you, God.* Andre, in his massive werewolf body, leading the small band of werewolves as they circled Malchance security agents, sinking their teeth into any bit of flesh they could find.

A fierce wind began to blow, and the temperature dropped. The bonfire sizzled as rain poured down.

The air was rent with a banshee scream as Malfeur shot up in height at least ten more feet, towering above the battle. He plucked up a wolf and brutally flung it over his shoulder. He scooped up three of the *bokors'* dark attackers and twisted them in half, dropping the pieces into the steaming bonfire.

Then he reached for Pat-as-Jean-Marc.

"No!" Izzy cried. She made a palm strike, felt the heat, and hurled a fireball at the demon. His eyes widened and he laughed heartily, bending down to catch it in his mouth.

She tried again. For the first time in her life, she succeeded in creating a second fireball after the first.

Malfeur consumed that one, too, rolling with laughter that made the trees shake, as if they were playing a game.

So she aimed her palm at Luc instead. He was standing beside the huge, gaping maw of the conduit, urging a second multihorned, taloned demon to come through the portal.

Nothing came from her palm.

Then Luc turned, wagged his finger at her and said, "Uh-

uh-uh!" in a mock-stern voice. Then he formed a palm strike at her, sending red crackles of energy directly at—

—the Malchance operative holding her left arm.

The electricity sizzled over the body as he morphed…into Jean Marc. His dark, curly hair tumbled over the Devereaux body armor that appeared as his glamour disappeared. His dark eyes drank in the sight of Izzy before they rolled back in his head.

The other Jean-Marc morphed as well.

Into Pat. Terribly, horribly beaten.

Another jolt from Luc had the real Jean-Marc on his knees.

A third, on the ground.

"No!" Izzy screamed. "Stop it!"

"Bring him!" Luc ordered, twirling the Medusa above his head. He was laughing hysterically. "This is just so crazy-mad! It's like Mardi Gras!"

Izzy's sadistic handler let go of her arm and grabbed both wrists of the real Jean-Marc's. He dragged him to Luc and dropped him in a heap at Luc's feet.

In the rain and the wind, he bent down and shouted a loud incantation.

"Barbarus est magnus—"

Red light blazed around him. His hands turned deep red.

"Cason magnus dux—"

He laid the Medusa on the police-officer's chest, plunged his hands into Jean-Marc's skull and yanked out his soul.

Holding the glowing mass in his left hand, Luc picked up Aristide's athame and smiled at Izzy.

"No! No! No!" she shrieked, kicking and screaming, fighting with everything in her to get free.

Luc waited one dramatic moment, and then cut it.

Izzy was speechless. She hadn't thought he would be able to do it. Something would stop him. It was too horrible.

He placed the glowing white mass into the chalice at his elbow, and laid the knife across it.

"Done," he said.

Her anger and desperation gave way to adrenaline-induced strength. She tore free and charged Luc. He countered every kick, every punch. But Izzy was beyond thought or reason.

"I will kill you!" she shrieked. "You are dead!"

Then she felt it behind her, the demon she had called. A block of icy hatred in her soul, a flashfire of rage, blazing with murder.

She heard the ops screaming. The voodoo drums stopped.

Staring past Izzy's shoulder, Luc calmly reached down and the Medusa was in his hand.

The shadow of her creation played across his face. Izzy did not look. She didn't want to see it. She only wanted it to kill him.

He backhanded her with the Medusa, snapping back her head as she fell backward against Jean-Marc, who was inert.

Kill Luc. Kill him, Izzy told her monster.

A roar shook the ground.

"There are still five .357s in the cylinder," Luc said to Izzy. "Enough for five demons."

Luc made a tripod of his arms, a smile on his lips as he pulled the Medusa's trigger.

Izzy held her breath.

Nothing happened.

The gun did not go off.

"*Merde*," Luc swore, as hands the size of assault rifles reached over Izzy's head and plucked him up. He yelled; Izzy reached up and grabbed the gun.

Then Izzy whirled around and saw her demon as it brought Luc toward its mouth. It was female, a huge, naked woman with enormous breasts and rows of skulls on necklaces. Her eyes were Izzy's eyes, but red, like glowing coals. Her teeth were yellowed, jagged, enormous, and she was about rip into Luc's chest with them.

Jehanne said to her, *Deny it. Deny this evil you have created. Or I will abandon you, my daughter.*

"*Malfeur!*" Luc screamed. "*Au secours, mon père!*"

From his location on the other side of the clearing, huge demon Malfeur flew at the female demon. They were about to collide.

But just before the moment of contact, a cloud of sparkling gray mist dropped down from the sky and enveloped Malfeur like a net. Malfeur batted at it, but it held him fast, lifted him up and threw him into the hole.

The conduit exploded. Fragments of green light burst outward like fireworks, zinging and sizzling in the rain. Vibrations shot through Izzy; she threw herself protectively over Jean-Marc's body.

There was another shockwave. And another. The portal became a sphere, and then a dot and then…nothing.

The gray mist evaporated as quickly and silently as it had arrived.

And then a scream from Luc, a horrible scream, as the demon opened her mouth again.

Deny it, said the voice inside her head.

Izzy looked down at the Medusa, flipped it open and examined the bullets. Was something wrong with them? Had someone put a spell on them to render them useless? She ripped open Jean-Marc's cargo pockets. Found another box of ammo.

Deny it!

Dumped out the cartridges, crammed in one.

Aimed.

Fired.

Izzy's demon exploded into hundreds of red fragments. It was like the supernova of a sun. Izzy shielded her eyes.

Luc slammed to the ground beside her.

His eyes were wide open.

He was dead.

And the chalice containing Jean-Marc's soul was gone.

Epilogue

In the aftermath of the bayou attack, Andre and Caresse tended to their dead and to Alain. Izzy bent over Pat, whose heart was barely beating. He was horribly beaten.

If I had slept with Jean-Marc again, I might have the power now to heal him, she thought in despair. But she hadn't. She would have to find the power inside herself.

An image of Jehanne filled her mind:

Bound to the stake as the flames rose, she had begun to call a curse down on all her enemies, all the traitors, on the men who had brought her to this day.

She hated them. She hated them all.

And then…one brave English soldier fashioned a cross for her of two pieces of burning wood. And one brave priest raised a cross on a staff for her to seek.

Kindnesses. Grace.

And her terrible rage transformed to love—the healing power of the universe.

Izzy bent over Pat and pressed her lips against his. Tears fell freely.

"*Je t'aime,*" she whispered.

He exhaled, and his eyes closed.

"Pat?" she asked in a high-pitched voice.

Then Alain stood beside her. He said, "I think he will live."

"He has to," Izzy murmured. Then she let him help her up and together they walked to Jean-Marc's twitching, quivering body. His eyes were wide and crazy.

"They took his soul," Alain said. "One of Luc's people."

"We'll get it back," Izzy said. "Alain, I swear to you we'll get it back."

He touched his cousin's face, and Jean-Marc jerked and mumbled under his breath.

"What is he saying?" Izzy asked.

"It sounds like a name," Alain replied.

She leaned down and pressed her ear against his lips.

He said, "Lilliane."

Izzy froze. She knew that name. From a lifetime before this one, from the moment of her birth:

Haiti

Lilliane de Malchance stared down in disbelief at the operative who knelt before her, the Chalice of the Blood in his hands. The glowing mass of the soul of Jean-Marc de Devereaux shifted in the cup.

"He's *dead?*" Her voice shook. She began to tremble. "My husband, Luc, is dead?"

"*Oui, madame,*" the operative said anxiously. Before she came completely unhinged, he hurried on. "But I have good news." He held his breath, hoping that what he had to say would keep him intact.

"Your twin sister, Isabelle, is alive."

Screaming with hatred and loss, Lilliane grabbed the chalice with both hands and flung it hard at the stone wall.

But the chalice landed upright on the edge of the wall. Jean-Marc's soul glimmered inside it like the holiest of Grails.

* * * * *

Coming soon
DAUGHTER OF THE SHADOWS
by Nancy Holder.
Available in June 2007,
wherever Silhouette Books are sold.

Experience entertaining women's fiction for every woman
who has wondered "what's next?" in her life.

Turn the page for a sneak preview of a new book
from Harlequin NEXT,
WHY IS MURDER ON THE MENU, ANYWAY?
by Stevi Mittman

On sale December 26, wherever books are sold.

Ambience is everything. Imagine eating a foie gras at a luncheonette counter or a side of coleslaw at Le Cirque. It's not a matter of food but one of atmosphere. Remember that when planning your dining room design.

—Tips from *Teddi.com*

"Now that's the kind of man you should be looking for," my mother, the self-appointed keeper of my shelf-life stamp, says. She points with her fork at a man in the corner of the Steak-Out Restaurant, a dive I've just been hired to redecorate. Making this restaurant look four-star will be hard, but not half as hard as getting through lunch without strangling the woman across the table from me. "*He* would make a good husband."

"Oh, you can tell that from across the room?" I ask, wondering how it is she can forget that when we had trouble getting rid of my last husband, she shot him. "Besides being ten minutes away from death if he actually eats all that steak, he's twenty years too old for me and—shallow woman that I am—twenty pounds too heavy. Besides, I am *so* not looking for another husband here. I'm looking to design a new image for this place, looking for some sense of ambience, some feeling, something I can build a proposal on for them."

My mother studies the man in the corner, tilting her head, the better to gauge his age, I suppose. I think she's grimacing, but with all the Botox and Restylane injected into that face, it's hard to tell. She takes another bite of her steak salad, chews slowly so that I don't miss the fact that the steak is a poor cut and tougher than it should be. "You're concentrating on the wrong kind of proposal," she says finally. "Just look at this place, Teddi. It's a dive. There are hardly any other diners. What does *that* tell you about the food?"

"That they cater to a dinner crowd and it's lunchtime," I tell her.

I don't know what I was thinking bringing her here with me. I suppose I thought it would be better than eating alone. There really are days when my common sense goes on vacation. Clearly, this is one of them. I mean, really, did I not resolve less than three weeks ago that I would not let my mother get to me anymore?

What good are New Year's resolutions, anyway?

Mario approaches the man's table and my mother studies him while they converse. Eventually Mario leaves the table with a huff, after which the diner glances up and meets my mother's gaze. I think she's smiling at him. That or she's got indigestion. They size each other up.

I concentrate on making sketches in my notebook and try to ignore the fact that my mother is flirting. At nearly seventy, she's developed an unhealthy interest in members of the opposite sex to whom she isn't married.

According to my father, who has broken the TMI rule and given me Too Much Information, she has no interest in sex with him. Better, I suppose, to be clued in on what they aren't doing in the bedroom than have to hear what they might be doing.

"He's not so old," my mother says, noticing that I have barely touched the Chinese chicken salad she warned me not to get. "He's got about as many years on you as you have on your little cop friend."

She does this to make me crazy. I know it, but it works all the same. "Drew Scoones is not my little 'friend.' He's a detective with whom I—"

"Screwed around," my mother says. I must look shocked, because my mother laughs at me and asks if I think she doesn't know the "lingo."

What I thought she didn't know was that Drew and I actually tangled in the sheets. And, since it's possible she's just fishing, I sidestep the issue and tell her that Drew is just a couple of years younger than me and that I don't need reminding. I dig into my salad with renewed vigor, determined to show my mother that Chinese chicken salad in a steak place was not the stupid choice it's proving to be.

After a few more minutes of my picking at the wilted leaves on my plate, the man my mother has me nearly engaged to pays his bill and heads past us toward the back of the restaurant. I watch my mother take in his shoes, his suit and the diamond pinkie ring that seems to be cutting off the circulation in his little finger.

"Such nice hands," she says after the man is out of sight. "Manicured." She and I both stare at my hands. I have two popped acrylics that are being held on at weird angles by bandages. My cuticles are ragged and there's marker decorating my right hand from measuring carelessly when I did a drawing for a customer.

Twenty minutes later she's disappointed that he managed to leave the restaurant without our noticing. He will join the list of the ones I let get away. I will hear about him twenty years from now when—according to my mother—my children will be grown and I will still be single, living pathetically alone with several dogs and cats.

After my ex, that sounds good to me.

The waitress tells us that our meal has been taken care of by the management and, after thanking Mario, the owner, complimenting him on the wonderful meal and assuring him that once I have redecorated his place people will be flocking here in droves (I actually use those words and ignore my mother when she rolls her eyes), my mother and I head for the restroom.

My father—unfortunately not with us today—has the patience of a saint. He got it over the years of living with my mother. She, perhaps as a result, figures he has the patience for both of them, and feels justified having none. For her, no rules apply, and a little thing like a picture of a man on the door to a public restroom is certainly no barrier to using the john. In all fairness, it does seem silly to stand and wait for the ladies' room if no one is using the men's room.

Still, it's the idea that rules don't apply to her, signs don't apply to her, conventions don't apply to her. She knocks on the door to the men's room. When no one answers she gestures to me to go in ahead. I tell her that I can certainly wait for the ladies' room to be free and she shrugs and goes in herself.

Not a minute later there is a bloodcurdling scream from behind the men's room door.

"Mom!" I yell. "Are you all right?"

Mario comes running over, the waitress on his heels. Two customers head our way while my mother continues to scream.

I try the door, but it is locked. I yell for her to open it and she fumbles with the knob. When she finally manages to unlock and open it, she is white behind her two streaks of blush, but she is on her feet and appears shaken but not stirred.

"What happened?" I ask her. So do Mario and the waitress and the few customers who have migrated to the back of the place.

She points toward the bathroom and I go in, thinking it serves her right for using the men's room. But I see nothing amiss.

She gestures toward the stall, and, like any self-respecting and suspicious woman, I poke the door open with one finger, expecting the worst.

What I find is worse than the worst.

The husband my mother picked out for me is sitting on the toilet. His pants are puddled around his ankles, his hands are hanging at his sides. Pinned to his chest is some sort of Health Department certificate.

Oh, and there is a large, round, bloodless bullet hole between his eyes.

Four Nassau County police officers are securing the area, waiting for the detectives and crime scene personnel to show up. They are trying, though not very hard, to comfort my mother, who in another era would be considered to be suffering from the vapors. Less tactful in the twenty-first century,

I'd say she was losing it. That is, if I didn't know her better, know she was milking it for everything it was worth.

My mother loves attention. As it begins to flag, she swoons and claims to feel faint. Despite four No Smoking signs, my mother insists it's all right for her to light up because, after all, she's in shock. Not to mention that signs, as we know, don't apply to her.

When asked not to smoke, she collapses mournfully in a chair and lets her head loll to the side, all without mussing her hair.

Eventually, the detectives show up to find the four patrolmen all circled around her, debating whether to administer CPR, smelling salts or simply call the paramedics. I, however, know just what will snap her to attention.

"Detective Scoones," I say loudly. My mother parts the sea of cops.

"We have to stop meeting like this," he says lightly to me, but I can feel him checking me over with his eyes, making sure I'm all right while pretending not to care.

"What have you got in those pants?" my mother asks him, coming to her feet and staring at his crotch accusingly. "*Baydar?* Everywhere we Bayers are, you turn up. You don't expect me to buy that this is a coincidence, I hope."

Drew tells my mother that it's nice to see her, too, and asks if it's his fault that her daughter seems to attract disasters.

Charming to be made to feel like the bearer of a plague.

He asks how I am.

"Just peachy," I tell him. "I seem to be making a habit of finding dead bodies, my mother is driving me crazy and the catering hall I booked two freakin' years ago for Dana's bat mitzvah has just been shut down by the Board of Health!"

"Glad to see your luck's finally changing," he says, giving

me a quick squeeze around the shoulders before turning his attention to the patrolmen, asking what they've got, whether they've taken any statements, moved anything, all the sort of stuff you see on TV, without any of the drama. That is, if you don't count my mother's threats to faint every few minutes when she senses no one's paying attention to her.

Mario tells his waitstaff to bring everyone espresso, which I decline because I'm wired enough. Drew pulls him aside and a minute later I'm handed a cup of coffee that smells divinely of Kahlúa.

The man knows me well. Too well.

His partner, whom I've met once or twice, says he'll interview the kitchen staff. Drew asks Mario if he minds if he takes statements from the patrons first and gets to him and the waitstaff afterward.

"No, no," Mario tells him. "Do the patrons first." Drew raises his eyebrow at me like he wants to know if I get the double entendre. I try to look bored.

"What is it with you and murder victims?" he asks me when we sit down at a table in the corner.

I search them out so that I can see you again, I almost say, but I'm afraid it will sound desperate instead of sarcastic.

My mother, lighting up and daring him with a look to tell her not to, reminds him that *she* was the one to find the body.

Drew asks what happened *this time*. My mother tells him how the man in the john was "taken" with me, couldn't take his eyes off me and blatantly flirted with both of us. To his credit, Drew doesn't laugh, but his smirk is undeniable to the trained eye. And I've had my eye trained on him for nearly a year now.

"While he was noticing you," he asks me, "did *you* notice anything about him? Was he waiting for anyone? Watching for anything?"

I tell him that he didn't appear to be waiting or watching. That he made no phone calls, was fairly intent on eating and did, indeed, flirt with my mother. This last bit Drew takes with a grain of salt, which was the way it was intended.

"And he had a short conversation with Mario," I tell him. "I think he might have been unhappy with the food, though he didn't send it back."

Drew asks what makes me think he was dissatisfied, and I tell him that the discussion seemed acrimonious and that Mario looked distressed when he left the table. Drew makes a note and says he'll look into it and asks about anyone else in the restaurant. Did I see anyone who didn't seem to belong, anyone who was watching the victim, anyone looking suspicious?

"Besides my mother?" I ask him, and Mom huffs and blows her cigarette smoke in my direction.

I tell him that there were several deliveries, the kitchen staff going in and out the back door to grab a smoke. He stops me and asks what I was doing checking out the back door of the restaurant.

Proudly—because, while he was off forgetting me, dropping by only once in a while to say hi to Jesse, my son, or drop something by for one of my daughters that he thought they might like, I was getting on with my life—I tell him that I'm decorating the place.

He looks genuinely impressed. "Commercial customers? That's great," he says. Okay, that's what he *ought* to say. What he actually says is "Whatever pays the bills."

"Howard Rosen, the famous restaurant critic, got her the job," my mother says. "You met him—the good-looking, distinguished gentleman with the *real* job, something to be proud of. I guess you've never read his reviews in *Newsday*."

Drew, without missing a beat, tells her that Howard's reviews are on the top of his list, as soon as he learns how to read.

"I only meant—" my mother starts, but both of us assure her that we know just what she meant.

"So," Drew says. "Deliveries?"

I tell him that Mario would know better than I, but that I saw vegetables come in, maybe fish and linens.

"This is the second restaurant job Howard's got her," my mother tells Drew.

"At least she's getting *something* out of the relationship," he says.

"If he were here," my mother says, ignoring the insinuation, "he'd be comforting her instead of interrogating her. He'd be making sure we're both all right after such an ordeal."

"I'm sure he would," Drew agrees, then looks me in the eyes as if he's measuring my tolerance for shock. Quietly he adds, "But then maybe he doesn't know just what strong stuff your daughter's made of."

It's the closest thing to a tender moment I can expect from Drew Scoones. My mother breaks the spell. "She gets that from me," she says.

Both Drew and I take a minute, probably to pray that's all I inherited from her.

"I'm just trying to save you some time and effort," my mother tells him. "My money's on Howard."

Drew withers her with a look and mutters something that sounds suspiciously like "fool's gold." Then he excuses himself to go back to work.

I catch his sleeve and ask if it's all right for us to leave. He says sure, he knows where we live. I say goodbye to Mario. I assure him that I will have some sketches for him in a few days, all the while hoping that this murder doesn't cancel his redecorating plans. I need the money desperately, the alternative being borrowing from my parents and being strangled by the strings.

My mother is strangely quiet all the way to her house. She doesn't tell me what a loser Drew Scoones is—despite his good looks—and how I was obviously drooling over him. She doesn't ask me where Howard is taking me tonight or warn me not to tell my father about what happened because he will worry about us both and no doubt insist we see our respective psychiatrists.

She fidgets nervously, opening and closing her purse over and over again.

"You okay?" I ask her. After all, she's just found a dead man on the toilet, and tough as she is that's got to be upsetting.

When she doesn't answer me I pull over to the side of the road.

"Mom?" She refuses to meet my eyes. "You want me to take you to see Dr. Cohen?"

She looks out the window as if she's just realized we're on Broadway in Woodmere. "Aren't we near Marvin's Jewelers?" she asks, pulling something out of her purse.

"What have you got, Mother?" I ask, prying open her fingers to find the murdered man's ring.

"It was on the sink," she says in answer to my dropped jaw. "I was going to get his name and address and have you return it to him so that he could ask you out. I thought it was a sign that the two of you were meant to be together."

"He's dead, Mom. You understand that, right?" I ask. You never can tell when my mother is fine and when she's in la-la land.

"Well, I didn't know that," she shouts at me. "Not at the time."

I ask why she didn't give it to Drew, realize that she wouldn't give Drew the time in a clock shop and add, "...or one of the other policemen?"

"For heaven's sake," she tells me. "The man is dead, Teddi, and I took his ring. How would that look?"

Before I can tell her it looks just the way it is, she pulls out a cigarette and threatens to light it.

"I mean, really," she says, shaking her head like it's my brains that are loose. "What does he need with it now?"

nocturne™

**WAS HE HER SAVIOR
OR HER NIGHTMARE?**

HAUNTED
LISA CHILDS

Years ago, Ariel and her sisters were separated for
their own protection. Now the man who vowed
revenge on her family has resumed the hunt, and
Ariel must warn her sisters before it's too late.
The closer she comes to finding them, the more
secretive her fiancé becomes. Can she trust the man
she plans to spend eternity with? Or has he been
waiting for the perfect moment to destroy her?

On sale December 2006.

AleX Archer
THE CHOSEN

Archaeologist Annja Creed believes there's more to
the apparitions of Santo Niño—the Holy Child—luring
thousands of pilgrims to Santa Fe. But she is not alone in
her quest to separate reliquaries from unholy minds who
dare to harness sinister power. A dangerous yet enigmatic
Jesuit, a brilliant young artist and a famed monster
hunter are the keys to the
secrets that lie in the heart
of Los Alamos—and
unlocking the door to the
very fabric of time itself....

**Available January 2007
wherever books are sold.**

GRA4

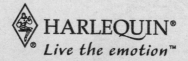

BOMBSHELL™

COMING NEXT MONTH

#121 SEVENTH KEY—Evelyn Vaughn
The Madonna Key
In her heyday, Professor Maggi Sanger had harnessed the powers of her female ancestors to fight evil; now she had her hands full raising a daughter. But when her archenemies kidnapped members of the Marian sisterhood and their children and imprisoned them in Naples, Maggi had no choice but to fight for their legacy...and the future of the world. Did she hold the key to salvation—or would she unlock the door to apocalypse instead?

#122 THE MEDUSA PROPHECY—Cindy Dees
The Medusa Project
When Captain Karen Tucker and her all-female Special Forces group, the Medusas, uncovered a drug lab during an arctic training mission, the situation got hot enough to melt a polar ice cap. Exposed to a deadly mind-altering drug, Karen now had to help her team put the pushers out of business while she struggled to stay alive. And stay sane enough not to kill handsome allied soldier Anders Larson *and* her fellow Medusas...

#123 DEAD IS THE NEW BLACK—Harper Allen
Darkheart & Crosse
For Tashya Crosse, being a vampire wasn't a difficult cross to bear—she got to stay young forever, the male vamps were *hot* and she could still go out in the sun, provided she wore SPF 60 lotion. But the other two Crosse triplets—a slayer and a healer—were hardly amused by her new identity. And when a deadly enemy arrived in town, Tashya had to choose between vamping it up and saving her sisters from certain destruction.

#124 STAYING ALIVE—Debra Webb
All Claire Grant wanted was peace and quiet when she settled down as an elementary school teacher in Seattle. But the day terrorists took her classroom hostage—and she successfully fought back—she became a prime target for one of the most wanted, deadly men on earth. Soon the FBI's legendary and ultrasexy antiterror agent Luke Krueger stepped in with a new plan to take out the terrorists—using Claire as bait.

SBCNM1206